They can't concentrate, can't eat or
sleep, and it's only getting worse.
The Parrish sisters must have…

BABY
Fever

Join Catherine, Elly and Abby as they
make their way down the exciting—
but sometimes bumpy—road
to motherhood!

Dear Reader

I cannot begin to tell you how delighted I was to be asked to write this set of stories—or how much fun I had writing it!

Creating the characters was a pure joy, and then 'matchmaking' Catherine, Elly and Abby with their perfect mates was rather like finding the perfect puzzle pieces that completed a picture you could see in your head, and now saw right there, taking shape in front of you.

Of course, every good story of motherhood needs a mummy, and Susie Parrish is a conglomeration of every 'Mum' ever born. Loving to her husband, protective of her daughters and only wanting what's best for everyone—and, naturally, *knowing* what is best for everyone.

Having visited Las Vegas, the location—with its romantic reputation and many wedding chapels—also seemed perfect. Certainly Susie thought so! Especially if a mum wanted her daughters to start thinking about romance…and marriage…and giving their anxious parents a few grandchildren to love.

Such obedient children—as you'll see when you read *Baby Fever*. Enjoy!

BABY
Fever

KASEY MICHAELS

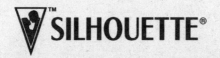

*All the characters in this book have no existence outside the imagination
of the author, and have no relation whatsoever to anyone bearing the
same name or names. They are not even distantly inspired by any
individual known or unknown to the author, and all the incidents are
pure invention.*

*First published in Great Britain 2000
Silhouette Books, Eton House, 18-24 Paradise Road,
Richmond, Surrey TW9 1SR*

© Kasey Michaels 1999

ISBN 0 373 48380 5

030-0004

*Printed and bound in Spain
by Litografia Rosés S.A., Barcelona*

To Tony Cross, and all the great
gang at Tony's Coplay Family Restaurant.
Bless you all for feeding my family while
I spin stories!

Kasey Michaels is a *New York Times* bestselling author of more than fifty books and has long been known as one of the premier authors in romance. Ms Michaels has been honoured with the *Romantic Times Magazine* Career Achievement Award for Regency Historical novels, and is also a recipient of the Romance Writers of America RITA Award, as well as several others. Her career has been the subject of a TV programme. Ms Michaels enjoys hearing from her readers, and you may write to her care of Silhouette® Books.

Prologue

Jim Parrish watched as his wife set down the glass of lemonade on the table beside him, then walked away.

It was the walk that warned him.

His Susie had the sweetest walk, always had. But when she put that special little "come-hither" hitch into it, he knew he was about to agree to do something he hadn't had the faintest notion of doing five seconds earlier.

Still, and just for the moment, he decided to pretend he hadn't seen the come-hither hitch. Instead, he rested his head against the soft cushion of the lounge chair, crossed his bare feet and slowly surveyed his surroundings.

Nevada. What a place! A three-bedroom ranch house with its own pool. No lawn to mow, no snow to plow, not even any leaves to rake. Cactus was nice, cactus was good. Cactus didn't shed.

Doctor James Parrish had fallen in love with Nevada the moment he and his Susie had stepped off the plane in Las Vegas. They'd flown out from Pennsylvania to see their middle daughter, Elly, who'd landed a plum job as a dancer in one of those elaborate casino productions.

Elly had been spectacular. Las Vegas had been equally wonderful. Jim had seen the city first as a playground for grown-ups, but Elly had insisted on giving her parents the grand tour. Soon Jim had seen another side to Las Vegas—what, in Pennsylvania, he would have called "the suburbs."

Within two years he had sold his family-medicine practice in Allentown and he and Susie had relocated to their ranch house in Summerlin. He'd opened a new practice, just to keep his hand in until the day retirement sounded more like fun than a chore, and after three years neither he nor Susie had regretted the move for a moment.

Of course, if Elly hadn't married Rob and moved to New York, and if Catherine hadn't refused to leave Allentown, and if Abby would—for crying out loud— settle herself *somewhere,* Susie would probably be even happier.

Jim shifted his gaze to his wife, admiring her small, trim figure as she walked the length of the pool surround, netted skimmer in hand. Oh, yes. She was still doing the walk. It was coming. Any minute now…

"Jim?"

Ah, his master's voice. Fluid, sweet and totally innocent. He was a dead man. "Yes, darling?"

"You do know what next Thursday is, don't you?"

Thursday. Thursday. What the devil was next Thursday? He stood up, walked toward his darling five-foot-two, eyes-of-green, blond wife whom he outweighed by one hundred pounds—not to mention the fact that he was nearly a full foot taller. But size wasn't everything. He knew he could end up in the pool if he didn't come up with the right answer. Fast.

Her bottom lip was just pushing forward in a pout when the dawn broke. Next Thursday. Of course! He slipped his arms around Susie's waist, then bent to nibble at her ear. "Thirty years, darling," he breathed as she relaxed against him. "Thirty deliriously happy, glorious years. I can only pray we have at least thirty more ahead of us."

"You're so right, darling, and *so* lucky." She lifted her head and he thought he was to be rewarded with a kiss for his brilliance. A kiss, maybe more than a single kiss. Maybe even a stroll to the bedroom? It was, after all, Saturday afternoon, and lazy weekend afternoons had become their favorite delight.

He'd forgotten the little hitch.

Susie slipped away from him, leaving him standing with his empty arms and the dawning knowledge that Sue, the Velvet Barracuda, was about to come in for the kill.

"And I was thinking, darling," she said, shrugging out of her short white cover-up to reveal an electric blue tank suit and a body that could have launched a thousand ships, "that thirty years is something of a milestone. I mean, it's not every year that two people are married for thirty years. And I turned fifty last month. Another milestone."

"And I'll be fifty-five this August," Jim said as he watched Susie stuff her blond curls beneath a snug white bathing cap. She was the only woman he knew who could look sexy as hell in a bathing cap. "We're just chock-full of milestones this year, aren't we?"

"Except for one," Susie said, and the pout was back. "You know, Jim, I didn't really look forward to being fifty, but now that I am, I've realized that it isn't so bad. I mean, I don't *feel* fifty."

"Or look it," he all but growled, reaching for her playfully.

"Oh, I've trained you so well, darling. And don't interrupt," she warned, grinning. "Anyway, I've decided that a woman of fifty, with three grown daughters and thirty years of marriage under her belt, is more than ready to become a grandmother."

That was it? Susie wanted to be a grandmother? Well, damn. How was he supposed to help with that? "I suppose you'll have to discuss that with Elly," he suggested carefully, "considering that she's the only one of our three who's married."

Susie looked away, hiding her expression. "Yes. Elly." Then she brightened. "And Catherine is creeping up on thirty in another two years. I had her when I was twenty-two, Jim. What on earth is she waiting for?"

"A husband?" he offered carefully, knowing his oldest daughter would not be pleased with this conversation.

"And Abby? I despair of her ever settling down," Susie went on quickly. "Living wherever she pleases, going wherever whim takes her, seeing life as one huge adventure. I can't imagine where she got that from."

Jim bit the inside of his bottom lip, hard, to keep from smiling. Abby was his Susie all over again, not that he was foolish enough to point that out at the moment. "Can't imagine," he offered commiseratingly.

"They need roots, Jim. They need husbands. I need grandchildren."

"Uh-huh," he said, then waited. Because it was coming. The coup de grace. He'd had the windup, and now he was going to see the follow-through. He decided to be agreeable, feed her the lines she needed. "You're absolutely right, babe. We need grandchildren."

"Yes, we do. I *knew* you'd understand, darling. We've waited long enough for our daughters to come to their senses on their own. We have every right to take matters into our own hands, point them in the right direction, teach by example. So it's all settled. I've already sent the girls their plane tickets. Next Thursday, my dearest love, you and I are going to get *married!*" Susie said brightly, her voice filled with Susie Parrish logic—always a frightening prospect. She dropped her gold watch onto the table, then skipped straight past her openmouthed husband and neatly dived into the pool.

BOOK I
CATHERINE

Chapter 1

"**S**he wants an Elvis theme," Catherine Parrish said before closing her lips around the straw and taking a long drink of her soda. She hated airport soda in paper cups. Hated paper cups. Wasn't all that damn fond of airports.

"Elvis? Really? Cool! Mom's always been a hoot."

Catherine looked at her baby sister levelly. Abby was their mother in looks, in personality—their mother down to Susan Parrish's last, lovable quirk. "Yeah, right, Abigail. A hoot. Mom and Dad renewing their wedding vows in some Elvis chapel while a guy in a white spandex suit and beer belly croaks out "Love Me Tender." I knew you'd like that. It's a real class act."

Abby hitched up an invisible collar, lowered her voice and said, "Thank you...thank-you-very-much.'' Then she gave Catherine's arm a playful tap, threw back her head and laughed aloud. ''Oh, come on, Teach, school's out. Lighten up, for goodness sake. It's going to be fun.''

Catherine fought to retain her bad mood, and failed as she felt the corners of her mouth curving into a reluctant smile. Abby was her baby sister, blond, bubbly and bouncy. Just the sort of irrepressible child who wrapped other people around her little finger without even trying. Catherine had been her slave since the day Abby was born. ''Okay, okay,'' she said, spreading her hands in surrender. ''I guess it could be fun.''

''Only *fun?*'' Abby asked, raising her eyebrows.

''All right, so it could be hilarious. I've never been inside one of those Vegas wedding chapels, have you? They're probably not all that bad, except maybe for the ones that put up signs saying 'Over Five Million Served.'''

''They do that?'' Abby's green eyes went wide, then narrowed. ''God, I fall for it every time, don't I? Twenty-five, and I still fall for every joke you and Elly pull on me.'' She looked over her shoulder, as if able to take in the entire terminal. The sound of quarters dropping from one of the slot machines in the center of the terminal came to their ears. ''When's their plane getting in? Man, I haven't seen Elly and Rob for nearly a year, do you know that? I mean, first I was in Hawaii, and then Ireland, and now I'm just finding my way around Miami. I should have stopped off in New York, I guess.''

''Or Allentown,'' Catherine suggested, knowing she hadn't seen her sister in a year as well. ''But thanks for the souvenirs,'' she added, remembering the swivel-hipped hula dancer doll and the over-stuffed leprechaun-faced pillow, both gifts still in their boxes and stuffed in the back of her hall closet. She checked her watch. "All three of our planes have been nearly an hour apart, so Elly and Rob should be landing in about five minutes. Which is a good thing, because I think I've had enough of this terminal to last me for a while. Are you sure you shouldn't have picked up your luggage on the carousel? How long do they let it circle there before they haul it away to Luggage Limbo?"

"I'm fine, I'm fine. I do this all the time," Abby assured her, looking at Catherine's neatly stacked luggage standing next to their table. "Somebody always finds it for me."

"Ah, to be young," Catherine said with an exaggerated sigh, then wondered when it was that she had begun to feel so old. Was it when her seventh grade students had stopped calling her Miz Parrish and begun addressing her as ma'am? Had it been that day last year, when she'd broken down and had her light brown hair streaked with golden highlights meant to cover the first hints of gray? Or maybe it had been seeing all her friends at her class reunion, and spending endless hours smiling over other people's baby pictures.

Not that she had been the only unmarried woman at the reunion. Not that she needed to be married, felt incomplete without a man.

But a baby? She really did want a baby. In fact, one of the reasons she'd accepted her mother's invitation—she refused to call it a demand—to come to Nevada in the first place was because she really did want a baby. If she could swear her father to secrecy, that was—

"Do you remember how I used to dress you up and take you for walks in your stroller?" she asked Abby suddenly. "Even when you were too big, so that I had to stuff you into the thing."

Abby, not being one to ask where a question came from, even when it arrived without warning from left field, grinned, resting her chin in her hands as she looked toward the nearest gate, and at the crowd of people just entering the terminal. "Little Mother," she said. "That's what Mom called you. Always taking care of us, always in charge. You bandaged our knees, wiped our noses, told us how to chew with our mouths closed, helped us with our homework. God, you could be a pain in the—oh, look! Here comes Elly!" She stood up, waved both her arms over her head. "Here we are, here we are! Over here!"

A half dozen men between the ages of twenty and eighty stopped dead in their tracks, clearly believing their own private god had just granted them the wish of a lifetime. One even went so far as to wave back and call out, "I'll be right there, darlin'!"

"Nice try!" Abby countered, giggling, then blew him a kiss before Elly could thread her way through the crowd, where she was caught up in her baby sister's warm embrace. "Oh, Elly, I'm so glad to see you!" said Abby. She disengaged herself from her much taller sister and looked across the terminal. "Where's Rob?"

Catherine was thinking the same thing. She was also thinking that her middle sister looked a little too tired, even after a fairly long flight. Her Mother Hen instincts went on red alert as she inspected Jim and

Susie Parrish's middle daughter. Mom had been right,
something was wrong with Elly. Her mother's con-
cern was, in fact, just one more reason she'd agreed
to rethink her plans for her first week of vacation at
the end of the school term and come to Vegas. But,
then, that was Mom. She always knew what strings
to pull.

Catherine stood up, opened her arms, and Elly
walked straight into them, the two exchanging fierce
hugs. Catherine, although a good five inches taller
than Abby, was still two inches shorter than her dancer sister, Elly. And at least fifteen pounds heavier.
She frowned as she rubbed her hands up and down
Elly's back, feeling the tenseness in her sister's muscles, able to discern her ribs under those muscles. Oh,
yeah, Mom had been right. Something was wrong.

"Where's Rob?" Abby asked again as the three
sat down and Elly reached out to take a sip of Catherine's soda.

"I left him," she said baldly, then looked at Catherine with sad, eloquent green eyes.

Abby stood up once more, scanning the terminal.
"Left him where? I still don't see him."

Catherine rolled her eyes. "We could draw her a
diagram, I suppose," she said, trying to smile.

"What joke are you pulling on me now? I
mean—" Abby sat down with a small thump. "Oh.
You *left* him. You *left* Rob? Oh, you poor baby!"
She pulled Elly into her arms, motherlike, which was
an affectionate, comforting gesture except for the fact
that Elly continued to sit ramrod straight, staring at
Catherine.

"Catherine?" Abby asked a moment later, also
looking at her.

Why did they always do that? Catherine wondered. Did they think she had an answer to every problem tattooed on her forehead?

What was she supposed to do? To say? She couldn't kiss it, make it all better. "I-I'm sorry, Elly," she said at last, reaching out a hand across the table, squeezing her sister's hand. Her ice-cold hand. "Do you want to talk about it, babe?"

"Not particularly," Elly said, standing up, a signal that all three of them should get up, gather luggage, be on their way. "Besides, Mom is going to tie me down until she's gotten the whole story out of me, and I'd rather not have to run through it twice."

"Good point," Catherine agreed, adjusting the handle of her roll-along luggage, then falling into step between her two sisters as they made their way down the length of the terminal.

"Just tell me this," Abby said, skipping in front of them so that she could look at Elly. "Do we want him back—or do we want him dead? Just so I know how to respond when you tell us this story we're going to hear."

Catherine settled herself behind the wheel of the rental car and strapped herself into the seat belt. She looked to her right, to where Elly was sitting with her perfect dancer's posture. "All right now?"

Her sister nodded. "Sorry I made such a fool of myself." Elly had broken down in the terminal, laughing and crying after Abby's innocently provoking question, but she seemed to be in control again, although it was a brittle control that would probably break all over again once Susie Parrish had taken one look at her, then gathered her into a hug.

"It's okay, Elly," Abby chirped from the back seat, where she had shoved her small body into a space only big enough for someone as tiny as she was, leaving the rest of the seat for the small mountain of luggage Elly had brought with her. "I do it all the time, myself. It's good for the soul, even if it does play hell with the mascara."

"Meaning that I look like a raccoon?" Elly asked, flipping down the sunshield to inspect herself in the mirror hanging behind it. "Oh good," she said, digging in her purse for yet another tissue and wiping at her eyes. "Mom will take one look and hire a hit man to murder Rob." She finished with the tissue, replaced it in her purse. "I cannot tell you guys how much I'm not looking forward to this. Thank God Dad talked her out of driving in to meet our planes, not that he could have gotten all our luggage into that little red sports car he's in lust with right now. He even sent us pictures. Did you guys get pictures?"

"You mean the ones with Mom draped over the front of the thing, like a hood ornament?" Catherine grinned. "Those are two sick puppies, you know. I can't imagine how they ever managed to raise three normal adults."

"Two," Abby piped up from the back seat. "I think the jury's still out on me, or at least that's what Mom says when I phone home." Catherine looked in the rearview mirror to see her sister wrinkling up her pert nose. "I don't see it. What's wrong with the way I live?"

"How long does the ride to Summerlin take?" Catherine asked, laughing. "Elly? Do you think we have time to answer Abby's question?"

Elly gave one final watery sniff, squared her chin

and said brightly, "How is our Abby *Ab*normal? Let me count the ways..."

"Oh, knock it off," Abby said, giggling. "I know I'm crazy, but it's a fun crazy, and I even make money. That should count for something."

"Abigail Parrish," Catherine intoned solemnly, "the world's gift to the harried homemaker. Doling out advice and recipes and how-to Halloween costume patterns twice weekly in all the major newspapers. Do you think any of them know you can't cook? Or sew? Or follow directions on a spray bottle? An honest person would tell them, you know. You've got millions of women believing you know what you're talking about, when you haven't got a clue."

"What, tell them, and spoil my image?" Abby shot back at her, laughing. "I should say not! And I've picked up a monthly column in *Matters Domestic* magazine, I'll have you know. Why, some people are even talking television show." She frowned. "The only thing holding me back is that I burn myself each time I pick up a glue gun, so I can't see how I'm going to swing television, can you?"

"Oh, God!" Elly was searching her purse for another tissue, this time to wipe away tears of laughter. "I'm so glad we're doing this. I don't remember the last time I laughed."

Catherine turned out of the rental lot and decided they had time for a quick ride down the Strip before heading out to Summerlin and the folks. Elly needed more time to collect herself, for one thing, as she certainly seemed to be riding a roller coaster of emotions—which wasn't like Elly at all.

Besides, they hadn't been in Las Vegas in two years, as her parents had come east on their vacation last summer, stopping off with each daughter for two weeks, catching up with Abby in Chicago, or someplace Abby had thought interesting at the time. There were probably six new casinos lining the Strip since their last visit.

What Catherine saw as they inched along in heavy midday traffic, however, was not the new casinos. What she saw were billboards. And benches at bus stops. And more billboards.

All of them advertising the fact that someone by the name of Griff Edwards owned five—count 'em, five—car dealerships in the Las Vegas area. Actually, the billboards and painted benches seemed to advertise Griff Edwards, because his grinning face was plastered all over them.

There was his smiling face, stuck to a bench. There was his smiling face and all of his body, twenty feet high and straddling a motorcycle. A person couldn't drive more than a mile without seeing Griff Edwards leering at her from somewhere.

"Talk about having a case on yourself," Catherine grumbled as they neared the Treasure Island casino.

"What?" Elly asked, as she and Abby had been talking about a new musical now on Broadway, with Elly waxing almost poetic over the lead performer's dancing ability.

Catherine pointed to the billboard on the far side of the intersection as they sat at a red light. "Him," she said, making a dismissive gesture with her hand. "Haven't you noticed? He's everywhere, like chicken droppings. Some people sell cars, you know. This guy? He's selling Griff Edwards. It's disgusting."

Abby leaned her arms on the back of the front seat, then nestled her chin against one forearm as she peered through the front windshield. "Hubba-hubba," she said, waggling her eyebrows. "He could sell me sand in a desert. Look at those soulful brown eyes under those absolutely fantastic eyebrows. Tom Cruise-ish, Elly, don't you think? And that hair, the way it sort of slides down over his forehead? And those teeth? That smile? I take it back. He could sell me used kitty litter in a desert."

"Do you have any tissues left, Elly?" Catherine asked in disgust. "I think we need to wipe the drool off baby sis's chin."

"What? You don't think he's handsome?" Abby asked teasingly. "How old are you, anyway, Teach?"

"Not funny," Catherine responded, knowing she was being unreasonable. But she couldn't help it. She was getting very nervous about her age and the rut she seemed to have fallen into without even noticing the drop. She gave one last, searing look at the billboard, saw the light turn green out of the corner of her eye—thought she saw the light turn green—and stepped on the accelerator.

A moment later the bumper of the rental car made contact with the bumper of the brand-new Porsche in front of her.

Catherine laid her forehead on the steering wheel and muttered a few words her seventh-graders had never heard her say. She watched as the green Porsche moved forward through the intersection, then turned into a small side street and pulled to a stop at the curb.

"You'd better follow him," Elly said as the drivers in line behind their car started blowing their horns. "Do you think there's much damage? You didn't hit all that hard."

"It's a sports car, Elly," Catherine grumbled as she pulled forward, then turned in behind the Porsche. "A scratched bumper probably costs five thousand dollars."

She turned off the engine, released her seat belt and opened the door.

And quickly closed it again in self-defense.

"It's him," she said, her voice coming out in an embarrassing squeak as a long male body uncoiled itself from the driver's seat of the Porsche and began walking toward her side of the car. "Can you believe this? If I didn't have bad luck, I'd have no luck at all."

"It *is* him!" Abby piped up from the back seat, where she had been rearranging the mountain of luggage that had come tumbling down during the slightly rocking impact. "And he's smiling. Look at those teeth. Do you think those are real? Oh, they've got to be real. Only nature could make that smile. Catherine, you'll have to get out, talk to him. I'd do it for you, except I can't stand up. My kneecaps just melted. And you know, if it's just the rubber bumper, there are several good products on the market that will rub any small discoloration right out. You know, maybe I should go out there. Hmm? What do you think?"

Catherine pushed at her huge, round tortoise-shell sunglasses and ran a hand over her pulled-back hair— then cursed herself for even considering her appearance. "Gag her, Elly. Tie her up if you have to," she said shortly, then took a deep breath and opened the door before Griff Edwards could do it for her.

He was tall. Very tall. Built like a man who loved sports, loved to play. His black knit shirt showed off the muscles in his arms, the flatness of his stomach;

his frayed, cutoff jeans shorts fit him like a second skin. He had a tan deep enough to turn the hair on his forearms and legs a sparkling gold, and it didn't seem the least bit unusual to Catherine that the man had been driving through the city in bare feet.

His smile was confident, his brown eyes seemed to laugh as he raised his mirrored sunglasses for a moment, then let them slide back into place so that Catherine could see her own reflection in the lenses. A slight breeze ruffled his dark brown hair as he looked down at her, smiled down at her.

He was so perfect he made Catherine's teeth ache.

"Hi," he said easily as he held out his right hand, his voice as smooth as his approach, which bordered on that of a god coming down from the heavens to grant a distressed damsel three wishes of her choice. "I'm Griff Edwards, whiplash victim. And you'd be…?"

Catherine tried to ignore his smile, his outstretched hand. She failed in both exercises. Taking his hand in hers, feeling the dry warmth of it, the callused strength of it, she answered, "I'm Catherine Parrish, Mr. Edwards, idiot driver. I'm really sorry." She withdrew her hand, felt a chill in the warm Las Vegas sun. "Are you really hurt? I didn't think I hit you that hard, but if you want to go to the hospital, I'll—"

"Just kidding. I'm not hurt, Ms. Parrish," he said quickly. "See?" He moved his head from side to side, then spread his arms as if he'd just given proof to his statement. "No harm, no foul. Shall we check on our cars?"

"Hmm? Oh. Oh, yes, our cars." Catherine followed after Griff as he walked back to the front of her car, then bent down to inspect the bumper. She took a moment to order her heart to stop its erratic gallop. What was the matter with her? The last time she'd felt bowled over by a smiling male face was when Timmy Smithers had apologized for putting gum on her chair by presenting her with a shiny red apple with a bow tied to its stem. She'd fallen for Timmy's apology, for his boyish smile—and ended up with gum on her chair again the next morning. There was nothing quite so dazzling, or more likely to mean trouble, than a male smile.

"See anything?" she asked, removing her sunglasses and squinting as the sun sparkled off the shiny white rental car. "I bought the insurance, so if there is—"

"No need to report this to your insurance company. There's nothing here I can't fix," Griff said, standing up once more. "The same goes for my car."

"But—"

He held up his hands and she fell silent. "No, really. I want to do this, and it's no problem. Just give me your address and I'll drop around later and take your car in to the shop, touch up that scrape near the bumper. I've got paint that will match perfectly."

"It's white," Catherine said, trying to regain her equilibrium. "Anybody could have paint that matches it perfectly. I'll just find a dealership and..." Her voice dropped off and she turned away, looking directly into the smiling face of Griff Edwards as it leered down at her from the billboard.

"Yeah," he said, almost sheepishly, Catherine thought. "That would probably be my dealership you'd go looking for, Ms. Parrish. So, like I said, let me save you a trip. Consider it part of the welcome-to-Vegas courtesy we locals all pride ourselves on, all right? Now, what hotel are you in?''

''We're not tourists, Mr. Edwards,'' Abby chirped from somewhere behind Catherine, her melted knees obviously having made a sterling comeback from their jellylike state. ''We're here to visit our parents in Summerlin. Catherine, give him the address. Elly says he can join us for dinner if he wants so much to fix our bumper, and then Mom won't be able to get her teeth into her until tonight. Tomorrow, if Elly can manage to escape to her room, complaining about jet lag.''

Catherine looked past Abby, into the front seat, where Elly was slinking toward the floor, trying her best to make her five-foot, nine-inch body disappear. ''I doubt she told you to say all of that, Abigail,'' she said tightly.

Abby, being Abby, ignored Catherine, stepping past her, hand outstretched, to introduce herself to Griff Edwards and give him their parents' home address, all without taking a breath. He pulled a piece of paper out of his pocket and wrote down that address as Catherine stood by, steaming.

''No,'' Catherine said, quickly stepping in front of Abby, a move which was beginning to look as if they were playing some demented form of leapfrog. ''This isn't necessary. I hit you, Mr. Edwards, remember? You're not obligated in any way. I am.''

Melting kneecaps must be contagious, because Catherine felt hers beginning to dissolve as Griff Edwards lifted up his sunglasses again and smiled at her with his eyes. ''Yes, you are, aren't you? Obligated, that is. But don't worry, I'm easily satisfied, and dinner tonight sounds just about right. Will there be dessert, or shall I bring something along with me?''

''Just your handsome self,'' Abby chirped, then quickly ducked back into the back seat when Catherine turned to glare at her.

''You'll have to excuse my sister, Mr. Edwards,'' Catherine said with a sigh. ''She was dropped on her head as a child. Repeatedly. Sadly, it didn't help.''

Griff threw back his head and laughed. He had a wonderful laugh, Catherine thought. Shivery, full-bodied. Sexy. If only the man didn't obviously have such a case on himself that he felt the world needed to see his face every five minutes or else go into Griff Edwards withdrawal. Catherine raised her eyes, wished the light standard above them would fall on his head.

''Why do you do it?'' she asked him without thinking, then winced as she heard her own words spilling out of her mouth.

''Pardon? Why do I do what?''

Catherine pointed to the billboard across the street, figuring she may as well get her insult out of the way before the man seriously believed he was expected at the Parrish household for dinner. ''That,'' she said. ''And that,'' she added, grimacing as a cab passed by them, a miniaturized version of the billboard riding on its roof. ''Siegfried and Roy use less advertising space for their animal act at the Mirage.''

''You don't like it?'' Griff asked, obviously refusing to believe that, no, she didn't like it. ''You don't think the photographer captured my best side?''

''That's not what I meant,'' Catherine said sharply, then shook her head. The man had an ego larger than the MGM Grand lion they'd passed by earlier, taller than the Luxor pyramid, wider than…than…well, wider than anything she could think of at the moment. ''Never mind. Just forget it. I shouldn't have said anything. I mean, it's not as if it's any of my business if you want to see your own face plastered from one end of Vegas to the other.'' Even if that damn face on that damn billboard had gotten her into this mess in the first place. ''And now, if you don't mind, we'll be on our way.''

''And I'll see you tonight,'' Griff said amicably, already moving toward his car. ''Around six? I'm really looking forward to it. Truly.''

''I'll just bet you are,'' Catherine ground out from between clenched teeth, then followed after him, walking with her best schoolmarm stride, the one that meant business and brooked no interference. ''Now, look,'' she began, once she believed she was out of earshot of her two interested sisters. ''Fun's fun and all that, and I know Abby is cute as a button, but I think this has gone far enough, don't you? Because I know your type, Griff Edwards. Handsome, smooth and probably with a libido that would level Detroit. Well, not with my sister. Okay?''

Griff lifted his sunglasses onto his head and smiled down at her, raked her body with his warm brown gaze so that she could feel her flesh begin to tingle. ''Abby? You think I'm interested in Abby? Really? Catherine Parrish, shame on you. Don't you own any mirrors?''

And then he was gone. Before she could close her mouth, before she could open it again to say anything remotely comprehensible, he and his damn green Porsche were gone.

Leaving Catherine to stomp back to her rental car,

fuming with anger and at the same time wondering what she'd packed that might not be too wrinkled to wear for dinner without having to drag out her mother's ironing board.

"Not a word, Abigail Parrish," she warned as she slid beneath the steering wheel and turned the ignition, the engine roaring to life. "Not a single, solitary word. You've said more than enough already."

Out of the corner of her eyes, Catherine could see Elly's left hand raised slightly, as if only half hoping to be called upon by the teacher. "If I might say something?" she inquired, a hint of laughter in her voice.

"If I say no?"

"If you say no, Teach, I'll just ignore you," Elly said, patting Catherine's arm. "Sorry. But he is a handsome one, isn't he?"

"And taller than Tom Cruise," Abby piped up from the back seat. "Elly says he was looking at you as if you were made out of pudding and he was contemplating where to dab the whipped cream."

Catherine groaned as she made an illegal U-turn and pulled back onto the Strip. "Oh, that's good, Eleanor, corrupt the child, why don't you?"

"Corrupt Abby?" Elly laughed, shook her head. "Hell, Catherine, she told me he was looking at you like you were a lollipop he wanted to lick all over. I thought my observation was much more creative. But, either way, I'd say the man is interested. Definitely interested."

"Well, that makes one of us," Catherine grumbled, staring daggers at the taxi in front of her, and the smiling face of Griff Edwards attached to a panel on its trunk. "Just do me a favor, guys, and don't share your thoughts with our maternal unit, as you call her, Abby. I have enough problems as it is, listening to her tell me she can hear my biological clock ticking away like a time bomb.''

''You, too?'' Abby asked, rolling her eyes as Catherine looked at her in the rearview mirror. '''When are you going to settle down, Abigail?''' she mimicked perfectly. '''I had two babies by the time I was your age. You don't even have a full set of dinnerware.' Jeez! Is she after the two of you the way she's after me? I mean, I'm the *baby,* and she's acting as if I'll be an old maid tomorrow if I don't soon find myself a husband and bear three kids in two years. Is that possible? Oh, wait—twins. It is possible. Son of a gun.''

Catherine smiled at her youngest sister's silliness, then looked at Elly. Her smile faded as she saw tears rising again in Eleanor's eyes. ''Elly? You all right?''

Her sister tried to summon a smile, failing badly. ''Yeah. Yeah, Catherine, I'm all right. Just promise me you'll call Mom off if she starts talking baby bootees, okay? Both of you.''

Knowing her own plans, Catherine quickly agreed. As Abby leaned forward against the back of the front seat once more, to make her own promise to Elly, Catherine thought of the brochures stuffed into her luggage, and wondered how fast she could get rid of Griff Edwards so that she and her father could have a nice long private talk.

Chapter 2

Catherine Parrish was a knockout.

Blue eyes the exact shade of a perfect Vegas sky. Naturally curly honey- and gold-streaked hair whose waves couldn't be hidden even as she'd scraped it all back into a no-nonsense ponytail at her nape. A full, wide mouth that begged to be kissed. Skin with the texture of finest cream.

And that body? Perfect posture, high breasts, long legs only partially hidden beneath her flowered, flirty skirt.

And the best, the absolute best, was that the woman had absolutely no idea that she was gorgeous.

Griff Edwards had met a lot of gorgeous women. A lot. Met them, romanced them, left them. Las Vegas was up to its glittering neck in gorgeous women. But they all knew they were gorgeous, and insisted on acting the part.

Catherine Parrish was as uptight as a virgin, as intimidating as his third-grade teacher, and gave off an aura that warned him she'd be about as touchable as a cactus.

Man, but he loved a challenge!

Griff pulled the Porsche into his reserved spot at the main office of his five-dealership, seventy-five-acre place of business and cut off the engine. Land was expensive in Vegas, but his had come down to him through his great-grandfather, and he'd made the best use of it, at least to his own mind. Too far off the Strip to consider going into the casino business, he'd found himself another gamble. Cars. Lots and lots of cars.

You wanted American made? Griff Edwards had American made. You wanted a foreign import? Griff Edwards was your man. New cars, used cars. Trucks. Suburban utility vehicles. From soup to nuts, from *A* to *Z*, from three-owner beaters to the top of the automobile food chain, if Griff Edwards didn't have it, hey, you probably didn't want it anyway.

He stepped away from the Porsche, put his hands on his hips, spread his legs and surveyed his domain. He had to squint, even behind his sunglasses, as the Vegas sun glinted off row after row of windshields. He listened to the wind slapping at miles of plastic red, white and blue banners, heard the squawk of the loudspeaker calling salesmen to the phones. He took a deep breath of desert air mixed with the smell of grease, exhaust and fresh paint. And money. The air was full of money.

Okay. So he was proud of all he'd accomplished. Damn proud. He'd put in his share of eighty-hour weeks, had even slept on the battered couch in his first office inside a used trailer because he hadn't been able to afford to hire enough salesmen to cover each shift. He'd lived on stale doughnuts and bad coffee and done every job from mechanic to lot boy, even washing the car he'd just sold before the customer claimed it.

And he'd found his own gold mine without having to buy a shovel. Built his own fortune without a single craps table or slot machine.

So, yeah. He'd okayed the billboards. Posed for the billboards. He'd put his face right out there with the public, put a face to the name, let his confident smile become the first thing his customers would think of when they were considering making a purchase, plunking down their hard-earned cash for the second most expensive buy they'd ever make.

And Catherine Parrish had turned up her fine, aristocratic nose at his latest, most lucrative advertising campaign, even asked him *why* he'd done it.

"Obviously not to impress her," Griff muttered. He rubbed at the back of his neck, then turned toward his office as he heard his name being called over the squawk box, wondering just what might impress Ms. Catherine Parrish.

Catherine stepped out of the bathroom, her body wrapped in one huge bath towel, her wet hair hidden inside a smaller towel she'd fashioned into a make-shift turban.

She felt good again, clean again after the long flight from Allentown that had included a stopover in Detroit. She'd scrubbed and conditioned her hair, then drizzled baby oil over her still-wet body before toweling herself dry. She loved the soft feel of her skin after the baby oil treatments, loved the smell of the oil even better.

The towel dropped onto the carpet as Catherine chose fresh underwear, deciding on a soft beige silk bra and matching panties she'd bought in her most recent dash through the local mall. Some people indulged themselves with upscale clothing or fancy jewelry. Catherine bought underwear. Scads of it.

She slipped her arms into an ankle-length, flowered bathrobe and glared into the closet. Maybe she should have taken time to buy at least a few new clothes. Something with a little dash, a little flair. Not the long cotton dresses, flowered skirts and summer sweaters she'd worn the last two months of school. They were all so…so…so unlike anything Griff Edwards would like.

Just the thought had Catherine reaching out blindly for the closest hanger, and she was soon dressed in pantyhose, flat sandals, and a high-waisted, A-line, tan-on-tan flowered dress with cap sleeves, a modest scoop neckline, and a hem that skimmed her ankles.

Sexy as a bran muffin, that was Catherine Parrish.

Which left her with her hair, now rapidly drying beneath the makeshift turban. Not that it mattered. No matter what she did with the shoulder-length dark blond hair, it curled its own way, went where it wanted, all ringlets and corkscrews, unless she ruthlessly captured the entire thick, heavy mop of it in an elastic band.

She blew at the tousled mop with her hair dryer and was just pushing one heavy corkscrewed lock out of her eyes as she rummaged through the top drawer for an elastic band when her mother bounced into the room.

"Oh, don't do that, darling," Susie protested as she sat in the middle of the single bed, her legs crossed in front of her like a child, her petite body so full of energy she made Catherine rethink her earlier decision not to take a nap. "You were going to hide all that lovely, shining glory in a rubber band, weren't you?" She wrinkled up her small, pert nose. "Definitely, definitely a no, my sweet. Especially with that handsome Griff Edwards coming to dinner." She rolled her eyes mischievously. "Goodness, what a hunk!"

Catherine rolled her eyes as well, not at all mischievously, but gave up her search for an elastic band. If her mother wanted her to look like Shirley Temple, she'd look like Shirley Temple. But she'd be damned if she'd tap dance!

"Mom," she said, perching herself on the end of the bed as she pushed her hair out of her face once more, "Dad is a hunk. Harrison Ford is a hunk. Sean Connery is a hunk, and he's older than God. Griff Edwards is—" she hesitated, searching her brain for a good description "—well, he's a hot-fudge sundae."

Susie blinked. "A hot-fudge sundae? What on earth does that mean?"

"I'm not sure," Catherine admitted. "I guess it's that he might look really good, taste really good, but he'll soon be gone and all you're left with is a memory and another five pounds you didn't need."

Susie laughed, gave her oldest daughter's shoulder a friendly poke. "You could use another five pounds, darling, although you look just fine in that dress. Rather like a butterscotch sundae, now that I think of it. And Abby tells me Griff looked quite hungry when he looked at you.''

Making a mental note to strangle her baby sister, Catherine only sighed, began picking at her skirt. ''He's not my type.''

''Not your type? Well, my goodness, Catherine, I would have thought he's every girl's type. I mean, I've seen the billboards, and the television ads. He's handsome as sin, and with a smile that could corrupt an angel. What's not to like?''

''Well, that's it, then, isn't it?'' Catherine said brightly, too brightly. ''I'm here for two months, just long enough to have a mad, wild fling with a Las Vegas Adonis. Better yet, I have my mother's blessing. It's not every girl who can say that, right? What do you think, Mom? Should I seduce him during the main course, or wait until after dessert?''

''After dessert, I think,'' Susie responded, unruffled by her daughter's sarcasm. She stood up, dropped a kiss on Catherine's cheek, and headed out of the room, stopping at the door to add, ''And, between the two of you, darling, I'd have the most deliciously *beautiful* grandchildren.''

''Yeah, right,'' Catherine grumbled as the door closed behind her mother. ''Don't hold your breath.''

She sighed, stood and picked up her suitcase, laying it on top of the bed. She'd unpacked two hours earlier, but she'd kept the brochures firmly zipped inside the case. Not that her mother was the peeking and poking around sort, but Catherine wasn't going to take any chances.

She unzipped the suitcase and took out the brochures, fanning them on the bedspread with the titles face-up. ''Artificial Insemination: A Practical

Choice." "A Consumer's Guide to Artificial Insemination." "Choosing Donor Sperm." "Insemination
Services: Southwestern United States."

Catherine gathered up the brochures as she heard
footsteps coming down the hallway, knowing either
of her sisters could come barging into her bedroom
without so much as a single knock or even a quick
"May I come in?" She shoved them back into the
suitcase, zipped it closed, placed it back in the corner.

And then Catherine Parrish sat back down on the
bed, hearing her mother's voice repeating inside her
head: *And, between the two of you, darling, I'd have
the most deliciously* beautiful *grandchildren.*

"No," she told herself firmly. "I couldn't do that.
I wouldn't do that. It would be...dishonest."

But he had found her attractive. He'd as much as
told her so. Even Elly and Abby had noticed.

Catherine stood up, walked over to the mirror that
hung above the dresser, turned her head this way and
that, pushed at her hair, the mass of tumbling curls
that made her look somehow younger, almost touchable. Not at all like a spinsterish, seventh-grade
teacher rapidly approaching her thirtieth birthday.

"No," she repeated, staring at her own reflection
as she lifted her hair with both hands, filling her head
with curls, exposing the long line of her throat. "I
just couldn't do it. Not even to Mr. Humongous Ego.
It simply wouldn't be right. Or fair." She dropped
her hands to her sides, watched her curls fall against
her neck, turning her back into Shirley Temple about
to take off on the "Good Ship Lollipop." "Or possible," she ended, sighing as her mother reentered the
room. "Forgot something?" she asked as Susie
plunked herself down on the bed once more.

"Yes," Susie said, her sigh twice as heartfelt as Catherine's had been. "I forgot that I've raised a trio of very stubborn daughters. You will leave your hair down tonight, won't you, darling? I'd hate to think I struck out with all three of you."

Catherine laughed out loud. Lord, but her mother was cute. Fifty years old, with the look of a woman a third her age. Bubbly, bouncy, sometimes bordering on the precocious. And yet every inch the perfect mother. The rambling colonial house in Allentown had been filled with love and laughter and every neighborhood kid who could find an excuse to sit at Susie Parrish's kitchen table and have her fuss over them. As the girls grew, that kitchen table had been the scene of more parties, more laughter, more tears, more broken hearts, more late-night secrets than any other ten houses on the block.

There had been, in fact, times when Catherine had been jealous of her mother, believing her friends courted her only so that she'd bring them home to Susie, who bandaged their knees, fed their bellies and listened to their sorrows and triumphs.

Susie Parrish was a born mother, a born listener, a woman with a heart large enough to love the entire world.

And she was a conniving, organizing, suggestive, persuasive, managing little Napoleon—it was just that she hid her iron hand inside a velvet glove.

"What's the matter, Mom," Catherine said now, sitting down beside Susie, laying a comforting arm over her shoulders. "The little beggars won't see that you know what's best for them? Imagine that."

"Oh, Abby's not so bad," Susie said, releasing her breath on a sigh. "She says she'll think about it, con-

sider it. She says, yeah, that sounds like a good idea,
I can't imagine why I didn't think of it myself. And
then she goes off whistling, blithely forgetting every
word I've said."

"You want her to move back to Vegas, don't
you?"

Susie pulled away from Catherine, looked up at
her—it was the very devil, finding yourself five
inches taller than your own mother. "Would that be
so terrible? I mean, it's wonderful that she's traveled
so much, seen so much of the world. It's wonderful
that she has the sort of career that allows her to be
wherever she wants to be."

"So?"

"So," Susie said, getting up, beginning to pace,
"that's all well and good. For a while. But a person
needs to put down roots, too. At least establish some
sort of home base. Catherine, do you know that
Grandmother Parrish's dining room set is stored in a
warehouse in Seattle? She *thinks!* She isn't sure." She
threw out her hands in disgust. "I've raised a grasshopper. Yes, that's it—I've raised a *grasshopper!* She
doesn't think more than a single day ahead, doesn't
plan, doesn't even consider the future."

"You want me to have a talk with her?" Catherine
asked, praying her mother said no.

Susie shook her head, her blond curls, so like her
youngest daughter's, dancing around her head. "Your
father promised to do it, after the wedding." She
looked at Catherine, smiled. "He agreed in exchange
for not having to wear a stand-up collar with his tuxedo. Poor man. As if I'd want to see him in one of
those awful, starched things."

Catherine uncoiled her long legs from the bed,

stood up and gave her mother a quick hug and kiss. "I can only aspire to be as conniving as you are, Mom. My hat's off to you, even as my sympathies are with Dad. Now, what did Elly say to upset you?"

Susie drifted over to the dresser, picked up Catherine's brush, ran her thumb across the bristles. "I think you already know," she said quietly. "I told you I was concerned, when I phoned you last week, but I wasn't sure until the phone rang last night and Rob was on the other end." She turned away from the dresser, looked at Catherine, tears standing in her expressive green eyes. "He's devastated, Catherine. Absolutely devastated. He hadn't had the slightest idea Elly was coming here until he found her note, then realized that she'd taken every stitch of clothing with her."

Catherine sank back onto the edge of the bed. "Oh, brother. I knew it was bad, but at least I thought they were *talking* to each other. But if she didn't even tell him she was leaving?" She shook her head. "Do you mean to tell me that Rob had no inkling that anything was wrong?"

"I didn't say that," Susie told her, absently running the brush through her curls. "He knew Elly was unhappy, but he thought it was because they haven't been able to conceive." Her bottom lip trembled as she fought back tears. "I didn't know they were even trying, let alone having trouble—seeing fertility specialists. When I think of how I've been hinting to her about wanting grandchildren? My every word, every phone call, must have broken her heart."

"Ah, Mom," Catherine said, once more rising to gather the smaller woman into her arms. "Don't beat yourself up over this. We all know Elly. She's a sphinx when it comes to talking about herself, always has been. But she's here now, because she needs to be here, needs to be with her family, with her mom. We'll just have to go slow, let Elly work through this in her own way." She put her hands on Susie's shoulders, eased her away so she could look down into her face. "You *can* do that, can't you?"

"It'll probably kill me but, yes, I can do that. I've already talked Rob out of hopping the next plane out of New York. Because you're right, Catherine, as always." She lifted a hand, caressed her oldest daughter's cheek. "My dear, sweet, practical Catherine. At least I can count on you never to do anything impulsive."

Catherine suppressed a wince, then hugged her mother once more. Oh, yeah. That was her, all right. The practical one. The careful one. The one who never did anything impulsively. That's why the brochures were in her suitcase. Because she'd thought and thought, and researched and researched. She weighed the pros, the cons. Made her decision, taken steps to implement her decision.

And then she'd bumped into Griff Edwards. Literally. Would she ever get her mother's tantalizing words out of her head?

between the two of you, darling, I'd have the most deliciously beautiful *grandchildren.*

Griff pulled up in front of the low ranch house that looked much the same as the others on the street, then grinned as he saw the pair of exaggeratedly cross-eyed pink flamingos standing in the front garden.

Okay. He was going to like it here.

He also liked seeing the low-slung red sports car

sandwiched between the white rental car and a top-of-the-line minivan in the driveway. Both Parrish vehicles wore Griff Edwards logos on the trunk. If Catherine had noticed, she was probably still locked up in her room, grinding her teeth.

Griff adjusted his ''Save the Children'' tie and checked the collar of his navy blue blazer before exiting the just-traded Mercedes he'd driven off the lot a half hour earlier. It was one of his favorite perks, test-driving the pre-owned cars of his choice. Pre-owned. Never used. Not when the word following used was Mercedes.

He walked around to open the passenger door and retrieved the bouquet of pink roses and the five-pound box of Godiva chocolates he'd commissioned Betty, his secretary, to purchase for him. Flowers for Catherine, candy for the mother and sisters. They both had seemed good ideas at the time. They still seemed like good ideas, along with the bottle of wine he'd personally selected from his own wine cellar.

Armed with his gifts, Griff strolled up the curving cement path to the wide, covered front porch and juggled bottle and bouquet as he shifted the chocolates under his arm and pressed the doorbell.

The door opened and a tall, ruggedly handsome man in his mid-fifties extended a hand, saying, ''You must be Griff Edwards. I recognize you from your advertisements. I'm Catherine's father, Jim Parrish. Please come in.''

Griff took the man's hand in his and they exchanged a firm, assessing handshake before he crossed the threshold, to see a living room decorated in comfortable Southwestern furniture and to smell the unmistakable aroma of roast beef wafting toward him from the unseen kitchen. He smiled, feeling very much at home. And then Catherine Parrish appeared in the room, her smile tentative, her eyes interested, and he felt his heart pick up a beat.

It had begun. Day One of The Siege.

"Catherine," he said, stepping forward to hand her the roses. "I want to thank you again for inviting me to dinner tonight."

"I didn't invite you," she answered quietly as Jim Parrish walked toward the back of the house, still admiring the bottle of wine Griff had handed him. "Abby invited you. Elly invited you. If it were up to me we'd have exchanged insurance cards and I would never have had to see you again—if I decided to go live in a cave, that is. Oh, and I saw your television ad this afternoon."

"Yes?" Griff inquired, knowing Catherine had made a fatal mistake. Every word she uttered, warning him away, only seemed to draw him closer, make him more interested. It might be perverse, but that's how it seemed to be working.

He followed Catherine into the dining room as she retrieved a vase from the bottom of a large, glass-fronted china cabinet. "Pitiful," she said as she left the dining room, headed for the kitchen he could now see to his left. "Jingles ought to be outlawed, don't you think?"

"You didn't like it?" Griff smiled at Catherine's ramrod-straight backbone as she filled the vase at the sink, jammed the roses into the water with more force than art.

"Do you?" she asked, turning around, leaning against the sink counter. "Cars might rhyme with stars, and deal and steal might go together in some instances—but 'Take my drift, folks, and deal with Griff'? Pitiful!''

"Yeah," Griff agreed, "it is pretty pitiful. But it sells cars, and you can't argue with that."

Her eyelids narrowed. "How can you be sure? How can you be sure your cars don't sell in *spite* of those tacky ads and that juvenile jingle? That maybe, just maybe, people are smarter than you think, and it's the product that they like."

"I like the jingle, personally," Jim Parrish offered as he drifted into the room, then rummaged in a bottom cabinet until he found the ice bucket. "And the slogan. 'Deal here with certitude.' Anyone could have said confidence, or assurance. But certitude? I don't know. It just makes me feel good. Well…yes…well, I'll be going now," he said as he looked at Catherine, who was glaring at him as if he'd just told her he'd always liked Elly and Abby best. "Leave you two kids alone, to get better acquainted. Catherine? We're all outside, on the patio. Join us whenever you want."

Catherine stared daggers at Griff, then stomped past him, the vase in her hands, heading for the living room once more. He followed her with his eyes, admiring her long strides, the way her legs moved so fluidly from the hip, the way she held her head, her shoulders.

He joined her in the living room, sitting down beside her on the green-and-white-checked couch. She stared straight ahead, refusing to acknowledge him. "So, I guess this means we aren't going to be making mad passionate love to each other tonight? Maybe tomorrow night?"

Her shoulders slumped and she turned her head, looked at him. "I'm sorry," she said, smiling slightly.

"I don't know why I was so insulting, so cutting. But I most certainly was, wasn't I?"

"I'm bleeding from about a dozen wounds, but I'll recover," he told her, taking her unresisting hand in his, lifting it to his lips. "Now, do you think you can tell me why you're so upset about my billboards, my television ads?"

She pulled her hand away, not sharply, but she pulled it away nonetheless. Laced her fingers together in her lap, stared at the almost surrealistic painting of Red Rocks hanging on the far wall. "They're why we had the accident today, why I hit your car."

"Come again?"

She looked at him, rolled her eyes in what seemed to be a cross between embarrassment and chagrin. "I was looking at one of those damn billboards of yours," she said with some heat. "One of the million. You do know that you're too handsome for your own good, don't you? Too handsome for *my* good."

Griff sat back, smiled. "Well, that was honest."

"Yes. Yes, it was. Entirely too honest." She stood up, walked across the room to stand in front of the painting. "Being in the automobile business, you're probably more accustomed to deception. Oh! Now I've done it again." She ran her hands through the mass of curls he'd been admiring ever since she walked into the room. "I don't know what's wrong with me. I'm not like this, not at all. But there's something about you, Griff Edwards, something that makes me want to…to…"

"Throw yourself into my arms, kiss me passionately?" he offered, rising from the couch and crossing the room in unhurried strides that hid his increasing interest, his definitely rising passion.

"Toss you out of here on your ear before I do something stupid," she ended for him. "I'm entirely too old to do something stupid."

Griff lifted a hand, stroked her bare arm from the bottom of her cap sleeve to her fingertips. "We're never too old to do something stupid, Catherine. Besides, I see nothing stupid about this, do you?"

He put his hands on her shoulders, turned her toward him, then lowered his mouth onto hers. Lightly. Tentatively. But not without passion. He kissed her once, twice, a third time. He tasted orange juice on her lips, smelled the honey of her hair.

And then he stepped back, watched and waited.

"It…it's a physical attraction," Catherine said at last, her voice small, quiet.

"It would have to be, wouldn't it," Griff agreed, "considering the fact that we know next to nothing about each other. But we can remedy that. Do you think your parents would mind if we skipped dinner, went for a drive?"

Catherine looked tempted. Very tempted. "Oh. Oh, no. We can't do that. Mom's been fussing for hours, and Dad is going to want to corner you and talk about spark plugs or something."

Griff put a finger under her chin, lifted her face to his. "But you want to? Don't you, Cat?"

She pushed his hand away, stepped back a pace. "Yes, damn you, I do want to. God, but you're smug!"

"Confident," he corrected. "There's a difference. And damned attracted to you. Physically attracted to you. I want to know if there's anything else, anything more. I'm telling you this because I stopped playing games in high school. I see what I want, and I go after it. Right now, Cat, I want you. I most definitely want you. It's as simple as that.''

She avoided his eyes. "Nothing's that simple," she said, then cocked her head, looked at him. "You say you want me. I can tell you that I'm interested. You may be straightforward, an up-front sort of person, but how do you know I am? I could be chock-full of ulterior motives."

He smiled, feeling confident, feeling lucky. "Oh, I doubt that, Cat. You'll talk to your parents, tell them we've had a change of plans and won't be joining them for dinner?"

She looked at him for a long time, measuring him, assessing him, examining her own reactions to him. "This is crazy," she said at last, then left him where he stood and walked through the dining room and out onto the patio, toward the sound of voices raised in conversation.

A minute later she was back, still glaring at him as she walked to the front door, opened it. "Well? Are you having second thoughts? God knows I am."

"Never," he said, taking her arm as they walked outside, headed toward the Mercedes parked at the curb. "Relax, Cat, we're going to be just fine."

"Don't call me Cat," she said, looking up at him as she settled into the leather seat, strapped on her seat belt. "Nobody has ever called me Cat."

"Really? Are all the men in your hometown blind?" He closed the door before she could answer, then smiled broadly as he walked around the back of the car, heading for the driver's door. "Oh, Edwards," he congratulated himself, "you're good. Damn, but you're good!"

Chapter 3

Catherine sat back in her chair, looking up at the marvelously created rain forest that surrounded the main entry and cocktail lounge in the Mirage casino. So many trees, so many flowers. An oasis of calm in the middle of the city that played all day, played all night.

"How did you know?" she asked as she picked up her simple glass of white zinfandel, looked across the table at Griff.

"That this would be your favorite spot in town? I didn't. But you did mention Siegfried and Roy this afternoon, so I figured you might have been here before, caught their show. Knowing this place, I also figured that you couldn't have seen it and not liked it. So I took a shot."

"Good aim," Catherine said, watching as one of the hostesses came by, giving Griff an "if you want it, if you want anything at all, all you have to do is ask'' look. He seemed to be oblivious to the very pretty woman. To Catherine, this was as good as a compliment, and she relaxed a little, deciding that maybe she hadn't entirely lost her mind. Griff Edwards was attracted to her. Now if she only knew *why*....

She watched as he leaned his elbows on the table. He'd left his tie and sports jacket in the car and rolled up the sleeves on his white dress shirt, opened the collar button. She found herself gazing at his strong forearms, the ones with the glorious tan and golden hairs.

"Tell me about yourself, Catherine," he asked, looking at her, looking truly interested. "Where you live, what you do. Your hopes, your dreams. Why you're still afraid of me."

"I'm not afraid of you," she answered quickly, too quickly. "I wouldn't be here if I were afraid of you."

His smile had to be illegal in at least three states. "If you say so, Cat."

"And don't call me—" She shook her head. Smiled. What was the use? The man did something to her, really did something to her. "I'm a teacher," she said instead. "Seventh grade, in Allentown, Pennsylvania."

"You're a teacher? Really?" If anything, his smile grew wider, crinkled up the skin beside his dangerous brown eyes. "I should have known," he said, picking up his glass of beer, taking a sip as he looked at her over the rim of the glass. "I've never quite gotten over my crush on Miss Del Vecchio, my third-grade teacher. I used to misbehave, just so she'd notice me, maybe keep me after school to clap erasers."

"Timmy Smithers," Catherine said, returning his smile, relaxing yet another notch.

"Who?"

"Oh, nothing. It's just that there's at least one in every class. I'll bet Miss Del Vecchio still remembers you, too."

"Yeah, she does. Except she's Mrs. Ruggerio now, and I just sold a car to her for her sixteen-year-old. Needless to say, she got a very good deal. After all, the woman did teach me long division."

"Timmy Smithers will probably be making the license plate for my car in ten years—from prison—if he doesn't straighten up. Either that, or he'll be the youngest state representative for Pennsylvania," Catherine said, her voice full of affection for her most fractious, yet most promising student of the past year.

"Yes, Pennsylvania," Griff said, drawing the conversation back to her. "Have you lived there long?"

"All my life, actually," she answered, knowing that must sound incredibly dull and boring. "We were raised there, my sisters and I, and then Elly took off for Las Vegas and a career in dancing, and Mom and Dad visited, fell in love with the desert, and that was that. Dad's got a family practice here now—he's a doctor, you know—and they plan to retire here in a few years. Elly lives in New York now, with her husband, and Abby lives wherever her latest whim takes her. I'm the only one who stayed behind. No spirit of adventure, I guess."

Griff reached out a hand, took hold of hers. "None?" he asked, his voice soft, intimate. He stroked his thumb across her palm. "You're here with me, aren't you?"

"You know," she said honestly, even as her ears

began to buzz, "if you want me to stop being nervous you're really going to have to stop doing that."

His smile bordered on evil, except that his eyes were dancing. "Doing what?"

Catherine was getting a slight crick in her neck, but she didn't mind. She loved the Freemont Street Experience, watching the canopy over the downtown street light up, dance, blast off, swing, go a little country, a little rock and roll. The music was perfect, the computer images fantastic as they appeared above her head.

And Griff was holding her hand. That was enough to make anyone dizzy.

He'd been holding her hand all night. He'd held her hand as they'd walked through the rest of the Mirage, made faces at Siegfried and Roy's famous white tigers who yawned and stretched behind thick glass, in an environment fit for jungle royalty. He was still holding her hand as they'd stood outside the Treasure Island casino, watching as an English man-of-war sailed into view and the pirates prepared to do battle.

She had been faintly disappointed when he'd let go of her long enough for them to grab a makeshift dinner out of samplings from a chili contest held right here, on Freemont Street.

The last space ship flew down the Freemont Street canopy as the last notes of music died away and the neon lights blinked back on over each casino, turning night back into day. Griff let go of her hand, but only so that he could slip his arm around her waist, turn her slightly into him so that her head pressed against his shoulder as they began walking once more.

He smelled of soap, and aftershave, and slightly of chili sauce, and Catherine felt herself falling in step with his strides, at peace with herself, in love with the world. She slipped her arm around his waist, the move feeling natural, if not quite safe.

"This is nice," she told him as they walked slowly, allowing the multitude of eager gamblers carrying plastic buckets of quarters to hurry past them, as mothers pushing strollers and fathers carrying sleepy toddlers wended their way back to their rental cars and resort hotels after the free downtown show. "And it could be any time, couldn't it? I mean, I know it's after eleven, but it's as if there's no time here. No problems, no worries, no reason to go to bed early, get up even earlier. Las Vegas is its own world. A fantasy land."

"It's a lot more than that, Catherine, although most people who come here on vacation don't have the time to see what I see, what your parents saw. This," he said, gesturing with his free hand, "well, this is the playground. But there's a lot more. There's a reason we're one of the fastest-growing cities in the country, and the jobs provided by the casinos and hotels are only one small part of it. This is a good town, a family town."

She looked up at him, saw his serious expression. "Planning on running for mayor, are you? Anything you can do to get your mug on a billboard, huh?" she teased, earning herself a grin and quick squeeze of his arm before he steered her toward the doors leading into the Golden Nugget Casino.

"Just for that, young lady," he said, holding open the door for her, so that the sound of slot machines either being fed or disgorging coins came out to meet

her, "I should let you go home without experiencing
the very best treat in all of Vegas."

Catherine stopped just inside the door, looked
around, saw the oversize slot machine just to her left.
Oversize? That was an understatement. The thing was
huge! "This?" she asked, watching as a man pulled
on the large lever with both hands, then stepped back
to watch the four tremendous reels spin around, settle
into place one by one. He couldn't have won, because
he just shook his head, laughed at something the
woman with him said, then walked away.

Catherine had never been attracted to gambling, but
this didn't seem like gambling. The machine looked
like a giant's toy, and appeared to be a whole lot of
fun. "Is this what you meant? May I try it?"

Griff grinned down at her. "Sure, why not," he
said, reaching into his pocket and pulling out a folded
wad of bills.

"Oh, no," she said, reaching into her purse. "I'll
pay for my own vices, thank you."

He seemed ready to protest, then replaced the bills
and waved her toward the slot machine. "Don't we
all, Cat?" he said, then took the twenty-dollar bill
from her and fed it into the machine. "You have to
play three coins at a time to win the jackpot," he told
her, then laughed out loud as she felt her eyes growing wide in her head.

"Three dollars at a time?" She couldn't help it,
she'd actually gasped out the question. "That's ob-
scene!"

"Yeah," he said, giving one of her spiral curls a
gentle tug, "you're a schoolmarm all right. Tell you
what, Catherine, I'll put in a twenty myself, increase

our odds a little with more plays, and then we can split the winnings.''

Catherine noticed that a small group of people had stopped to watch the big reels go around, and she didn't really care to be part of a show, which she would be if she protested Griff's idea. "All right," she said reluctantly, then stood by while he fed yet another twenty dollars into the machine. "What do I do now?''

Griff reached around her and pressed the lit button three times. "There you go. Now say the magic words and pull the lever.''

She stepped forward, took hold of the huge, black ball-topped lever with both hands, then stopped, looked at him over her shoulder. "Magic words?'' When she saw his unholy grin, she could feel her cheeks turning pink with embarrassment. "Oh, very funny. I hope Miss Del Vecchio had you clapping erasers every day of the school year.''

And then she pulled the lever, stepped back, and watched the reels spin. And stop, one by one.

Nothing. No bells went off, no whistles split the air, no cheers were heard from the crowd. Nothing.

"This is supposed to be fun?'' she asked incredulously, punching the lit button three times, watching as the coin counter on the machine dropped to thirty-four.

"You didn't use enough body English,'' Griff explained, his expression now one of complete innocence. "One more gold bar and we would have won ten bucks. Try to do better this time, okay?''

Aware of the crowd that still stood there, watching, listening, Catherine gritted her teeth and gave the lever another pull.

Nothing. She hit the button again, and the coin counter blinked onto thirty-one coins. No. Not coins. Dollars. She'd just spent nine dollars in less than two minutes. "You pull the lever this time," she told Griff, backing away from the machine as if it had just devoured her life's savings and had begun greedily nibbling at her 401K plan.

"Only if you give me a kiss for luck."

Catherine looked at the dozen or so interested spectators, some there to watch, some there to patiently wait their turn to pull the lever on the ridiculously huge machine. "You're kidding, right?"

"Nope," he said brightly, waggling his eyebrows at her in a way that could goad a Pennsylvania Quaker to violence.

"Oh, kiss him, honey," someone called out from the crowd. "Nobody's looking. Except us of course."

Everyone laughed, including Catherine, who finally saw the ridiculousness in the entire situation. This was Vegas, that was a slot machine and, damn it, it was time to let her hair down in more ways than one, have herself some fun. She held out her arms to Griff, said, "C'mere, big boy."

Griff Edwards was nothing if not obedient, nothing if not a showman. A man so sure of himself that he could plaster his face from one end of Las Vegas to the other couldn't possibly know the meaning of the word *insecure. Flamboyant,* however, he knew. In spades.

The next thing Catherine knew, she was in Griff's arms, being bent backward over his arm so that her hands came up to grip his shoulders, her right leg lifted instinctively so that she could keep her balance, and she was being thoroughly—very thoroughly—kissed.

People should always smile when they kiss, a small voice said from somewhere in the back of her head. Curved lips were happy lips, tasty lips, exciting lips. Why, she even giggled as Griff all but mashed their mouths together, making silly grunting noises as he stole her breath, stole her heart.

Stole her heart? Did she really just think that?

Somehow, as the shock of what had just happened began to hit her, Catherine was standing on her own once more, her lips throbbing, her heart pounding, and Griff was taking a silly, elaborate bow as the crowd around them clapped and hooted in appreciation.

She was going to kill him, she decided as she pushed her ridiculous curls out of her eyes, glared at his bent back. Definitely. The man deserved to die. Slowly. And then she smiled, relaxed, decided that a temporary delicious madness was definitely an option in Las Vegas. But he still had to die, damn it. Maybe she'd kiss him to death....

Griff turned, blew her a kiss, then stepped forward, rubbing his hands together as he faced the slot machine. He pulled the lever, stepped back, slid his arm around her waist. Waited.

The first reel stopped with some sort of symbol positioning itself right on the line drawn across the center of the glass in front the reels. The second reel repeated the action of the first.

Catherine felt her knees bend as Griff pulled her into some sort of weaving, bouncing motion that she supposed was the requisite body English for making the third reel match up with the other two.

It worked.

Now only the fourth reel was spinning, slowing. The crowd around them grew quiet and the reel kept moving, dragging out the agony of waiting until Catherine at last understood the appeal to be found in anticipating a run of good luck, a jackpot.

And then it happened. The fourth reel stopped, a lovely looking black and gold symbol sliding neatly into place, and the bells began to ring. The crowd cheered.

And then Griff Edwards kissed her until she began to believe not just in good luck, but in small miracles as well.

Catherine watched the pile of bills growing in front of her as Griff doled them out—one for him, one for her. She couldn't believe it, couldn't comprehend quite how it had happened, but that didn't mean she didn't fold the stack of bills and slide them into her purse.

"I'll never gamble again," she said, sitting back in her chair in the Carson Street Café inside the Golden Nugget. "I mean, why try, when I could never possibly top this?"

"You suppose you'll be able to wipe that grin off your face before Christmas?" Griff asked, pocketing his share of their winnings.

She propped her elbows on the table, grinned at him. "Nope. And I don't see you sitting there all sophisticated and jaded, either. Was that your first jackpot?"

He reached across the table, took her hand in his. "Nope. My second of the day, actually," he said quietly, then kissed her palm.

She pulled her hand free, folded both her hands in her lap.

"You're right, Cat," he said, settling back in his own chair. "I'm going too fast. Sorry." Then he brightened, a man who found it impossible to nurse a sad thought. "Are you ready for my surprise?"

"Surprise?" Catherine shook her head, not understanding. "Oh, wait. You did bring me into this place to show me something, didn't you? I forgot. What is it?"

The waiter stepped up to the table and Griff smiled up at him, waving away his offer of menus. "Two hot-fudge sundaes, please," he said with a typical Griff Edwards smile, the one he used to dazzle both sexes, and probably little children and dogs. And cats. The man could probably charm Siegfried and Roy's tigers into believing they were domestic cats. "Heavy on the fudge, okay?" Then he turned back to Catherine, who was having a very difficult time keeping herself from running out of the cafe as quickly as her legs could carry her.

"Hot-fudge sundaes?" she asked, all but squeaked, remembering what she'd said to her mother earlier. "That's your surprise?"

"It worked didn't it? Because you sure do look surprised. They make the best sundae in Las Vegas right here. I try to limit myself to one a month, but tonight's a special occasion."

"A special occasion?" Catherine parroted, wishing her ears would stop pounding as her heart beat inside them, drumming out a warning to her brain. "How so?"

"Then I'm wrong? You don't feel what I feel? That physical attraction we both admitted to earlier? The attraction I felt the moment you stepped out of your car, looking mad as hell and more delicious than honey on vanilla?''

"Butterscotch," Catherine mumbled under her breath, then gave herself a mental shake as the waiter placed two huge hot-fudge sundaes in front of them. "You were right earlier, Griff," she told him. "This is going too fast. We're going too fast. I don't know a thing about you—or you about me. Not really. If I were sitting in front of me in class, I'd be hearing my yearly warning about acting first and only thinking later."

Griff dipped his spoon into the small mountain of whipped cream in front of him, then offered it to Catherine. She opened her mouth without protest, felt the cool cream begin to melt on her tongue. "Do we really want to think now, Cat? I sure as hell know I don't.''

It had been the longest night of her life. The shortest. The best. The worst. The most magical. The most frightening.

And now it was over.

The Mercedes was parked in front of her parents' house once more, its engine cut, the silence of the night surrounding Catherine and Griff as she laid her hand on the door handle, only to find she didn't have the strength to activate it.

"I had fun tonight," she said lamely, staring out the windshield, looking at the stars that seemed so much brighter here in Nevada than they did in the Pennsylvania sky. Maybe it was the tears in her eyes, the tears she was determined not to shed, that made those stars so bright, so glittering.

"I'm glad, and sorry it's over," Griff said from five hundred miles away, but not so far that she couldn't hear a tinge of real regret in his voice.

"Look," she said impulsively, turning on the seat, facing him head-on, facing his perfect profile, seeing the lock of hair she'd dared to brush from his forehead more than once that night. "This isn't fair. Not to either of us. It's all been too soon, too sudden. Too much. For all I know, you could be the greatest playboy of the Western world, and for all you know I could be a scheming, manipulating woman with an agenda all my own."

He laid a hand on her arm, sent shivers of desire racing through her body with the simple gesture. "A seventh-grade teacher with a scheming, manipulating agenda? That's a bit of a reach, don't you think, Cat?"

"Why?" she countered, trying to find refuge in anger. "Don't you think I'm capable of it?"

He raised his hands to her shoulders, drew her close, moved toward her at the same time. "No, Catherine, I do not. Any more than you believe I'm the greatest playboy of the Western world. Just like you know now—at least I hope you know—that having my face stuck all over Las Vegas is an advertising campaign, not a massive ego trip."

"I know," she said, sighing. "I'll never mention it again, promise." Although, she knew, she'd probably go mad for the next two months, seeing his face everywhere she looked. Because, after tonight, she would not, could not, see Griff Edwards in the flesh again. He was just too dangerous.

He released her shoulders, turned away. "Come on. I'll walk you to the door."

She sat on the front seat, furious with herself for feeling so disappointed that he hadn't tried to kiss her again, hadn't taken a quick shot at a little mindless seduction. Had she been right? Was that all he'd wanted? And now, now that she'd put on the brakes a little, had he lost interest, given up?

She took his offered hand as he helped her out of the car, then walked ahead of him up the narrow cement walkway, only turning to him once they were both standing on the porch. Here, with the twin porch lights shining down on them, she could see his expression, read it as one of confidence only slightly mingled with humor. "What?" she said, stepping back a pace.

"You're angry that I didn't kiss you back there, in the car," he said, putting his hands on either side of her waist, easing closer to her. "Aren't you?"

"I am not!"

"Liar," he said quietly, lowering his head, blocking out the porch light behind him, blocking out all common sense as she tasted the sweetness of hot-fudge sundae on his lips. He kissed her lightly, teasingly. Once. Twice. A third time. The man had the short, seductive kiss down to a science.

"I could really learn to hate you," she said, looking into his eyes, drowning in his eyes. "I never should have admitted I was attracted to you. You don't play fair."

"A good salesman uses every advantage," he said, bending to kiss her throat, run the tip of his tongue tantalizingly along its length. "I pride myself on being a very good salesman." His voice dropped to a husky whisper as he breathed into her ear. "Tomorrow? We'll have the whole day. We can do tourist things. Tour Red Rocks. Drive out to see the dam. Go to my house and make wild, passionate love to each other until we figure out what the hell's going on between the two of us.''

It would be easy, so easy. So wrong.

Because Griff Edwards was the sort of man who would make a great lover, Catherine was sure of it. He wasn't, she was equally sure, the sort of man who would ever be content to have skateboards in his foyer or a basketball hoop on the side of his driveway. She couldn't see him with baby drool on his shoulder or a soggy toddler on his lap.

He was one of those larger-than-life creatures. Too handsome. Too rich. Too absolutely wonderful.

Too wonderful to take advantage of, to *use*.

''I...I have to go in now. Truly.'' Catherine stepped back, avoiding Griff's suddenly confused gaze. She dug in her purse for her key. ''Tomorrow,'' she said quickly, inserting the key in the door. ''Call me tomorrow.''

Two heartbeats later she leaned against the closed door, taking in air in deep, painful gulps, knowing she'd just thrown away her mother's big chance for the best-looking grandchild in the whole world.

''Hello, darling.''

''Mom?'' Catherine said, squinting until her eyes adjusted to the dim light shining from the kitchen. There she was, sitting on the couch, her legs drawn up beneath a pink, ruffled bathrobe that would have looked silly on anyone else Susie's age, but looked great on her. ''It's after two. What are you doing up?''

''Drinking decaffeinated tea and waiting for you,'' Susie answered easily, patting the space next to her so that Catherine had no choice but to join her on the couch. "Did you have a nice time?"

"Yeah," Catherine answered quickly, too quickly. "Yeah, I did. He's a nice man."

"That's what your father said. I, of course, didn't get the chance to meet him, not that I'm complaining. I trust your father's judgment. You'll be seeing him again, of course."

"No—yes—oh, damn it, Mom, what answer do you want? I know you haven't been sitting here in the dark just in the hope I'd invite Griff in for a nightcap so that you could inspect him for yourself."

Susie patted her daughter's knee. "You're right, darling, I haven't. But it hasn't been an easy evening around here one way or the other, and I didn't want my tossing and turning to wake Dad, as he's on call early tomorrow at the hospital."

"Elly?" Catherine asked, immediately concerned for her sister. "What happened? Did Rob call again? You warned him away for now—didn't he have the sense to listen to you?"

"Rob didn't call. But Elly and I did have a long talk, a rather unhappy talk. The poor thing is miserable, and won't listen to reason."

Catherine smiled in the dimly lit room. "She won't listen to *you,* you mean."

Susie Parrish shrugged her slim shoulders. "Same thing," she said, gifting her daughter with the ghost of a smile. "Five minutes, Catherine. That's all those two need. Five minutes of sitting down, *listening* to each other." She gave out a heartfelt sigh. "But maybe Elly's right. First they both need to be alone for a while, think things out. I'm going to give her a few weeks for that, good mother that I am. But after that, well, I'm not making any promises."

"You're the best," Catherine said, leaning over to kiss her mother's cheek.

"And then there's Abby," Susie went on, having accepted Catherine's praise as only reasonable. "How does she do it? Dragging computer and fax and all sorts of things around with her—along with some of the most outlandish clothing I've ever seen. And she's much too friendly and trusting for her own good. She's a beautiful girl, Catherine. A beautiful girl living alone, traveling alone, believing every stranger is a friend she just hasn't met yet." She sighed again. "I can't help it. I worry about her."

"Abby's got a guardian angel hovering over her, Mom, and always has. She'll be all right. Even if she is slightly nuts," Catherine ended on a smile.

"That's one thing you've never been, Catherine. Not that Abby's nuts—such a crude word. You've always been my stable one, my level-headed, dependable child. You never gave me a moment's worry. I didn't like leaving you behind in Allentown when we moved out here, but I knew you'd be all right."

"Because I'm sensible," Catherine said dully, thinking of how uncharacteristically *unsensible* she'd been earlier that night, how damnably sensible she'd been at the end of it. "Yeah, Mom, that's me all over, isn't it? I don't even have a nickname. Abby does, Elly does. But not me. No one has ever called me Cathy, or Cath…or Cat. I wonder why. Probably because I'm just so damn sensible, huh? You know, Mom, that's almost depressing."

"Really? Don't you like being sensible, darling?"

"I did, I used to," Catherine answered slowly.

"Maybe I'm just having my rebellious teenage years a little late, that's all, trying to cram a little life into my life before I stumble into middle-age."

"Could be, could be," Susie said, taking up Catherine's hand, pressing it against her cheek. "Darling, there's something we have to talk about, all right?"

Catherine was suddenly all attention, her nerves turning on to full alert. "What is it? Is it Dad? You? Are one of you ill?"

"My, you *do* think like an old woman, don't you, darling?" Susie smiled, rather sadly. "But it's not us, Catherine. It's you."

Catherine sat very still, listened very closely, because her mother's voice sounded so reluctant, yet so very determined to be heard.

"I was in your room earlier, darling," she began slowly, and Catherine's heart immediately skipped several beats. "You're always very neat and orderly, but I wanted to bring you some fresh towels and, well, I saw your suitcase standing in the corner and thought I'd just lift it onto the shelf in the closet. Do I need to go on?"

Catherine could only nod, her tongue stuck to the roof of her mouth, her stomach having relocated itself to somewhere in the region of her ankles.

"I heard something slide inside the suitcase as I lifted it, and thought you'd missed unpacking something. A book. A magazine." Susie's hands fluttered in the air a moment, resettled in her lap. "So I opened the suitcase."

"Oh, God." Catherine closed her eyes.

"Oh, God? Then you are serious about this, aren't you, Catherine? And it's all my fault!"

Catherine roused from her mingled anger and anguish. This wasn't how she'd planned to let her mother know what she was about to do. "What? How is this *your* fault?"

Susie moved on the cushions, faced her daughter head-on. "Because I'm the one who's been nagging and hinting—nagging mostly, I suppose—telling you girls how much I want grandchildren. Elly's separated from her husband because of it—at least partially because of it. You're contemplating—well, you know what you're contemplating. Difficult as it is to believe, Abby seems to be the only one of the three of you who isn't jumping off the cliff I put in front of you all with my stupid, selfish wish to have a few grandchildren to spoil in my old age."

"Oh, Mom," Catherine said, gathering her mother close, kissing her forehead. Comforting her, as her mother had comforted her years ago. "Elly's been married for several years, long enough to have wanted babies without you putting the idea into her head. And I'm twenty-eight, Mom, certainly old enough to make my own choices, my own decisions. I want a baby for me. If that gives you a grandchild, hey, that's a bonus, and one very lucky grandchild. But I'm doing this for me. Honest."

Susie pulled a tissue from her pocket, wiped at her eyes. "Are you sure? Really, really sure?"

Catherine nodded. "Completely and absolutely."

"And...and meeting someone like Griff Edwards hasn't changed your mind, made you realize that you're a sweet, wonderful, desirable girl who should have men falling over themselves to marry you? Have you really given up on finding a man who loves you and having babies the old-fashioned way?"

Catherine put her fingertips to her temples, rubbed

small, tight circles against her skin. "I can't count on that, Mom. I don't even want to. Besides, I wouldn't sleep with a man, marry a man, just so that he could give me babies."

Catherine really wanted to believe that. Had believed that, through all her years of dating, even through the one fairly serious relationship she'd had three years earlier and finally broken off, knowing it hadn't been right for her. She was more than willing to fashion a life without a man in it, had begun to believe she wasn't cut out to love a man, cut out for marriage and the conventional Happily Ever After.

So why did she have to run into Griff Edwards? Why did he have to make her heart go wild and mushy at the same time? Why did she only have to close her eyes to see his smile, taste his mouth on hers...and want more, so much more? In only one night, she already knew that calling what she felt for him physical attraction was not an explanation. It was an excuse.

"No, of course you wouldn't try to use a man, do anything remotely like that," Susie was saying, patting Catherine's knee once more as she stood up, stretched. "However, if you were to unexpectedly stumble onto someone wonderful, well, wouldn't that be nice? And your father says that Griff Edwards couldn't seem to be able to wait to get you alone. That's a determined man, a confident man. He'd have to be, to be so successful at such a young age. And he's attracted, Catherine. I'm sure of it."

Catherine looked up at her mother, her fingertips still pressing against her throbbing temples. "We've had one casual date and you're hearing wedding bells? I thought you might have given up on suggesting how we all run our lives, Mom. I guess not, huh?''

Catherine felt herself being pulled against her mother's stomach, her head cradled in her mother's loving arms. ''I'm not going to try to push you into anything you don't want, anything that doesn't happen naturally, on its own. At the same time, darling, I don't want to see you rush into this single motherhood thing, either, no matter how well you've researched it, no matter how reasonable and logical it may seem to you now. I want you to talk to Dad about it, I want you to listen to him because he's a doctor, because he loves you. I just want you to promise you'll think about all of this a little while longer, not do anything you might regret a month from now, two months from now. Not because of Griff Edwards and one, as you call it, casual date. Because I love you. All right?''

Catherine disengaged herself from her mother's embrace, stood up, laid her arm around Susie's shoulders as the two of them walked toward the hallway leading to the bedrooms. ''All right, Mom,'' she heard herself say, knowing she'd go to bed tonight thinking about Griff's call tomorrow. About when it would come. About if it would come. ''I'll talk to Dad. I promise.''

They stopped outside Catherine's bedroom door and kissed good-night. She was just opening her door when her mother said in that sweetly suggestive voice Jim Parrish had learned to respect, ''You know, darling, your father proposed to me only a week after we met.''

''Meaning?'' Catherine asked, turning her head to glare at her mother.

"Meaning nothing at all," Susie said brightly. "Except maybe that you haven't got a bit of lipstick on, and you came home tonight looking thoroughly kissed and deliciously confused. Well, good night, darling. Happy dreams."

Chapter 4

The first excuse had been her having to tag along with her sisters all day as their mother hunted down the perfect dress for her renewal of vows ceremony.

Griff had bought that one.

He'd sent Catherine a dozen pink roses that day.

The second excuse had been that she'd promised to help her father clean the pool.

That one had been a little iffy.

He'd doubled his rose order, added a box of double-dipped, chocolate-covered cherries.

The third excuse had been that, well, she was tired from all that shopping and pool skimming.

It was a nice try, but Griff hadn't gotten to the top of the heap by not recognizing a stall when he saw it. The time had come for a little wheeling and dealing.

He showed up on the Parrish front porch before noon on the third day, holding four choice tickets for that night's show at the MGM Grand, tickets they'd been awarding with each new-car purchase at the dealership.

"Oh, wow—thank you! What a great idea, what a treat!" Abby exclaimed as she jumped up from her lounge chair on the patio and gave Griff a fierce, if rather damp, hug, as she'd only climbed out of the pool a few minutes earlier. "Does Catherine know?"

"Yes, thank you, Griff. I'll go see where she is," Elly suggested, rising from her chair at a round table sporting a green and white striped umbrella, so that she'd been resting in the shade rather than in the hot Nevada sun. It was a pity, Griff decided, as the young woman certainly looked like she could use a little color in her cheeks.

"I'll go with you," Abby said, quickly following her sister.

Which left Griff alone on the patio with Jim Parrish and his wife.

"You two look like twin sisters," he said as he sat down on the edge of a wooden bench, smiled at Susie Parrish. "You and Abby, I mean. It's almost uncanny."

"The tickets were enough, son," Jim Parrish said, his blue eyes twinkling with good humor. "Not that I hear Susie complaining, understand."

No, Susie Parrish wasn't complaining. She was, Griff had already noticed with some unease, inspecting him from head to toe, as if he were an object she might consider purchasing.

"I missed seeing you the other night, Griff," she said now, pouring him a glass of iced tea from a frosty pitcher. "And you've been busy? We haven't seen you again, that is."

Okay. The woman was a matchmaker. Griff could live with that, especially when his first reaction was to think, happily, that he might have a Griff sympathizer in the Parrish camp. "I called, several times, but Catherine was busy," he said, smiling at Susie. "I only came here today to see if I could pry her away for a few hours, if that's all right with you. She's working much too hard for someone on her vacation."

Susie sat down beside her husband, laid a hand on his arm. "Oh, I like this boy, Jim," she said, smiling at Griff. "He reminds me so much of you, darling. All take-charge and refuse to take no for an answer. No wonder Catherine's hiding. I always said she needs a masterful man."

"Susie…" Jim warned, giving Griff a man-to-man look that was half apology, half amusement with his wife's blatant matchmaking.

Griff decided a change of subject was in order, and quickly latched on to the vows renewal Jim and Susie were planning for the end of the week. "My parents renewed their vows last year," he told them. "Forty years of marriage. It's something to be proud of, especially in this day of easy divorce. My mother says it takes a great love and a lot of patience and forgiveness, to make a marriage work."

Griff turned as he heard a sharp, half-sobbed intake of breath, and saw Elly, who had just returned to the patio, all but spin on her heels and race back into the house.

"Did I cause that?" he asked, looking at Jim in confusion as Susie excused herself and then bounded to her feet to run after her daughter. "I'm sorry."

Jim sat back in his chair, smiled at Griff. "You

couldn't know, Griff. Elly's, well, she's going through a bit of a bad patch right now. But it will turn out all right in the end. I'm sure of that.'' He crossed his bare legs at the ankle, took a drink of iced tea. ''I've been outnumbered since Catherine was born, you know. You get used to these roller-coaster rides, raising three daughters through their teenage years.'' His gaze slid toward the patio doors. ''Although I thought Elly had outgrown tearful hysterics ten years ago. Funny,'' he ended thoughtfully.

''I'm an only child,'' Griff said, hoping to change the subject yet again. ''It's probably why I want at least three children of my own someday. At least they'll each have somebody else to blame when the loaf of bread has been left open to go stale or there's a broken vase and a baseball on the living room floor.''

Jim chuckled deep in his throat. ''Good point, Griff. I'd never thought about it that way. So, do your parents still live in Las Vegas?''

''Not in the city, no. In Henderson,'' he answered, relaxing a little, realizing he'd been feeling as nervous as he had at seventeen, while waiting for bouncy cheerleader Jennifer McConnell to rescue him from her father's questions so that they could head off to the Junior Prom. ''For half the year, that is. They have a condo in Vail they retreat to for the summer every year. They left just last week, as a matter of fact.''

''Vail?'' Abby Parrish said, walking back onto the patio. ''I spent three months there a few years ago, right after college, as a matter of fact. It's lovely there. By the way Catherine is helping Mom mop up Elly, Griff—they threw me out for some reason or another—so she'll be a couple of minutes.'' She wrinkled her nose, looking much like a mischievous pixie. "Make that an hour, considering that Catherine has a towel wrapped around her wet head and Lord only knows what *that* will look like by the time Elly's stopped sobbing into her shoulder while saying 'I don't want to talk about it!'"

"You've always been so good with sisterly secrets, Abby," her father said facetiously. "No wonder they used to draw straws for the privilege of murdering you."

"Yes, Daddy, but I'm the baby and you've always loved me best." Abby grinned, winked at Griff, and then lightly, gracefully, dove into the pool.

A man could get dizzy in the Parrish household, Griff decided, but he was beginning to think he liked dizzy. He glanced at his watch, decided he'd give Catherine an hour, and then go on a search and abduct mission through the house if he had to, knowing full well Jim Parrish would not only back him up, he'd probably give him directions.

"About this vows renewal, Mr. Parrish," he began, only to have the man cut him off, ask him to call him Jim. "Thank you, Jim," Griff amended easily. "Anyway, I was thinking that you and Mrs. Parrish might be willing to accept my gift of a Mercedes limousine for the day. You could all travel into town together that way, and not have to worry about driving through the heavy Strip traffic."

"Why, Griff, that's really thoughtful of you. Susie will be delighted. I accept, on one condition."

"And that would be?"

"Well," Jim said, standing up, motioning for Griff to follow him to the crushed-stone path leading around the side of the house. "My new baby's been running a little rough lately, hesitating a bit on turns. It could be the spark plugs, I guess, but if you'd be willing to give the engine a listen, give me your professional opinion before I take her to the garage?''

''I'd be delighted,'' Griff said, following after him. ''And then, if you want to, you can help me fix the bumper on Catherine's rental. I've got all we need in the trunk of my car. Rags, rubbing compound, paint, sealer. All that's lacking is a cold beer for each of us and a bit of elbow grease.''

Jim Parrish turned to him, fairly beamed his pleasure. ''Always knew we shouldn't have stopped at three, taken a chance on the fourth being a boy,'' he said, grinning as he retraced his steps, heading for the kitchen and those cold beers. ''Come on, Griff, this is going to be fun.''

Two hours later, Griff and Jim had bonded and were collapsed on the edge of the front porch. They were taking turns with the paint thinner as they cleaned their hands and admired their work as the white rental car sat in the driveway, looking as good as new, better than new. ''I think we've got more paint on ourselves than we did on the car,'' Jim said, shaking his head. ''But the car looks great now, especially since we rubbed out those other marks on the back bumper as well. Ah, and not a moment too soon,'' he said, craning his neck to look back over his head, toward the front door. ''Hello, Catherine, don't you look nice. Are the waterworks over? Is it safe to go back in the house?''

''The dam really broke this time, Dad,'' Catherine said, ignoring Griff. ''But I think we've got it all mopped up for now.'' Only after her father had shaken Griff's hand, thanked him again for the show tickets, and gone past her into the house, did she look at Griff, say hello.

He stood, held up his hands. "I need a sink and some soap, if you don't mind," he said, dropping a quick kiss on her cool, unresponsive lips as he passed by her, following Jim. "Then you can kill me, all right?"

Oh-boy-oh-boy-oh-boy! She looked gorgeous. Soft, warm, wonderful. Eminently kissable. Well, she would, Griff decided as he scrubbed his hands and forearms at the kitchen sink, dried off with paper towels, if she hadn't been glowering at him and his bare chest as if he'd just broken into her house and stolen all her toys.

He stepped out onto the porch once more, picked up his shirt and pulled it over his head, drew it down around his waist. "That's better, but I sure could use a shower. If I promise not to bite, will you come back to my house while I shower and change? Then we can take a drive out to Red Rocks. You can't come to Nevada and not see Red Rocks, Catherine. It's illegal."

"Why are you here?" she asked at last, even as he itched to pull the elastic band out of her hair so that it tumbled down onto her shoulders, drove her mad by falling into her eyes so that she had to push it behind her ears—a move he thought to be as sexy as all hell. "You're not a stupid man, Griff. You can take a hint. I didn't want to see you again. So, thank you for the tickets for my parents and sisters, but goodbye."

She turned to leave…leave him standing on her

front porch like some traveling salesman, trying, and failing, to sell her encyclopedias.

But she didn't get far.

He grabbed on to her arm at the elbow, swung her around so that they were standing thigh to thigh, chest to chest. "Look at me, Cat," he asked her quietly, searching her eyes and seeing fear there, which he didn't like to see. But he also saw a certain sadness, a sense of longing he'd begun to recognize in his own reflection every morning since they'd last seen each other, every night before he went to bed, alone. "Look at me, Cat, and tell me you don't want to go with me now, that you don't want to be with me as much as I want to be with you."

She bent her head, hid her gaze behind lowered lashes.

"Maybe it is only physical attraction," he said quietly, releasing her arm so that she could leave him, walk away, if she wanted. "Maybe it's just something chemical, some temporary madness, a fire that rages for a while and then just as quickly dies. But, Cat—don't you want to know for sure? Don't you *need* to know for sure?"

She sighed, looked up at him, so that he saw the tears standing in her eyes. "I didn't come here for this," she told him, her voice breaking slightly. "I came here because my mother's a romantic fool. I came here because Mom told me Elly probably needed all of us around her right now, and she does. I came here to present Abby with her yearly Goldie Hawn Award for Terminal Ditzyness, to see my mom, to talk with my dad. I did *not* come here for this."

Griff stroked a finger down her cheek, gathered up the single tear that had slipped onto it. "I won't let you run away, Cat. I'm a persistent salesman. You can send me away, but I'll be back. Again and again.''

''Offering me a deal?''

''I don't know what I'm offering, Cat,'' he said honestly. ''How can I?''

''You just want to take me out for a test drive,'' she said, sounding more sad than angry. ''I don't think so.''

''Neither do I,'' he told her seriously. ''So let's give up on the automobile analogies, okay? I saw you, Catherine Parrish, and I liked what I saw. I spent an evening with you and it was the best evening of my life. I wake up thinking about you, I go to bed wanting you. If you ask me to explain the why of it, Cat, I can't. I just know it's there. You're there, inside my head. Now, if you still want me to go away, I will. But I think you'd be making a big mistake.''

She looked at him, looked at him for a long time, while he held his breath. ''Wow,'' she said at last, a small smile playing around her full, generous mouth. ''No wonder you're so successful. That was some sales pitch.''

She reached up, kissed his cheek before he could react and then disappeared into the house, only to return a moment later, her purse draped over her shoulder. ''I told Mom not to wait up for me tonight,'' she said, slipping her hand into his. ''Then I left, before she could start doing handsprings across the living room.''

''I like your mother,'' Griff said, heading toward the street, beating down the impulse to skip for the entire length of the cement path.

''That's because she's on your side,'' Catherine

said as he helped her into the car. "I never thought
I'd live to see the day my mother would send one of
her daughters off to…to—well, never mind that."

"I take that back," Griff said, bending down to
kiss Catherine as he buckled the seat belt around his
precious cargo. "I *adore* your mother. Now, let's go.
First to my house, while I shower and change, and
then we'll do a little exploring."

The trip to Griff's house went as planned, though
both of them were a little quiet, a little on edge during
the drive. The shower and change of clothes went off
without a hitch.

The "exploring" idea, however, got shot down the
moment Griff walked out of his bedroom in clean
khaki shorts and a black knit shirt and saw Catherine
sitting in the living room, paging through a family
album his mother had given him for Christmas two
years earlier. He would have hidden the album if he'd
thought of it, but he'd never brought a woman into
his home before. He kept his home life and his love
life separate, had never before seen any need to join
them together. Until Catherine Parrish.

She looked so good. Good enough to eat. Her long
legs bare beneath a pair of loden-green cotton shorts,
her arms and a tantalizing bit of her midriff bare in a
white, sleeveless cotton shirt she'd tied at the waist.
He could have her hair out of that ponytail in five
seconds flat, except that it suited her somehow, made
her look both young and prim at the same time. Un-
touchable. Yet so appealing to the touch.

She looked up at him now as he sat down beside
her, smiled a rather watery smile that should have set
off warning bells in any bachelor's head, yet didn't.

"You were an adorable baby," she said, and he winced at that, especially when he remembered the requisite naked butt on a blanket pose that was his mother's pride and joy.

"Mom didn't have to tie a pork chop around my neck to get the dog to play with me at least," he offered, trying to close the album. "Let's go into the kitchen, get a cold drink, maybe some sandwiches, then pack them up and head out to Red Rocks."

"No, no, I've only gotten to the good stuff," she protested, slapping his hand away. "I've already seen *little Griffin* at six, on his first two-wheeler. You were even adorable with your front two teeth missing. And then there was *little Griffin* at ten, his arm in a sling and posing in front of the tree he tumbled out of after being warned not to climb it in the first place. But I think my favorite so far is *little Griffin* at thirteen— about the same age as my students at home—all spit-shined and polished in his blue suit and off to his very first dancing lesson. Your mother wrote the cutest captions."

"Oh, God, Miss Macon's ballroom dancing class. How could I forget?" Then he smiled. "But I can do a mean fox-trot, if it ever comes back into style." He looked down at the page, saw his younger self smiling back at him as he stood beside his very first car. A 1957 Chevy convertible. Cherry red, with a white convertible top. "Man, I loved that car," he said, pulling the album partially onto his own lap. "Rebuilt the engine with my dad, worked a summer job at the local dealership to earn enough money to replace the soft top—the Nevada sun is hell on convertible tops— spent my Saturdays waxing and polishing the thing until it gleamed in the sunlight."

"Is that how it started? Your love of cars, I mean?"

"Yeah," Griff answered reflectively as he leaned back against the couch, slid his arm across the cushions in anticipation of Catherine sitting back, as well. "I guess that was it. I worked at the dealership every summer from then on, all through college—I thought I wanted to be a mechanical engineer, if you can believe that—and then just couldn't leave."

Catherine closed the album, set it back on the coffee table, and did just as Griff had hoped, settled herself against the cushions, their legs touching from hip to knee. "And you worked and worked, then bought the dealership?"

He shook his head. "I worked and worked all right—salesmen put in a lot of hours. But it was my grandfather leaving me everything in his will when he died—that everything including a prime piece of real estate about five miles from here—that really got me started." He turned to her, smiled down into her face, her beautiful, interested, interesting face. "I've had a lot of luck, Catherine." He put out his hand, touched her cheek, ran a finger over her smiling mouth. "A lot of luck. More than I probably deserve."

He felt her fingers against his own cheek, felt her draw him closer as she smiled into his eyes. "I can't believe I'm going to say this, Griff Edwards, but I think that, if you want to, you're about to get a little luckier."

He didn't hesitate. Didn't ask, "Are you sure?" Didn't say a single word. He didn't want to give her a chance to reconsider, to perhaps realize that, yes, they were still going very fast. Probably too fast. He'd gone with his instincts all of his life, and he was going to go with his instincts now. And those instincts told him he'd regret it for the rest of his life if he didn't kiss Catherine Parrish, if he didn't hold her, learn her, make love to her.

She melted against him as he kissed her mouth, as he molded her shoulders with his hands, as he ran those same hands down her back, drew her closer. Closer.

He could feel her bare thigh against his, feel her full, firm breasts against his chest. Her lips opened on a sigh and he slid his tongue inside. Plundered gently, progressed slowly, carefully, afraid he might frighten her, frightened by his own reaction to her.

Slam, bam, thank you ma'am wasn't Griff's style, had never been. But now he felt a new gentleness inside him, a passion mixed with something more, something indescribable, something both thrilling and terrifying.

"Not here," he murmured against her throat even as his hands fumbled with the buttons on her shirt, the square knot she'd tied at the bottom of it. He'd been a Boy Scout years ago, but this knot totally defeated him.

He picked her up, held her high in his arms even as he continued to kiss her; kiss her mouth, her throat, her hair. And then, like a blind man totally acclimated to his surroundings, he made his way out of the living room, down the hallway, turning right, then left, then somehow finding his wide bed, laying Catherine down as if she were made of the finest crystal and he was afraid she'd shatter under his hands.

The room was dark, vertical blinds shuttering out the bright Nevada sun, but he could see Catherine clearly as he slipped out of his sneakers, lay down beside her on the bed, drew her close once more.

They lay face-to-face, his hand slowly, lightly tracing up and down the length of her smooth arm, his eyes on her as she bit her bottom lip for a moment, then tugged at the hem of his shirt, slid a hand beneath it, drew her fingers over his side, onto his lower back. His skin shivered in reaction, her touch doing something incredible to his insides that nearly made him laugh in surprise.

"I've never had a woman in this house before today, Cat," he told her, not knowing why it was so important that she know this, that she believe him. "No woman has ever been in this bed." He shifted his body slightly, so that he was propped on one elbow, looking down at her. "I don't know why in hell I feel I have to tell you that, but I do."

"Thank you," she breathed quietly as she slid a second hand under his shirt, as his nerves did another skittering dance, as his passion grew and his heart seemed to swell in his chest. She smiled up at him, a hint of mischief in her gorgeous blue eyes. "But now I'd like you to kiss me again, if you don't mind?"

The last of Griff's unaccustomed nervousness melted with that smile, and he lowered his head to hers, captured her mouth beneath his, felt her welcome, made his entry. His hands, which had fumbled earlier, were swift and sure as they untied the simple knot in her shirttails, slid the blouse from her shoulders, revealed the insane wisp of white satin and lace that whispered secrets about Catherine Parrish she seemed to find necessary to hide from the world.

Her skin was so smooth, so soft, smelled so good. Every inch of it. And, as he peeled away her shorts, kissed away her satin and lace panties, he kissed every inch of it. Worshiped every inch of it.

He didn't know how he'd gotten rid of his own shirt and shorts. He may have helped remove them, but his mind would always remain a blank on just how, just when. He only knew that they were both naked somehow, lying close together even as he lowered his mouth to her breast, took her nipple inside his mouth, felt her response as he ran his tongue in tight circles, as his hands cupped her, lifted her.

Her thigh was between his legs, pushing at him gently, suggestively, and Griff didn't need much suggestion to know what came next, what had to come next or else he was going to explode into a million jagged pieces.

He lifted his head even as he let his hand move lower, find her center, find her warm and wet and welcoming. "Cat? Are you on the pill?"

She stiffened beneath him, her hands stilling on his shoulders. "What?" Her face went white, her hands fell to her sides. Her breaths, that had been quick and shallow, grew deeper, harder, faster. "I...yes, I—no. No, Griff, I'm not on the pill," she ended, turning her head away from him.

He kissed her throat, her chin, her left ear. "I've got something in a dresser drawer. Which is about a million miles away from where I want to be right now. I'm sorry, Cat. Even if you were on the pill, I should go get it."

She only bit her bottom lip, nodded.

Something was wrong. Griff knew he didn't have to be a rocket scientist to know that something was very definitely wrong. But he tried to ignore it as he retrieved a packet from the dresser across the room, returned to the bed in time to see Catherine slipping beneath the covers she'd pulled down, hiding herself from him.

He slid beneath the covers, as well, dealt with the packet. He pulled her close to him, their heads lying on the same pillow. He'd have to start all over with her, which wasn't much of a hardship, because there wasn't anything else in the world he wanted to do than to touch Catherine, to taste her, to learn her, to love her.

Griff's hand stilled as he captured Catherine's breast once more. *Love her?* Wow, talk about your shots to the solar plexus! And then Catherine sighed, the sigh hitching in her throat, almost a small sob, and he looked at her. Really looked at her as she lay in his bed, her hair having somehow come loose from the elastic band, so that her honey- and champagne-streaked curls clustered on his pillow.

Yeah. All right. He might as well face facts. He loved her. Griffin Edwards loved Catherine Parrish. He hadn't needed three days to know that. He'd known that the first moment he'd looked at her as she'd stepped from the rental car, mad as hell at him and the whole world even as she tried to hide it behind a mask of calm sophistication. She was his Catherine, his Cat. He'd been waiting for her all of his life. And he'd be damned if he'd let her go.

He kissed her hair, kissed her trembling mouth, let his breath go in a ragged sigh as he felt her move toward him once more, as she made small, soft sounds in the back of her throat when he explored her intimately, stroked her until she began to lift herself off the bed, seeking out his touch.

"That's it," he whispered, lowering himself over

her, sinking into her. "Purr for me, Cat, purr for me."
He felt her legs circle around him as he began to
move inside her, gloried in the feel of her fingernails
pressing into his back.

And then he was lost, they were both lost. Lost in
a storm so passionate, so intense, that the rest of Nevada couldn't have been seen as overreacting if they
were to believe the government had resumed under-
ground nuclear testing and a tremor from one of the
explosions had just rumbled beneath the city.

Chapter 5

It was four in the morning, and Catherine sat curled up on one of the lounge chairs on the patio, a beach towel wrapped around her legs to fend off the cool night air. Griff had dropped her off only fifteen minutes earlier, after an afternoon and evening filled with loving and talking and more loving. They'd eaten microwave pizza at some point, shared a bottle of wine. She may even have eaten the pizza without first picking off the pepperoni, which she loathed; she really couldn't remember.

They'd kissed good-night a dozen times at the front door, Griff saying each kiss was the last, then only making it partway down the cement path before coming back, kissing her again. Neither one of them seemed able to say good-night and really mean it.

But now, at last, she was home. And alone. And the guilt was creeping in....

"Hi, honey," Jim Parrish said, and Catherine

looked up, startled, to see her father pulling over a chair from the table, sitting down beside her. "You can't sleep, either?"

Grateful for the darkness that hid her tears, Catherine only shook her head, surreptitiously wiped at her eyes with the edge of the towel. "Then...then you weren't just waiting up for me, the way you used to?"

Jim chuckled low in his throat. "Ah, those were the days, weren't they? Standing at the front window, waiting for headlights to appear on the street, then racing into the kitchen to sit down at the table and sip cold coffee and pretend I'd been there all along, thinking about a patient. Not really waiting up for you at all, not really worrying at all. But you saw right through me, didn't you?"

"And loved you for it," Catherine said, reaching out to squeeze her father's hand. "I love you, Dad, you and Mom both. Mom, for letting me fly and you for packing the parachute."

"You used to come to me in the old days, Catherine, talk to me, ask my advice. But I guess that all changes once a child grows up, becomes independent, lives on her own."

Catherine tipped up her head, looked up at the stars hanging overhead. "Hoo, boy," she said, shaking her head. "Mom showed you the brochures, didn't she? The pamphlets?"

"Oh, yeah," Jim said, sighing. "That she did, Catherine, that she did."

"I was going to show them to you, talk to you about them, ask your opinion. That's the only reason I brought them with me. Honest."

"I know, sweetheart. And if you want my opinion as a doctor, I'd be glad to give it to you. The procedure is safe, relatively painless, and I know of at least two of my associates who perform it all the time. It's a wonderful alternative for people who want a baby and, for one reason or another, are not able to conceive in the usual way.''

"But?" Catherine urged, as she had heard the implied *but* in her father's tone.

"Yes," Jim said, rubbing at his forehead, "there is a but, sweetheart.'' He turned to her, took her hand in his. "You're twenty-eight years old, Catherine. Twenty-eight. Do you really, truly believe you have no other options open to you? Do you really, truly believe that you'll never marry, never raise a family with your husband?"

"I thought so," Catherine said slowly. "I really thought so. I love kids, Dad. I wouldn't be a teacher if I didn't love kids. I think I'm ready to care for a child of my own. And I didn't want to marry some man I didn't really love, just so he could give me children. That wouldn't be fair."

"No, sweetheart, it wouldn't. Not to either of you. There'd be a lot fewer divorces if more people realized you don't marry for expectations, but for love, and love alone. Everything after that—a house, babies—they're all a bonus for loving and being loved, not a substitute. So, are you still so sure you know what you're going to do?"

"We're talking about Griff now, aren't we, Dad?"

Jim stood up, bent down to give her a kiss on the forehead. "No, sweetheart, we're not. That's your mother's department, although I've promised her a second honeymoon if she'll back off for at least another week, let you work this out on your own a little bit. I just want you to know that I'm behind you, one hundred percent, no matter what you decide to do."

Catherine's bottom lip began to tremble and she

felt fresh tears stinging her eyes. "I'm crazy about him, Dad. I've never felt this way abut a man before, never thought I could. The way I feel? It has nothing to do with babies, and everything to do with Griff. Only Griff. And now...now I have to tell him that I actually—just for a moment, Dad, no longer than that—considered using him as a sperm donor. I do have to tell him, Dad, don't I? I mean, if we're ever to have anything between us, if we're going to have a chance to find out where we are, where we might be going—well, I just have to tell him. I can't let this hang between us."

"I know, sweetheart," Jim said, helping her to her feet, putting his arm around her as they walked into the kitchen. "If it helps any, I think the guy's head-over-heels in love with you. Just don't let this drag on, all right? The sooner you get this off your chest, the sooner you'll know whether or not Griff's the one for you."

"You like him, don't you?" Catherine asked as they walked down the hallway, toward the bedrooms.

"Yes, I do." Jim smiled as they stood under the hallway light, so that Catherine could see the twinkle in his eyes. "Any man who can make my baby purr can't be all that bad."

Catherine felt all the blood running out of her cheeks. "What?"

"My car, Catherine," Jim said, looking confused. "He tuned her up for me, right outside in the driveway. Had her purring like a kitten in no time. The boy's good with his hands. Really good."

Catherine's smile was half relief, half genuine amusement. "Yeah, Dad. He is." Then she went up on tiptoe and kissed Jim's cheek. "Thank you, Dad. I love you. I love you very, very much."

* * *

Catherine waited until noon, then drove to the car dealership and proceeded to get thoroughly lost among the snaking lines of cars and trucks surrounding a hub of five showrooms, five huge repair shops, a body shop the size of a football field and a half dozen other buildings she couldn't recognize because there were no signs on them to tell her just what in hell purpose they served.

At last, just when she was beginning to think the gods were telling her she had made a mistake in coming here in the first place, she saw Griff's Porsche parked beside one of the anonymous buildings and pulled her rental car into the empty space next to it.

The Nevada air was dry and hot after the coolness of the air-conditioned car as Catherine stood on the burning asphalt, cupped a hand over her eyes, and looked out over the acres and acres that made up Griff's dealership.

A fairly stiff breeze had set the miles of red, white and blue plastic flags to snapping, and she winced as some loud, disembodied voice told someone named Bob Stevens to "Pick up on line two."

She could hear the sound of hammering from the body shop, the whir of a drill from the repair shop closest to her. A thousand noises assailed her, the smells of oil, of grease, of gasoline, swirled around her. And that damn voice was back, shouting above the crackle of the wires: "Body Shop, pick up on line seven."

It was a very exciting place to be, no doubt about it.

And she was impressed. Griff's dealership wasn't just a car lot, it was a small city. And, even though he said he owed it all to his inheritance from his grandfather, Catherine knew it was one thing to get your foot in the door. It was something else entirely to keep that foot there, build on what you've been given, use your brains and your guts and your talent to take what you have and make it into a success. No wonder Griff had his face plastered all over the place. He *was* Griff Edwards Dealerships. And she was *so* proud of him!

''Hi,'' she heard from behind her, and turned around to see Griff smiling at her. ''I thought I saw you out here. I was just about to call you, ask you if you wanted to go to dinner tonight at the Carson Street Café. I figured a second hot-fudge sundae this month couldn't hurt.''

Lord, but the man did something to her insides. Melted them, actually. He had on a linen sports coat and matching slacks, his paisley tie contrasting well with the snow-white of his crisp dress shirt, his golden tan. She watched as he raked a hand through his hair, looking almost nervous as he tried, unsuccessfully, to push back that one unruly dark brown lock she'd come to adore.

''Cat?'' he prompted, and Catherine belatedly realized that she'd been standing there, mute, not answering him, not reacting at all. ''Is something wrong? Is everything all right back at your parents' house?''

''Yes, um—yes, of course. Everything's fine, Griff,'' she said, doing her best to summon a smile. ''And dinner tonight would…would be fine. Just fine.''

''Well, good,'' he answered, looking to his right and left, then stepping closer to her. ''Now, would it be all right if I nibbled on your ear while I tell you what I was thinking when I first saw you standing out here, the wind blowing that incredibly sexy sundress against your legs?''

"Griff, um, excuse me," Catherine heard from behind her, so that she turned around to see one of Griff's employees standing about ten feet away, looking torn between duty and the certainty that his boss didn't want to be disturbed. "I guess you didn't hear the page. There's some guy named Jack Matthews on line one. Something about the golf tournament you're running for the Kidney Foundation next month? I had the call transferred to the front office, if that's all right."

"Yeah, Paul, thanks. You're right, I do have to take this call." Griff put his hands on Catherine's shoulders, turned her in the direction of the closest building. "Do you see that door, Cat? It leads to my private office. There's a small refrigerator built under the cabinets—get yourself a cold drink if you want. I'll meet you there in ten minutes, okay, and we can continue our *discussion.*" Then he kissed her mouth, a short yet wildly satisfying kiss, and turned to trot toward another door at the front of the building.

Ten minutes turned into twenty, and still Griff hadn't joined her in the office. Catherine had half convinced herself that she had more chance of having a private conversation with Griff in the middle of Freemont Street as computer-imaged cowgirls danced over their heads than she did here, on his own turf.

But she stayed, waited. And learned even more about the man she had slept with, had made love with, had held and kissed and later, when she was alone, cried over.

He was a golfer; the trophies on the credenza against the back wall of his office proved that.

He had gotten his sherry-brown eyes from his mother and his thick, unruly hair from his father, and she'd seen the photographs in his album, and now those on Griff's desk, that proved it.

He also, she thought with a smile, had the messiest, most disorganized desk she'd ever seen. There were files everywhere, papers everywhere. Adding machine tapes snaked here and there amid piles of papers, sat coiled into tight circles in others. There were slick, colorful brochures showing off dozens of automobiles of different types, different models. A large combination desk blotter and calendar, barely visible beneath yellow legal pads covered in doodles and rows of addition, was nearly black with scribbled phone numbers, names and appointments.

But what kept her waiting rather than writing him a note, promising to see him later, was the thick yellow elastic band she saw hanging from the gooseneck desk lamp. It was the one she'd worn last night, then lost somewhere in Griff's bed.

She was pacing the office, winding the elastic band around and around her index fingers, when the door opened and Griff came in, apologizing for keeping her waiting even as he headed for the small refrigerator and pulled out two soda cans. She quickly stuffed the band into her pocket and smiled at him as he walked past her.

"Thanks," she said, accepting one of the icy-cold cans after Griff had pulled the tab top. "This place really hops, doesn't it?"

"Nine to nine weekdays, nine to seven on Saturday," he told her with a grin, collapsing onto the burgundy leather, tufted couch, resting his legs on the brochure-cluttered coffee table in front of it and then gesturing that she join him. "But all work and no play makes Griff a dull boy, so I've got a dozen great managers, another dozen great teams working their own areas of the dealership. One person can't fool themselves into thinking they can run a show like this. In fact, since the other day, I've begun to worship the word *delegate*.''

Catherine sat down beside him, snuggled against him because she couldn't be this close to him and not want to be closer. ''Do you usually work all those hours?''

''I did, for a lot of years, but not anymore. One day last year I realized that ten years of my life are little more than a blur to me, so I got smart, hired a few more good men, and went hunting for a life.'' He lifted his arm, resettled it behind her back as he let his hand drift through her loose curls. ''Ahh, soft and warm, just as I remember.''

Catherine laid a hand on his flat stomach, rested her head against his shoulder. ''And did you find it?'' she asked, hating the tremor in her voice. ''That life you went looking for?''

She felt his hand under her chin, lifting it, so that she couldn't avoid his eyes. His wonderful, tender, smiling eyes. ''Yeah,'' he said, lowering his mouth to hers. ''It took a while, but I think I did.''

He eased into the kiss, but Catherine didn't want tender. She didn't want trusting and loving. She wanted the hot heat of him, wanted to feel his arms around her, his hands on her. Because she might never be this close to him again.

''I love you,'' Griff breathed against her hair, as he kissed her throat, her cheek, her faintly trembling lips. ''God, but I love you, Cat.''

She heard the words, gloried in them even as they

broke her heart. And then she pushed him away, stood up, put the large, messy desk between them.

"Catherine?" he asked, levering his feet to the floor and sitting forward, then stopping as she motioned for him to stay seated, to stay where he was. "Still going too fast, huh?" He smiled ruefully, shook his head. "I should know better. I guess I'm not as good at this love business as I should be. I'm sorry, Cat. I thought, hoped—well, I guess you know what I hoped. All right, I'll slow down, give you more time. I could still grow on you, you know."

She couldn't stand it. Couldn't stand to watch the light go out of his eyes, couldn't bear having him believe she didn't love him, wouldn't love him forever, even though they couldn't be together. Not after she told him the truth.

"Griff," she began slowly, then sighed, tried to marshal her thoughts. "You're a wonderful person…"

"Wow," he said, rolling his eyes. "This is worse than I thought. I haven't heard that one since college. I really was seeing only what I wanted to see, wasn't I, Cat? Please, if you can, don't tell me you want to be my friend. I mean, there's a pretty sharp letter opener somewhere on my desk, and the 'let's be friends' line might push me straight into slitting my wrists."

Catherine slammed her fists onto her hips, leaned forward, the teacher about to punish whoever had thrown that last paper airplane by her while her back was turned. "Would you knock it off…be serious?" she demanded. "This is difficult enough without you making me feel like you really do love me. Which you couldn't…which I couldn't. Not really. I mean, even if Dad did propose to Mom a week after he met her—that doesn't mean everybody falls in love at first sight. Why, I'll bet, statistically, it only happens one in every ten thousand times. Maybe one in every hundred thousand times.''

Something she'd said had made Griff smile, either that or she might have just protested too much to sound convincing. "Maybe, Cat," he said with that small smile growing wider, tugging at the corners of his mouth, and she longed to pick up one of his golf trophies and brain him with it. "Personally, I like to think of you as one in a million.''

"Griff, stop," she pleaded, searching her pocket for the elastic band. "Please." She turned away from him, ran her hands through her hair, gathering it at her nape, then ruthlessly wrapped the elastic band around it, pulling it into a ponytail. Tried to pull herself together at the same time. Then she turned around once more, feeling more like Catherine Parrish, teacher, and less like one of her silly, romantic students.

"Griff," she began carefully, still avoiding his eyes, "I came out here to see my parents, spend the summer with them. But that's not the only reason. Although I certainly didn't come out here to fall in love.''

"Fall in love, Cat? This gets better and better. Go on, I'm listening." Griff the lover was suddenly gone, and Griff the super salesman had taken his place on the couch. She could hear it in his voice, see it in his eyes as she finally dared to look at him. He was waiting, watching her, hoping for some sign, some opening he would then use to his advantage. She loved him, loved him dearly, but she'd decided with the first delivery of roses that the man simply didn't always play fair.

"I came out here to ask my father's help in finding a good artificial insemination clinic," she blurted out, then brought both hands to her mouth, unable to believe she'd said it so bluntly, without once saying how much she'd wanted a child to love, how long and hard she had considered what she had then planned to do.

Griff collapsed all at once against the cushioned back of the couch, the room so silent Catherine could hear the soft hiss of air as the leather protested beneath his weight, breathed out a sigh of its own.

"Last night," Griff began slowly, and she believed she could now hear the well-oiled gears in his brain beginning to turn. She knew it wouldn't take him long to add one and one and make three. "Last night, when I asked you if you were on the pill..." He looked up at her, searched her expression. "You almost said yes, didn't you, Catherine?"

She nodded, unable to speak.

He rubbed at his chin, still looking at her. "Well, I'll be damned."

"Not you, Griff. Me. I'll be damned. I think I already am."

And then she picked up her purse and walked out of the office, into the bright sunshine. There shouldn't have been sunshine. In Pennsylvania there was a good chance it would be raining.

By tonight, as she stepped off the plane in Allentown, she'd know for herself.

Abby plopped down on the bed, swinging the lid of the suitcase closed with one hand as she did so. "You can't go."

"I can't stay," Catherine said, throwing open the suitcase once more and tossing in a stack of bras.

"You're an idiot."

"I'm worse than an idiot."

"And you're going to break Mom's heart. As the oldest, you're supposed to be her maid of honor, remember? Or are you too busy thinking about yourself to think about that? Man, and they say I'm flighty."

Catherine turned her back on her sister, knowing Abby was right, and only turned around again when Abby said, "Hey, what are you doing with these?"

Her blood running cold, Catherine whirled around to see that Abby had been busily unpacking her suitcase—and had stumbled on the brochures and pamphlets tucked into a side pocket. "Give me those," she said, making a quick swipe at them only to watch as Abby neatly rolled off the opposite side of the bed, out of reach.

"You're really going to do this?" Abby asked, leafing through the brochures. "Cool!"

"I've changed my mind. I'm not going to do it, at least not right now," Catherine said, replacing the items Abby had tossed out of the suitcase. "It's like Dad told me—it's a good thing, but it's not for everybody. I've decided that it's not for me. At least not yet."

"Uh-huh," Abby said, her nose already in one of the pamphlets. "Can I keep these?"

Catherine didn't care what her sister did, as long as they could drop the subject. She walked over to the dresser and stopped halfway there, as a car was being parked at the curb in front of the house and she could see it through the window. "Griff," she breathed, her heart leaping into her throat.

Abby pulled back the sheer curtains and looked outside for herself. "Yup, that's him all right, and it's about time," she said, grinning at Catherine. "Did I tell you that there are about a zillion roses lined up on the dining room table? Red ones, pink ones, white ones, yellow—hey, where are you going? I thought you had a six-o'clock flight?''

Catherine ran out of the bedroom, trying desperately to push her hands through her tangled curls, arrange them into something even vaguely resembling order, then skidded to a halt at the end of the hallway, took a deep breath and walked into the living room.

Griff was standing there, looking at the painting of Red Rocks. His linen sports coat was gone, his tie was loosened, he'd opened the top button of his white dress shirt. Abby had been wrong. He didn't look anything like Tom Cruise. Compared to Griff, Tom Cruise *would* have to tie a pork chop around his neck to get his dog to play with him.

As if he sensed her presence, Griff turned toward her, smiled that smile that had the ability to curl her toes inside her sneakers. "Hi, again," he said, shoving his hands into his pockets. "Sorry it took me so long to get here, but I had a few things to do. Kicking myself all around my office took at least a half hour."

"Kicking yourself around the— Griff, what are you talking about?"

"You like the flowers? I know they're not all that original, but I was working on a deadline, especially after Abby called and told me you'd booked a seat on the six-o'clock plane out of here."

Catherine swallowed down hard, trying to find her voice. "The...the flowers are lovely. Thank you."

"You're welcome," he said, walking over to her, taking her hand. "I'd thought about simply buying you the biggest diamond in all of Las Vegas, but then I realized you probably wouldn't want the biggest one, and that I should let you pick out your own ring. But I did bring this."

He stepped to one side, and she saw the teddy bear sitting on the chair next to the front door. The huge, blue and white teddy bear sitting on the chair next to the front door. Some of her students weren't that big!

She looked at Griff, fought to understand. He should hate her. Didn't he know he should hate her? "Um…"

He put a finger against her lips, keeping her silent. "No, Cat, it's my turn now. All you have to do is nod, all right?"

She nodded, and he took his finger away, so that she opened her mouth once more.

"Ah-ah!" he warned, raising his hand. "Now, let's see if I've got this all straight, okay?"

Catherine pressed her lips together. Nodded.

"You came out here to visit your parents and, oh, by the way, to get pregnant."

She nodded once more, this time keeping her head lowered.

"And you—and please don't think I'm being flip, because I'm not—and you bumped into me. You were so bowled over by my smiling face as you looked at one of my billboards that you forgot to look where you were going and bumped straight into me. If I wanted to stretch things—and I'm game for anything that works—I might even say you fell in love with me at first sight. That probably made you really, really mad, huh, Cat?"

She didn't nod this time. She raised her head and glared at him.

"Right," he said, grinning. "We can hash out that business about billboards and my towering ego again later if you think it's necessary, but we'll let it go for now, all right? Hmmm, I guess a glare is as good as a nod. Okay, so we met, I either suffered some sort of wild mental whiplash or the mere sight of you knocked me clear into next week, and I wormed a dinner invitation out of you so I could see you again, as I had to know if you were real, if this feeling I had was real.''

He stopped speaking, frowned, then went on, "Actually, I think Elly and Abby had more to do with that dinner invitation than I did, although I would have thought of it myself, eventually. Give them some of these flowers, will you?"

Catherine heard a giggle from behind her and whirled around in time to see Abby racing back down the hallway.

"She's really cute, you know," Griff said. "But I never even saw her. Not once I'd looked at you."

"Griff, I—"

He held up his hands, warned her to silence. "I didn't mean to fall in love with you, Catherine. It just happened. And you probably didn't want to fall in love with me, either. God knows how I've complicated your well-ordered life, all your, I'm sure, carefully thought-out plans." He stepped closer, so it became nearly impossible for Catherine to breathe. "You do love me, Cat. If you didn't, you would have lied to me last night, you would have gone on lying until you got what you wanted from me. I'm right about that, aren't I?"

She couldn't blink the tears away any longer, and felt the first of them spill over, run down her cheeks.

She nodded.

The next thing she knew, Griff was down on one knee, holding both her hands in his. Her reaction was half laugh, half sob, as she tried to pull him to his feet, but he was a stubborn man, and a strong one. "Catherine Parrish, there's something I learned very early in my career. You can sweet-talk a customer, take that customer for a test drive to impress him, ply him with everything wonderful you can say about the product, try to second-guess him, anticipate needs before the customer states them. But at some point, be it sooner in the sale, be it later, a salesman has to ask for the order, ask for the sale.''

Catherine was trembling so badly she could barely stand. ''A car analogy, Griff? *Now?*''

''Oh, for goodness sake, Catherine Marie,'' she heard her mother call in from the kitchen. ''Stop complaining and tell him yes. I don't think your poor father and I can stand much more of this.''

''I get all of them, too, don't I?'' Griff asked as Catherine dropped to her knees, laughing and crying at the same time. ''I think I can handle that.'' He slipped his arms around her waist, pulled her close. ''So, Catherine Marie Parrish, will you marry me? Will you please, *please* marry me?''

Catherine nodded....

BOOK II
ABBY

Chapter 6

The Parrish kitchen was one of those U-shaped affairs, with grass green Formica counters and green and yellow accents against white cabinets. It was a pretty kitchen, with ceramic tile backsplashes that sported a large, hand-painted fruit bowl design behind the stove. Susie Parrish was very proud of her kitchen.

Which meant it was a good thing Susie was out shopping with Catherine, so that she didn't have to see what her daughter Abby had done to it.

It was funny, Abby thought, as she tossed a set of measuring spoons in the general direction of the sink. Today was to have been the day her parents renewed their wedding vows, and her mom had just blithely postponed the whole thing in order to go honeymoon trousseau shopping with Catherine. Her mother was planning something, that was for sure, and Abby wondered if the woman actually believed Catherine and Griff would consent to a double ceremony—although that might be kind of cute, in a hokey, sentimental, Susie Parrish sort of way....

"Abby! What in the world happened in here? Did the flour bag blow up? And why are my sneakers sticking to the floor?"

"Oh, hi, Elly." Abby tucked an errant blond curl behind her ear and then wiped a hand across her cheek, adding another flour smudge to those already there—and already she looked as if she was auditioning for the role of head ghost in the next *Casper* cartoon. She scanned the kitchen, then scrunched up her short, straight nose. "Wow, what a mess. Wanna help me clean up?"

"Fat chance, bucko." Elly walked past her, carefully picking her way across the sticky floor, and grabbed an apple out of the bowl of fruit sitting next to the refrigerator. "At least it smells good in here," she said, slipping onto one of the tall stools arranged around the breakfast bar built into one outside arm of the U. "Something cinnamon, right?"

Abby wet a handful of paper towels at the sink and began wiping the counters. "A cinnamon streusel breakfast cake, as a matter of fact, a recipe sent to me by dear Alvira Clampett from Wallback, West Virginia. I have to test all this stuff out before I put it in my column."

"Yeah," Elly said, dabbing at her chin with a paper napkin after taking a big bite out of the juicy apple. "You wouldn't want another fiasco like last year, with the homemade modeling clay and permanent dye."

"Don't remind me," Abby said, arranging her features into a comical grimace. "You know, it's remarkable how mean an eight-year-old with bright blue hands can get in a letter to the editor."

Elly laughed, and Abby smiled, happy to hear her sister's laughter, which no one had heard much of lately. As a matter of fact, Elly had been a great big downer ever since they'd all come to Nevada, and Catherine's happiness seemed to have lowered Elly another ten or so feet into her private pit of despair.

The stove timer beeped three times. Abby slipped her hands into two oven mitts, retrieved the finished cake and set it on a cooling rack. She leaned her head close and took a deep, satisfied sniff. ''Ah, I think we've got a winner. What do you think, Elly—do we play food taster to the king and try some now, while it's warm, the sugary cinnamon all sticky and gooey, or just wait until tonight and serve it for dessert?''

''Tonight is soon enough,'' Elly said tightly, and Abby turned to see her sister toss the half-eaten apple into the sink, then turn on the garbage disposal. ''I'm going to lie down a while, take a nap,'' she then said, heading out of the kitchen, her complexion having gone pale, with tinges of green around the edges. ''Try to get this place cleaned up before Mom comes home, okay?''

''Well, thanks a heap. And if you think that reaction passes for 'my compliments to the chef,' Miss Manners, I can tell you that it doesn't,'' Abby called after her, then hiked her petite self up onto the stool her much taller sister had just vacated, plunked her elbows on the counter and rested her chin in her hands.

She'd promised their mother and father she'd leave Elly alone, not try to find out what had happened between her sister and her brother-in-law, Rob. They were all to wait and be gentle, until Elly came to them on her own. Which was easier said than done, Abby knew, her heart breaking for her sister.

But, if she wasn't going to go running after Elly and sit on the bed while her sister cried but refused to talk, she'd better find something else to do. Not that she'd have to look far. Abby glared at the kitchen, at the mess she'd made, and tried to remember the series of articles she'd published last year on "Speed Cleaning: It *Is* Possible!"

"Why am I so good at writing about this stuff and so lousy about doing it myself?"

She'd fallen into her role of How To columnist at the newspaper she'd worked at during her college breaks, a small, regional newspaper chain that had then, most happily, been absorbed by a much larger chain. The girl who had graduated with a degree in journalism had hoped to become the next great investigative reporter. Suddenly she'd found herself not just putting in time until her "big break" came along, but having that big break served up to her, as it were, on a tarnish-free silver platter—"a good commercial polish and lots of elbow grease, then store the platter in tight plastic wrap."

Unfortunately, it had come with the How To column, and not an exposé of corruption in some high government office. The publisher had liked her columns on cooking and sewing costumes for children and nifty housecleaning tips and how to wallpaper behind toilets and six ways to make that same old chicken taste new again.

And yet, much as she'd never planned her life the way it was unfolding, the whole thing wasn't that bad. Once she'd established herself, the columns came to her, not the other way around. Her thousands and thousands of loyal readers sent her their own tips and hints, and all she had to do was write an opening to each column, then thank MaryEllen Bexler from Topeka, Kansas, for her great tip on how to wash a big dog and not drown yourself in the process, or give kudos to Jessica Glazer from Zanesville, Ohio, for having discovered the perfect way to clean up garden tools before storing them for the winter.

Within two years, Abby's column became syndicated in over eighty newspapers across the country; she'd been asked to do more in-depth articles for national women's magazines; and her last check-in with her answering service had told her that a New York publisher was interested in compiling some of her most popular columns in a book.

Not too shabby for a girl only four years out of college. Definitely not too shabby for a girl who still was only hazy on whether a person dusted first or vacuumed, and whose idea of gourmet food was having three pickles on her hamburger.

"Yeah, well, Abby, old girl," she told herself at last, heading for her mother's well-stocked cleaning closet, the bottoms of her sneakers making stick-sticking noises across the floor, "you know the old saying, don't you? 'Them what can't, teach.'"

They also lived a pretty good life, all things considered. Abby could travel anywhere she wanted, laptop computer in tow, her readers' letters and tips sent to her via fax from her supposed home base in Philadelphia. She could ski in Colorado, sunbathe in Miami, rollerblade in Venice Beach in California. And when she'd begun adding some of her personal travel experiences to her columns, her readership had gone up yet another notch. It was a great life, all things considered.

And yet, happy as Abby was with her career, she still sometimes wondered why her publisher considered "Abby's Answers and Anecdotes" as a human

interest column. A *humorous* human interest column
at that. She didn't think it was all that funny. She was
simply trying to help people like herself, people without a single clue as to what "first blanch the skin so
that it peels off easily" meant in a recipe, and then
wondered, in print, if Thelma Frickert from Homer-
ville, Georgia, was trying to put one by her by sending her a recipe she'd discovered in a book titled *Can-
nibalism Made Easy*.

She returned to the kitchen counter, kicking a plastic bucket along in front of her, plunked down three
different cleaning products in their nice spray bottles,
then pulled the sponge mop from under her arm and
propped it against the refrigerator. Where to start?
You had to divide big projects into small steps, she
knew, and the mess spread out all over the kitchen
was definitely a big project.

And then she smiled. Man, that cinnamon breakfast
cake surely did smell good. Step one decided upon,
she grabbed a knife from the drawer, sliced herself a
hefty wedge of the still-warm cake, laid it on a napkin, and then sat down at the breakfast bar. She
reached into her pocket and pulled out the miniature
tape recorder she always carried with her, pushed the
Record button and set it on the counter while she
sampled her first bite of the warm cake.

"Ummm," she mumbled in delight, wiping crumbs
from her lips as the tape recorder, set to begin re-
cording when she spoke, captured her reaction for
posterity. "Congratulations Alvira Clampett from
Wallback, West Virginia, your recipe has made the
cut."

The tape recorder stopped, waiting for Abby's next
words. She took another bite of cake as she surveyed
the kitchen once more. And then she smiled, knowing

how she'd begin her column. "Today, dear readers," she began slowly, licking her fingers as the tape in the recorder began to turn, "we're going to try a recipe for a delicious cinnamon breakfast cake. But first let's discuss, just for a moment, the proper way to open one of those pesky five-pound bags of flour...."

Two hours and two slices of Alvira Clampett's breakfast cake later, Abby was standing in front of the mirror in the bathroom, wiping away the steamy film on it with a hand towel. There was something a person could rub on, spray on, *something* on mirrors to keep them from steaming up, but she couldn't remember exactly what at the moment. She'd have to check the database on her laptop, then tell her mother about it.

In the meantime, she just leaned closer to the mirror, standing on tiptoe as she inserted a fresh disposable contact into each green eye, then stood back, blinked and smiled as the world came back into focus once more. She ran her spread fingers through her wet hair, satisfied when it fell into heavy waves she would let dry on their own. What difference did it make, when her hair had a will of its own and only went where it wanted to, anyway?

She stepped into bright red-and-white-striped cotton bikini panties, hooked her front-closing, fire-engine red bra, then dropped a dark emerald green sundress over her head. The dress skimmed her body to just above the knee, had a scooped neck, cap sleeves and a bright yellow Tweety Bird embroidered on the front of it. Just a nice, simple little dress. Or, to hear Elly tell it, just another fashion idea gone sadly wrong.

Still, and Elly was always the first to admit it, Abby

could carry off such nonsense. She was short, only two inches over five feet tall. She had wide green eyes, an innocent, "isn't it a lovely world?" smile and a riot of natural blond curls that bounced and moved when she walked and made her look like she was always racing forward, to embrace life. Of course, as Catherine had once grumbled good-naturedly, it also didn't hurt that Abby had a killer, if petite body, and that she'd probably be as alluring in a gunnysack as a designer original.

Slipping her feet into metallic-gold strap sandals, Abby stepped out of the bathroom, leaving behind her a shambles of wet towels, uncapped toothpaste and a sink counter cluttered with bottles and jars—and spilled baby powder. She seemed to be having a real problem with white powders today.

Oh, well, she'd clean it all up later. It wasn't as if her mother or sisters were going to come into her bedroom, her private bathroom, and clean up for her. That hadn't happened in, oh, at least five years. Until then, however, Abby had very much enjoyed the benefits of being the pampered, faintly spoiled baby of the family.

Not that being the baby didn't have its drawbacks. Too young to stay up late with her sisters, too young to "understand" whatever secrets Catherine and Elly whispered to each other, too young to tag along to the movies with them when Elly had reached that magic age of seventeen that allowed her in to see R-rated movies. Of course, Elly and Catherine had gotten into a lot of trouble on that one, when Abby had complained to their mother that she'd been sent to the other end of the multiplex to watch some G-rated movie about a bunch of talking dogs.

But now, at twenty-five, a person would think she'd

be treated as more of an adult. Sadly, except for no longer picking up after her, her sisters still seemed to believe that she was little more than a child. When were they, and her parents, ever going to believe that she was all grown-up now and capable of taking care of herself, making her own decisions? Why, they all still acted as if she should be handed milk and cookies every night, then be in bed by eight.

"Maybe Tweety Bird wasn't a good choice," she said to herself as she walked into the living room. "Yet, somehow, I don't think the Yosemite Sam one would have made a difference.... Oh, hi, Griff," she said easily as she saw her soon-to-be brother-in-law sitting on the couch, surrounded by bags and boxes, a rather bemused look on his face. "Don't tell me— Mom and Catherine dragged you along on their shopping trip. Oh, you poor boy. Do you want a cold beer?"

"Do you want a slave for life?" Griff answered, grinning at her, then getting up to follow her into the kitchen. "I never knew shopping was so exhausting, especially when all I got to do was chauffeuring-and-lugging-packages duty, then sit on my hands while Cat and Susie tore through three different malls on their seek-and-acquire mission. I think I saw the sun rise and set in the dome of the Caesar's Forum Shops ceiling three times."

Abby laughed, handed Griff a cold can from the refrigerator. "That bad, huh? Now you know why Daddy did his usual disappearing act this morning, claiming an emergency at the hospital. Just between you and me, Griff, Daddy had already arranged to have the day off, for the renewal of vows thingie, remember? I'll give you odds he comes home with the back of his neck freshly red from the sunburn he got on the golf course.''

"Smart man, your father," Griff said, taking a sip of cold beer as he wrapped his legs around one of the stools at the breakfast bar. "What are you doing tonight, Abby?" he then asked, pulling a small white envelope out of his back pocket. "I have four complimentary tickets to some dinner and show in town, but so far everyone else in your family has turned me down, and Catherine says she'd rather stay in tonight, so we can look through brochures I picked up from the travel agent. You want them? Maybe you could convince Elly to go along with you?"

Abby eyed the envelope, considering. Lord knew she had nothing planned, not that she believed Elly would look kindly on an invitation that included driving into Las Vegas at night. No, she'd rather sit in her room, listen to sad songs and read romance novels, then cry when the guy got the girl and they went off to live their happily-ever-after. Like she hadn't known that was going to happen? Jeez! "What sort of show? Do you think I'd like it?"

"I wouldn't count on that, actually. It's a revue of some sort, pretty far off the Strip. Probably more of an amateur night with a two-drink minimum." He moved to pick up the envelope. "Forget I even mentioned it."

"No, wait," Abby said, taking the envelope, pulling out a single ticket and sticking it in the front pocket of her sundress. "Since nobody else is going to use them, I might as well take one. I mean, at least it's a free dinner, right?"

"Yeah," Griff said, sounding reluctant, as if he'd opened his mouth, then realized he should have kept it shut. "But alone in Las Vegas, that far off the Strip? I don't know, Abby..."

"Oh, Griff, not you, too," Abby complained, sighing. "I'm a big girl now, and I can take care of myself. Honest."

He looked at her, his head tipped to one side as he ran his gaze over her from head to toe and back again. "What am I worried about?" he asked himself, grinning at her. "The bouncer isn't going to believe your ID, anyway."

"Ha-ha, Griff, very funny," Abby shot back at him, picking up the rental car keys from the counter. "Now I'm definitely going!" She snagged her purse from the chair she'd flung it on earlier, shoving the strap up onto her shoulder. "Tell everyone not to wait up. I do believe it's about time Abby does Vegas." Then she grinned. "Well, the G-rated version of *Abby Does Vegas* anyway."

She batted her long dark eyelashes at Griff. "Could you please tell me how many points I need to have at one of those blackjack thingies? You know, blackjack—except some people call it twenty-one, don't they? Oh!" she said, her eyes wide as Griff looked ready to put her over his knee and spank her. "Why, I'll just bet it has something to do with that number, doesn't it? Well, never mind. I'm sure the nice croupier will tell me how to play the game if I just ask him nicely."

"That's *dealer,* Abby, not croupier," Griff told her as she planted a big kiss on his cheek. "But you already know that, don't you? There's a smart, crafty lady hiding behind that goofy yellow bird with the big feet, isn't there? I think I should be more worried about what you're going to do to Vegas than what Vegas could do to you."

''Now you're talking, Griff,'' Abby said, laughing. ''Thanks for the ticket, okay? Oh, and don't forget to tell everybody not to wait up for me.''

Abby was having the time of her life, sitting in the front row of the smallish theater stuck into a back corner of the no-brand-name casino, digesting her rather good prime rib and Yorkshire pudding, nibbling on the complimentary lime sherbet that had come with the dinner.

Griff had been right, it had been amateur night in Vegas, that was for sure, but it had all been so much fun that she'd stayed around for the second, midnight performance, wondering if Jo-Jo the Laughing Poodle would return to the stage after that most embarrassing accident on his trainer's leg during the first show.

She'd clapped as hard as she could for the former Miss Pulaski County, Arkansas, as she'd taken her bows after singing ''Impossible Dream'' while twirling two fire-tipped batons. She'd laughed in real delight at the Elvis impersonator as he tried to woo her with his swiveling hips, and had honestly enjoyed the tap-dancing twins.

Not that it appeared anyone else had enjoyed themselves enough to stick around for the second show, and only about a half dozen new customers had seemed willing to leave the casino to see it, either. In fact, except for the guy at the next table, Abby was pretty much alone in the front of the theater.

She'd noticed him the moment she'd first walked into the place and was escorted to her front-row table. He was a handsome enough man, with a shock of dark blond hair and quite attractive green eyes behind his gold, wire-rimmed glasses.

He seemed tall, even slumped down in his chair,

with long legs she'd nearly tripped over as she walked past, not that he'd said "Excuse me" or anything. He'd just pulled his legs back under the chair long enough for her to pass by, then slumped down even lower on his spine.

She'd watched him out of the corner of her eye all through dinner. A dinner she ate, a dinner he ignored in favor of the scotch and water that had seemed to reappear in front of him without pause. It was strange. He didn't seem to like the drinks, still making a face after each sip, as if he couldn't quite get used to the taste. Not that he stopped drinking, or changed to a different poison.

Once the lights were lowered, she'd directed her attention to the stage, but she could actually *feel* the silence coming from the table next to her, a rather sad silence interrupted only by the clink of ice on glass as he lifted another scotch and water to his lips.

By the time the lights had been lowered for the second show, the man had rested his arms on the table and lowered his head into them, and Abby wondered if he had fallen asleep or simply passed out. The mother hen in her worried about him, which was silly, because he was a big, strong man, not a child. Except that he seemed so very much in need of comfort.

The already-thin crowd thinned out some more as the second show dragged on, enlivened only when Miss Pulaski County's baton came too close to the velvet curtain and a waiter in a white coat jumped onto the low stage, fire extinguisher in hand, to save the day.

By the time Marvin the Marvelous came onstage to pull a few more rabbits out of his hat, even Abby had seen enough and was ready to leave. She still worried about the guy at the next table, worried what would happen to him, left alone and drunk in this place, but she really was bored now and the excitement of the Strip was calling to her. She stood up, swung her purse over her right shoulder.

"And we have a volunteer, ladies and gentlemen!" Marvin the Marvelous exclaimed, hopping down from the stage and grabbing onto Abby's arm. "Ladies and gentlemen—a big hand for the little lady, if you please."

A very large man in the audience, wearing a very plaid shirt, put his fingers into the corners of his mouth and whistled, but that was about all the applause Abby got, considering that there were only about a dozen people in the room now, and most of them were either talking to each other or studying their drinks.

"No, really, I was just leav—" Abby began, trying to pull away as Marvin the Marvelous tugged her arm, moving her closer to the table beside her and the unconscious scotch and water drinker. "Hey, what are you doing?" she asked as the magician pulled out a set of handcuffs, linking one side of them around the man's wrist.

Before she knew it, the other half of the handcuffs was snapped shut around her left wrist and Marvin the Marvelous was taking a bow.

"Hey, just a cotton-picking minute here, bub," she complained as Plaid Man got off another ear-splitting whistle followed by a loud "I wish it could be me you picked, Marvin, instead of that drunk. Wow, what a looker!" Abby took a moment to smile at the man, a rather painful smile, then turned back to Marvelous Marv. "Um, look, Marvin—may I call you Marvin? Fun's fun and all that, but one of us isn't interested, and the other one doesn't even know he's become part of the act. So, what say you get on with the magic words and get us out of these things, okay?''

"Did you hear that, ladies and gentlemen?" Marvin the Marvelous shouted right beside Abby's abused ear, as if he was speaking to a crowd of thousands. "The little lady wants these cuffs off. Well, who could blame her?" he asked, reaching for the sleeping blond man—he had to be passed out, not just sleeping—and trying to boost him up higher in his chair. "Come on, fella," he said, patting the guy's chest, half lifting him in the chair. "Wake up. You don't know how lucky you just got."

Enough was enough, and too much was just too much! "Now, look, buster," Abby said through gritted teeth, wishing she wasn't sporting Tweety Bird on her dress and that she at least looked as if she could back up her words, "either uncuff us now or start thinking about how you'll chew steak with dentures."

"Play along with me, honey, please," the magician whispered in her ear. "If I don't pull off this trick the management is going to boot my ass straight out of here. I need the job, honey. I've got kids."

Abby didn't believe him. Oh, she believed management might be ready to give him the boot, as his magic tricks were older than dirt. But she didn't believe he had kids, at least none under the age of thirty, and they could darn well take care of themselves, in her opinion. "Two minutes, tops," she told him, then allowed him to raise her arm enough that the drunk's arm lifted up, showing their handcuffed wrists to the meager audience.

"And now, ladies and gentlemen," the magician said, dancing around like a bear in a tutu, "Marvin the Marvelous is going to place this silk cloth—" he produced a scarlet square of what looked like old rayon from the breast pocket of his tuxedo ''—and place it just so, over our volunteers' hands and wrists. Unless,'' he continued, leering down at Abby, ''you'd rather stay attached? You could think of it as a dating opportunity. What do you think, ladies and gentlemen? Could these two be a couple?''

''Yeah! Yeah!'' Plaid Shirt yelled, cupping his hands around his mouth, stomping his feet on the floor.

''Don't push me, Marv,'' Abby warned, gesturing toward the scarlet cloth, then glaring daggers at the magician. ''Do it—now! I mean it, Marv. If you don't soon…Marv? Hey, Marvin, what is it? You don't look so good all of a sudden.''

Marvin the Marvelous swayed where he stood, both hands to his chest as if he was in great pain. ''I…I don't think I feel so good,'' he said quietly, laying a hand on her shoulder, as if that would help him retain his balance.

''You want to sit down?'' Abby asked, feeling her knees beginning to buckle under Marvin's nearly dead weight. *Dead* weight? She winced, wishing she hadn't thought that. Even as she tried to hold on to him, the magician's body seemed to go all formless and liquid, sliding down her until he was half kneeling on the floor. ''Oh, okay, Marv,'' she squeaked out, definitely beginning to panic. ''That's it. Good idea. You just lie down. Right here, on the floor. That's fine.''

And then, with Marvin the Marvelous half lying on her right foot, and the dead weight of the drunk she was handcuffed to pulling her over so that she had to brace a hand against the tabletop or fall down, Abby yelled at the top of her voice, knowing it was a cliché, yet unable to think of anything else: "Is there a doctor? Is there a doctor in the house?"

The scotch and water drunk groaned, pressed his hands against the tabletop—a move that forced Abby to either sit on the table herself or fall on top of one or both men. In the end, she was somehow forced onto the tabletop itself, kneeling there, staring at the slowly rousing drunk. He raised his head, carefully, and obviously not without pain. Straightening his glasses, he looked at her blearily.

"I...I'm...I'm a doc...a doctor," he said, his words slurring. "An'...an' you're gor...you're gor—" He grinned at her, a silly, lopsided, drunken grin. "Pretty bird, pretty bird. I tawt I taw a puddy-tat," he said on a giggle, pointing at her dress, then put his head down once more, oblivious to the chaos going on around him.

"Well," Abby muttered as she felt herself sliding across the table, falling onto his lap, "at least he's a happy drunk...."

Chapter 7

There were memories. Vague ones. Probably dreams. Yapping dogs. Spinning fires. A one-hundred-pound canary. And then lots of voices, lots of noise and somebody singing "just put one foot in front of the other…" as he staggered along in the dark, his eyelids closed and feeling like lead.

He tried to open his eyes now, but his lids were still proving uncooperative. So was his neck, which didn't seem to want to support his head, so it was lolling sideways against the…against the…where the hell was he, anyway?

No matter. Whatever he was leaning against, it was soft. And warm. And it smelled good, sort of a mix between exotic roses and cotton candy. He grinned, thinking that last bit had been almost poetic. Funny. He wasn't a poetic sort of guy.

He was a drunk guy, that's what he was, he re-membered slowly as he forced his eyes open, forced himself to remember. He lifted a hand to his head, to his horribly throbbing head…and all hell broke loose.

First, his hand seemed to weigh a ton. Probably the effects of the scotch. But he persevered, yanking his hand and arm higher by sheer force of will. The next thing he knew, he was slipping sideways as a grumbled "Hey, watch it!" was followed by something solid landing across his lap.

Okay. His eyes were open now. Not that he could believe what he was seeing in the half-light of a Las Vegas dawn.

He was half lying in the back seat of a car. How in hell did he get into the back seat of a car? Whose car? He'd taken a cab to the show, he was sure of it.

The next thing he noticed was that there was a woman lying across his lap, pinning him to the seat, and most of his view was taken up by the sight of a pair of extremely well-shaped female legs. He groaned, lifted his hand once more and was once more warned to "Knock it off, for crying out crumbs. Put down your hand and let me sit up!"

Well, that got his attention. That voice, husky, yet feminine, and definitely not too pleased with something he was doing. The voice and the legs both had him struggling to clear his brain, react in some way.

The first thing he did was look at his right hand, the one he was having so much trouble keeping raised to his aching head.

Now, this was interesting. He had two right hands. How had that happened?

No. No, that wasn't it. Not unless he'd taken to wearing fire-engine red nail polish.

Then he noticed something else. A pair of handcuffs, one locked around his wrist, one attached to the wrist of the hand with the fire-engine red tipped fingers.

"Handcuffs?" he said, baffled.

"Congratulations, you got it. Now, let's see what prize is waiting for you behind door number two," the rather disembodied female voice grumbled, and he looked down to see a jumble of blond curls—the woman's face seemingly crushed against his midsection, her left arm raised, as it had to be as long as he kept his right hand pressed against his aching skull.

All right, all right, he'd gotten it now. He was in the back seat of a car—not his car—and he'd been sleeping on some strange woman's shoulder, which accounted for the soft and the warm and even the nice smells. He'd been quite comfortable. Until he'd awakened, that is, and tried to massage his hangover headache, at which time his movement had pulled the strange woman's body across his and he had lost his headrest, which had sent him toppling over onto the seat.

Made perfect sense.

He spread his fingers as wide as he could, rubbed at his temples with his thumb and middle finger. No. No, damn it, it didn't make perfect sense. It didn't make any sense at all!

"You're doing this on purpose, aren't you?" the woman asked, and he could feel her free hand digging into his thigh as she tried to lever herself back onto the seat even as she aimed her feet toward the floor of the car.

He quickly lowered his arm, realizing that, if she moved her hand just one more time, they could both end up a lot more embarrassed than he was sure each of them already were. At least, he was certainly embarrassed. "I'm sorry, miss," he said, lowering his arm at last, so that she could sit up.

"That's okay," she said, trying to push down her dress as she sat back against the seat, tugging at the emerald green material so it covered her kneecaps.

Which was a pity, because she had gorgeous thighs. "Perhaps if you were to, um, crawl over me?" he suggested, still finding it hard to believe any of this was happening as he looked at the woman. The girl. No, he'd been right the first time. The woman. The absolutely gorgeous woman.

Little Miss Gorgeous smiled at him. "Crawl over you? Oh, I don't think so, doc," she said, her perfect nose wrinkling delicately.

"No, really," he continued, raising his right hand, just a little, so that she didn't fall over him again. "Look. My right hand, your left hand. If you crawled over me, and I moved toward your side of the car a little—well, then we could both be more comfortable."

She looked at their joined wrists consideringly. "Well, how about that, doc? You're right," she said, grinning at him. "Last night I was so busy just trying to keep you on your feet, keep you moving, that I just kind of *pushed* you into the car and then fell in after you, too exhausted to move. All right. We'll change places."

A bit of clever and rather provocative maneuvering followed her agreement, until they were both leaning their heads against the back of the seat, breathing deeply after their exertion, but obviously more comfortable.

He turned his head, looked at her profile. Hungover or not, he'd been right. She was gorgeous. And at least he now knew where he'd seen that one-hundred pound canary before.

"Hi, again," he said politely as she rested her cheek on the fabric seat, looked at him with the biggest, most guile-free green eyes he'd ever seen. "Who the hell are you, and why are we handcuffed together in the back seat of this car?"

She giggled, obviously not upset at his question. "I'm Abby Parrish," she told him, then giggled again as he raised his eyebrows. "I know, doc, Abby Parrish. Sounds like a church, doesn't it? Daddy liked Abigail, you see. He just didn't plan ahead."

He raised his hand—his left hand this time—to his head once more, adjusted his glasses a millimeter higher on his nose. "I've fallen down a rabbit hole, haven't I?" he asked, silently vowing never, never ever, to drink again. He didn't even like to drink. He especially didn't like scotch. Vile stuff, scotch, and it definitely packed a punch. "Next thing I know that damned canary is going to disappear, leaving behind only his grin."

"The Cheshire Tweety-bird?" Abby Parrish returned, still grinning, still there, right beside him, and not acting at all like a figment of his imagination. Hell, his imagination had never been *this* good. "That's a funny one, doc."

"And there's another thing," he said, rubbing a hand over his chin, feeling the early-morning stubble. "I don't know you. I've never seen you before in my life. Believe me, you're not the sort of woman a man forgets, even if he is hungover and feeling like being run over by a very large truck could only improve his condition. So how do you know I'm a doctor? Because I am," he added, realizing he'd not yet told her his name. "Doctor Shaw. Doctor Peter Shaw."

"Pete? That's a nice name."

"Peter," he corrected automatically. "So, now that we know each other's names, Abby Parrish, maybe you can tell me the rest of it? Where we met, why we're handcuffed together, why we're sitting in the back of this car?"

"Mint?" she asked, searching in the pocket of her dress and coming out with a roll of peppermints. "I don't know about you, Pete, but I feel like something died in my mouth."

"Peter," he said, then took a mint, because he felt as if at least two somethings had died in his mouth.

And then, finally, Abigail Parrish sat back, took a deep breath, and began to explain.

"We were both inside that casino over there, watching the dinner show," she said, pointing across the street to the casino Pete vaguely remembered being dropped off at by the cabbie he'd asked to take him someplace nobody ever went so that he could be alone and drink himself to death. So far the cabbie had been proved only half-right. Peter definitely had been able to get a good start on drinking himself to death, but he sure hadn't ended up alone. He was, in fact, about as far from alone as a person could get.

"Uh-huh," he said, nodding. "Go on."

"Well, we were watching the show, as I said. Except that you weren't really watching, were you? You were drinking glass after glass of scotch and water on the rocks. I don't know why, because you certainly didn't seem to be enjoying the stuff. Anyway, I stayed for the second show, which was my first mistake— and partially your fault, Pete, because I really hated leaving you there alone, sleeping at your table. I mean, who knows what can happen to an unconscious person alone in Vegas after midnight."

"*Peter*. And you've certainly got a point, Abby," he said facetiously, lifting his right hand a little, so that the handcuffs clinked. "I could have ended up in some real trouble if you hadn't come along. You know, I doubt I'll ever be able to find the words to properly thank you."

She rolled her eyes and sighed dramatically. "You wouldn't happen to know my sisters would you? You sound just like them. Anyway," she went on cheerfully enough, and obviously difficult to intimidate, "I was just getting up to leave when Marvin the Marvelous thought I was volunteering, which I wasn't, and the next thing I knew you and I were handcuffed together and Marvin was clutching his chest and then dropping to the floor."

"You're kidding, right?"

"No. No, I'm not. I called for a doctor and you said you were a doctor, and then the big plaid person said he'd take Marvin to the hospital faster than any ambulance could, and it wasn't until after they were gone that I realized my purse was gone, too, and that either Marvin or the plaid man took it."

"Back up," Peter pleaded. "I think I can live without hearing more about this plaid person, but who's Marvin the Marvelous?"

"Oh, didn't I tell you that? Marv's a magician. At least he *says* he's a magician, but I really think he's a very bad one, and when he realized that he was probably going to be fired he and the plaid man made up this idea where they could steal my purse and then run away. At least that's what I think. If I'm wrong, then Marvin is in some Las Vegas hospital and my purse is safe. But I doubt that I'm wrong. I watch a lot of those real-crime shows on television, you know.''

As Abby paused to take a breath, Peter slipped his hands into his pockets, coming out with thirty-five cents and a pink, folded piece of paper scribbled with a two-day-old message to call his service. ''Not just your purse, Abby,'' he said, longing to kick himself. ''But my wallet, my keys, even my beeper. So you're right. Marvin the Marvelous isn't a magician—he's a damn pickpocket.''

''He got you, too? Really?'' she asked. ''How about that. And here I was, kind of hoping you'd be able to spring for the locksmith. Well, we'll have to think about this and how we're going to manage. In the meantime, do you want to hear the rest of it before I call my parents—they're bound to be awake by now and wondering where I am.''

''Probably not,'' he grumbled, ''but go ahead.''

''Well, here I was with you handcuffed to me—a doctor, no less—and I knew that if we didn't get out of that place the police would want to talk to us, and it couldn't be good for a doctor to be found drunk and handcuffed. And it certainly couldn't do *me* any good, because I'd never hear the end of it—trust me!—when the police drove me home and told the family what happened. Are you still with me,'' she asked, looking at him carefully, ''or should I slow down?''

''No, please,'' he told her, wondering what she'd do if his head just fell off and landed in her lap. ''Let's get this over with as quickly as we can, all right? I think, in our last episode, you were trying to save me? And yourself, of course.''

"Of course,'' she answered, not seeming to be in the least deflated by his sarcasm. "I knew we had to get out of there until we could be free of the handcuffs and until you sobered up—sorry, but you were really, really tying one on there, Pete. Definitely not good for your healer image and all of that. So I just yelled at you and slapped your cheeks—sorry about that, too—and somehow got you to your feet and the two of us safely out of there so that I could put you in my car and drive you home once you told me where home was.''

"Drive to *my* place? Not knowing me from Adam, you tried to save me? Wanted to drive me home? You're kidding, right?'' He shook his head, which hurt—a lot. "And they say Mary Poppins is a fictional character.''

"No, Pete, I'm not kidding,'' she said slowly, as if trying to explain something not all that terribly complicated to a young child. "I mean, I couldn't let anyone important either see you in your condition or read about it in tomorrow's newspapers, and I most certainly couldn't take you home to introduce you to Mom and Daddy in *my* current condition, now could I? I can see it now, can't you? Hi, Mums and Dad, look what I found! Oh, yeah, that'd work. You think these handcuffs are bad? I'd be kept on a leash until I was forty, for crying out loud. But I may have said some of this before, Pete. Try to pay attention, okay?''

"Sorry,'' Peter said, trying not to laugh. If he wasn't so miserable, he could really like this woman.

Really like her. Except he was miserable—for good reason—and she was a certifiable nutcase!

"Apology accepted," she told him, and the smile was back. She really had a great smile. "And it would have worked, Pete, except that it's my left hand and your right hand, so that I couldn't possibly drive, anyway, even if you woke up enough to give me directions, so I put you in the back seat—I'm still amazed I could do that—and figured I'd just wait until you woke up and then you could drive us to your place and call a locksmith or whatever so that I could go home and just say I'd lost my purse and no one would be the wiser, except that we can't even do that because the car keys were in my purse, and if I hadn't forgotten to lock the car doors we'd be in an even worse pickle than we're in now, and I fell asleep myself while waiting for you to wake up and help me figure out what to do next, so my parents and sisters are probably out dredging rivers someplace for my body, and I really, really think we're in a bit of a pickle, Pete, don't you?"

Peter looked at her for long moments, wondering how she could talk for so long without stopping to take a breath, then turned his head as he heard a sharp rap against the window. A very large Las Vegas bicycle patrol officer was standing beside the car, nattily dressed in a bright bumblebee-yellow shirt and black shorts.

"Yes, Abby," Peter said, sighing. "As a matter of fact, I do think we're in a bit of a pickle." He reached for the handle that rolled down the window. "But that's all right. I'll just let you tell the nice officer what happened, just like you told it to me. With any luck he'll run screaming back to his bicycle and not stop pedaling until he reaches the California border."

"Oh, *Gawd*," Abby groaned, sliding down in her seat. "Why does stuff like this always happen to *me?*"

Peter rubbed at his sore wrist, watching as Abby lifted a cup of tea in both hands, then drank from it, sighing as if she'd just tasted ambrosia. "You know," he said, "we're both pretty lucky Marvin the Marvelous is an honest man. The police could have pressed charges against the two of us. Well, you, anyway. Leaving the scene, obstructing justice, whatever. Me, I'm completely innocent. In fact, some could say you kidnapped me."

Abby set down her cup, sighed again. She'd just returned to their booth in the small restaurant after having talked with her parents on the phone for the third time in as many hours. Not a good conversation, obviously, but they'd get over it eventually, she'd told him, then said nothing else. "I'm just so shocked that I misread Marvin so badly, poor guy—and the plaid man. He really did take him to the hospital."

"And you really did leave your purse lying on the floor somewhere in the dark when you hijacked me," Peter said, wondering what was wrong with him that he was beginning to see the humor in all of this. "Marvin picked my pockets, yes, but it was all a part of the act. He just didn't get to finish the trick before that mild infarct knocked him down. They did an angioplasty on him last night, right in the emergency ward, by the way, just in case you didn't hear the officer tell me. He's going to be just fine."

"Yes," Abby said, trying to smile though her eyes

clouded. "Marvin's fine, the plaid man is a hero, you've got your wallet and stuff, I've got my purse and car keys." She sighed and collapsed against the bench seat in the booth. "So, Pete, where would you go, if you were going to run away from home?"

"That bad, huh?" He wished she would confide in him, because he could see she was really upset and sad that her family had been worried about her needlessly.

"Oh, not that bad," she answered. "Worse. The casino manager called the car rental place after seeing that my identification was out of state. The car company, recognizing the rental number or some such thing, called my parents' house at three o'clock this morning. Since then, Mom's been telling Daddy that I'd probably just forgotten my purse at the casino and I'll show up just fine and with a great story to tell everybody, and Daddy, according to my sister Catherine, has been making up scenarios about serial killers. Now that I've been found, safe and alive, he's thinking up ways to kill me himself. You just can't imagine how I dread going home."

"I see," Peter said, looking at her sympathetically. "Does this sort of thing happen often? Something you said earlier makes me believe it just might."

"Only when I'm around my parents and my sisters," she answered, sighing. "Oh, not that it happens often anymore. I mean, I *am* twenty-five now, a grown woman who has been living on her own for over three years. I have a career, not just a job. I'm taken seriously in that career. But I'm the baby of the Parrish family, you understand, and used to be a little, well, *flaky,* I guess you could say, so that everyone seems to just *expect* me to get into trouble. For some reason, even though I can walk and chew gum at the same time anywhere else, just put me down next to my family and I regress straight back to my own version of the *Perils of Pauline.*''

"Except that this time it was my fault," Peter said, reaching out to take her hand in his. His right hand felt rather lonely now, after being joined to her for all those long hours, while they waited for one of the police officers to go to the hospital and retrieve the keys to Marvin's handcuffs. "You were only trying to help me, Abby. And I appreciate it, I really do. So, how about you drive me back to my place while I shower and change, and then we can face the Parrish clan together?''

"Really?" Abby sat up, seemed to brighten a little. "You'd do that for me?" And then she frowned. "No, that wouldn't work," she said sadly. "I didn't tell you, but my dad's a doctor, Pete. Family practice. Not that he'd say anything, but I wouldn't want him to think that you, another doctor, was a…was a…"

"A drunk?" Pete finished for her. "So that explains it. As a doctor's daughter, I guess I can consider your rescue of me as a sort of professional courtesy?''

She pulled her hand away from his, took another long drink of the cooling tea. "I…I knew your reputation could have been hurt if the whole thing had gotten out, gotten into the newspapers. Patients don't like thinking their physicians are human, and fallible." She raised her head and looked at him levelly. "Besides, you didn't like the scotch, even as you kept pouring it down your throat. That was obvious. So I knew you didn't routinely get sloshed, that it wasn't something you just *did.* I knew there had to be a reason, a good reason. There was a good reason, wasn't there, Pete?''

Peter shifted his lower jaw to one side, nodded. ''Yeah. Yeah, Abby, there was a reason. But not a good one.''

''You lost a patient? My dad has had a drink-or-two too many a couple of times over the years, when he's lost a patient who had touched him particularly. And that doesn't make him or you a drunk, by the way. That makes you very human, and shows that you really care about your patients.''

He nodded his head, sighed as she took his hand in hers and began stroking the back of his hand with her thumb. He felt her compassion, her understanding. No pity, though. He couldn't have handled pity, and she seemed to know that.

''I'm a surgeon, Abby,'' he began slowly, quietly, then waited as the waitress topped off his coffee and walked away. ''A surgical resident, to be exact, in my last year. Yesterday…well, yesterday I was on call when they brought in one of our own interns. He'd been sideswiped on his motorcycle, so he'd ended up eating about a quarter mile of gravel on the side of the highway. He was a mess, unrecognizable, barely alive. I didn't even know it was Don, not until one of the emergency room nurses read the identification in his wallet. I'd cracked his chest by that time, had my fingers wrapped around his aorta, trying to plug the hole in it. It took two guys to pull me off him, make me realize that Don was gone, that I had to call it, call the time of death…''

Abby squeezed his hand. ''I'm so sorry. You don't have to talk about this. Really.''

He looked at her, tried to smile. ''No, Abby, I'm

sorry. Sorry I couldn't save Don, even though it was too late for him the moment his motorcycle was hit. Sorry Don hadn't been wearing a helmet, so that no matter what I did there really hadn't been much of Don left to save, anyway. Sorry I spent last night feeling sorry for myself because I'm not a miracle worker. Don wasn't the first patient I've ever lost. But, damn, he was a great kid. The whole thing was just such a stupid waste, you know?''

''I know,'' Abby said quietly, her lovely green eyes sparkling with unshed tears. ''I know.''

''Yeah, well, enough of that.'' He reached into his pocket, drew out a few bills, scattered them on the table. ''Now come on. Take me home so I can change, and then I'll stick my head in the lion's mouth along with you, explain that the whole thing was my fault and you were only being a Good Samaritan. It's the least I can do.''

They were all there, waiting in the living room of the sprawling ranch house in Summerlin. Jim and Susie Parrish. Catherine Parrish. Elly Parrish Lyndon. ''And you're Griff Edwards,'' Peter said, accepting the hand offered to him. ''I'd recognize that face anywhere.''

''That's because it *is* everywhere,'' the very pretty woman who'd been introduced as Catherine said, leaning her head against Griff Edwards's shoulder. ''He's thinking his next promotion should be trying to guess the number of Griff's billboards, taxi boards, bus boards, bus stop bench backs there are out there, and then presenting a new car to the person who comes closest. Aren't you, darling?''

Griff laughed. "It's a running gag Cat has going, Pete," he said. "Don't worry about it."

"Peter," Peter said, knowing he was fighting a losing battle. Abby had introduced him as Pete, and Pete he was probably going to be, at least in the Parrish household.

He set his shoulders and turned to Jim Parrish. "I made an ass of myself last night, and Abby, with all the best of intentions, rescued me. You've got a great, compassionate daughter, Dr. Parrish," he said sincerely, hoping the man wasn't the sort to hold a grudge. "So, if you're going to be angry, and I don't blame you if you are, please be angry with me. Abby was only a victim of circumstance."

"That's Jim, Pete, okay? And my youngest daughter is *always* a victim of circumstance," Jim said, motioning for him to follow along into the kitchen. "As a matter of fact, I think she considers getting into crazy situations like this her second career. Now, how about a glass of iced tea?"

"Anything nonalcoholic would be fine. I'm considering taking the pledge, as a matter of fact," Peter said as Griff also followed along to the kitchen, leaving the four women alone in the living room.

"I feel partly responsible for all of this," Griff said as they walked out onto the patio, each of them holding glasses of iced tea. "I gave the ticket to Abby, you know."

"And I appreciate it," Pete told him sincerely, looking through the sliding glass doors toward the living room, where three of the Parrish women were sitting, their heads close together as they talked. Abby, he assumed, had gone off to shower and change. "Abby was right, you know. I wouldn't want

to have been anywhere near the center of anyone's
attention last night. I was having a private pity party
and really tied one on.''

Jim nodded, immediately understanding. ''Lost a
patient, didn't you? Abby said you're a surgeon. Was
it that intern I read about in this morning's paper by
any chance? Damn shame. And it was a hit-and-run,
just to make things worse. I hope they find the guy
and lock him up for fifty years.''

''Yeah, at least fifty,'' Pete agreed, pressing the
cold glass against the side of his head. He was sober,
but his headache was still far from gone. ''And I'm
a surgical resident, Jim, just finishing up my final
year.''

''Really. What's your specialty?''

''Reconstructive surgery,'' Pete told him, settling
more comfortably into the wicker chair. ''For a long
time I wasn't sure what I wanted, but then this kid
came in during my rotation in the department. Another traffic accident. Face a mess. And we put him
back together. Kevin's got a great smile again, no
scarring—just one of the guys in second grade again,
you know? And I was hooked.''

Jim nodded. ''That's always how it happens. We
think we know why we go into medicine, and then
one case, one event, and we're hooked. Mine turned
out to be spending a month with a group of family
practitioners. I thought I'd be bored out of my skull—
runny noses, coughs, sprained ankles. But that's not
what it is. Every day is a new adventure in family
practice, and I liked getting to know my patients. So,
Pete, tell me—what do you think of Abby? I know
that sounds like a damn pushy question, but if I go

back in there without asking, Susie is probably going to hang me up by my ears.''

''He's not kidding,'' Griff said genially, saluting the absent Susie Parrish with his glass. ''She's little, but she's mighty.''

Pete leaned forward, looked toward the sliding glass doors once more, then grinned at Jim. What the hell—he might as well call it like he saw it. ''What do I think of Abby? I think she's kind and caring and just about the most beautiful woman I've ever awakened next to in the back seat of a car or anywhere else, bar none. I also think she's a bit of a space cadet.''

Griff, who had been in the process of drinking his iced tea toast to Susie, spluttered a fine spray of liquid out of his mouth before being caught up in a fit of choking laughter. ''Oh, Jim,'' he said between coughs, ''*this* is going to be fun!''

Pete looked at Griff, then at Jim, then sat back in his chair again, crossed his legs. Yeah. They were right. This *was* going to be fun. But that was all it was going to be, because he had a residency to finish and a career to begin. He didn't have time or room in his life for a woman like Abby Parrish, a woman who, he instinctively knew, was not the sort a man enjoyed, then walked away from with no regrets.

Chapter 8

One by one they followed Abby into the bedroom, each of them taking their turn, or their best shot, and then stepping back, courteously giving the next one room to take a couple of verbal swings.

With age came privileges, so Susie Parrish was the first to enter Abby's room, marching straight into the bathroom where her youngest daughter stood at the sink, a toothbrush stuck in her mouth.

"Wet towels get moldy if allowed to lie around on the floor," Susie said, stooping to pick up both this morning's wet towel and the one Abby had flung on the floor last night before leaving the house. "But I suppose you know how to remove mildew, so that's all right, isn't it?"

"Soap, water, dry the article outside in the sun, treat stubborn spots with lemon juice or a weak bleach solution," Abby grumbled around the tooth-brush, then rinsed and spit before reaching for the fresh hand towel her mother was holding out to her. "But I would have picked up my stuff last night, Mom, or first thing this morning. I'm usually very neat, considering the fact that I have to do the work sooner or later, anyway. I was just in a hurry last night, that's all."

"Yes, you were, weren't you?" Susie said, sitting down on the edge of the bathtub. "In a hurry to get out of the house before your father or I could forbid you to go into Las Vegas on your own."

"Forbid?" Abby opened a jar of face cream and dipped into it, then began rubbing the cream into her face with a lot more enthusiasm than the product makers recommended. "*Forbid?* Mom, do you hear yourself? Do you see this cream?" she asked, shoving the jar in her mother's direction. "It's one of those antiaging creams. The gal at the beauty counter told me that anyone who has passed the quarter-century mark has to start thinking about using stuff like this. I'm twenty-five, Mom, heading into my second quarter century. But to listen to you—and the rest of them, not just you—anyone would think I was sixteen, and you were about to ground me or something."

Susie took the jar from her and slipped a pair of half-lens reading glasses out of her skirt pocket before checking out the directions printed on the bottom of the jar. "My baby," she said quietly, "using antiaging creams. I imagine I should ask your father if he could bring home a walker for me, or at least a cane. I can't imagine how I'm still able to stumble around on my own, at my advanced age."

"Aw, Mom," Abby said, kneeling down to give her mother a hug. "You're younger than I am. And you've forgiven me, right? I'm really sorry the car rental place called and scared you guys, and I got to a phone as quickly as I could. After I woke up, that is, and the officer at the police station told me I was allowed one call,'' she ended, wincing at the memory of her recent brush with the long arm of the law.

Susie returned her daughter's hug. ''Oh, baby, you did scare us, and that's no lie.'' Then she put her hands on Abby's shoulders and pushed her away, grinning at her. ''So, he's cute, isn't he? And a doctor, too. You'd make a good doctor's wife, Abby. Independent, able to amuse yourself and with a career and interests of your own, aware that a doctor's time is not always *his* own.''

''She never quits, does she?'' Catherine said, standing at the doorway. ''My turn, Mom, now that you've done everything but congratulate Abby for ending up in another of her crazy escapades.''

Abby clung to her mother in exaggerated fear as she grinned up at her oldest sister. ''Oh, no! Don't let the bad lady take me, Mommy! I'll be good, I promise! I'll clean my plate every night—even the broccoli—and I'll make my own bed and everything.''

Susie laughed as she disengaged Abby's arms from around her neck and stood up. ''Catherine phoned Griff at three o'clock this morning and made his life a pure hell for letting you get away from him with that ticket, Abby. So, apologize to her, and then promise to apologize to Griff. Otherwise, well, I just don't think I can save you, this time.''

''See?'' Abby said, standing up and walking past Catherine, gathering up fresh underwear on her way to the walk-in closet, her bottom lip thrust out in an exaggerated pout. "I told you, Teach, mom always liked you best."

"Apology accepted," Catherine said wryly, picking up the bath sheet Abby let drop to the floor as she walked, naked, into the closet. "And mom's right, he is cute."

Abby stuck her head out of the closet, grinning as she stepped into pink-and-white polka-dot panties. "And she said I'd make a great doctor's wife, Catherine. Is she right about that, too?"

"That depends," Catherine quipped as her mother sat down on the chair in the corner. "Is he a pediatrician?"

"Ha-ha," Abby shot back at her as she slipped her arms through the thin straps of the matching pink-and-white polka-dot bra. "Mom, Catherine's picking on me. And where's Elly, anyway? You two usually prefer the tag-team approach to your Let's Pick on Abby routine. Ah—all present and accounted for," she ended as Elly walked into the room and sat down on the edge of the bed, gracefully crossing her long, dancer's legs.

"Did you two leave anything for me," she asked, "or am I just here to bandage up her wounds?"

"No wounds," Catherine said, shaking her head. "As always, she got off easy. So now we want to hear the details, and you're just in time. Come on, Abby," she urged as Abby walked out of the closet, now dressed in snow-white denim short-shorts and a hot pink blouse with long, full sleeves and a peasant neckline, "you owe us."

"Nope," she told them, heading for the bathroom once more to blow-dry her freshly washed hair at least a little bit. "Not this time. This one's private."

"Oh boy," Elly said, looking at her mother. "Abby, not sharing? What do you think, Mom? Catherine? Do you think we have a winner?"

"You guys are nuts. Pete's a nice man, that's all. Stop giving mom ideas, okay?" Abby grumbled, then turned on the hair dryer, shutting everyone out with the noise it made as she bent over from the waist and began drying her hair. After all, Pete was waiting for her.

"Nice car," Abby said as she leaned her head back against the leather seat of Pete's late-model convertible and let the wind run riot with her curls. "The guys at college used to call these things babe catchers."

"Yeah, at my college, too," Pete said, grinning over at her. "Although I don't think about it that way. Much," he added, waggling his eyebrows at her, so that she laughed at his silliness.

"Idiot," she said, then closed her eyes and enjoyed the ride.

She'd escaped from the house without saying anything more to her family about Pete. It wouldn't have been fair. Not when he'd confided in her, told her about his bad time in the emergency room. It had even been difficult to tease back and forth with her sisters, and that had never been difficult before. Funny thing about that...

Abby turned her head and looked at Pete Shaw. Really looked at him.

He was, as she'd already decided, one very handsome man. Tall, with rather shaggy, dark-blond hair in need of a cut. His eyes were as green as her own behind those gold-rimmed glasses that made him look sexy, not at all nerdy. And then there were his hands. She really liked his hands. Long, straight fingers, neatly clipped nails. The hands of a surgeon, the hands of an artist.

She already knew he was a reconstructive surgeon only a couple of months from his final license to practice in his speciality. She'd always thought of doctors like him as plastic surgeons—a remark she'd made as they were driving to his house earlier that had gotten her a swift but kind correction. "Call it cosmetic surgery if you have to, Abby," he'd told her with a smile. "But not plastic, okay? Makes me feel like I'll be repairing Barbie dolls. There's a lot more to it than that."

She didn't really care what he called what he did, what he wanted to do with his life. It was enough to know his was important work, and she already knew that much. Rebuilding lives as well as faces, healing wounds that refused to heal on their own, reconstructing bodies ravaged by necessary surgeries or accidents.

Yes, he had the hands of an artist. And she'd bet his bedside manner had to be the best in the hospital. How could he miss? Not with that smile, that's for sure.

"So, you've been pretty quiet," she said at last as they turned into the parking lot of a local restaurant. "Was it that bad?"

He pulled into a parking space, turned off the motor. "Wasn't what that bad?" he asked, then gifted her with another one of his really beautiful smiles. "Oh," he said, shaking his head, "now I understand. Jim challenged me to a duel, actually."

Abby giggled. "He what?"

"Oh, yes, Abby. A duel. A duel to the death. We're meeting, Jim and Griff and I, on the golf course next Friday for eighteen holes of cutthroat golf. Since I rarely have time to play anymore, I'm figuring it's going to be a massacre. Now, come on. I'm back on duty at eleven tonight, so let's grab some food while I listen to you tell me about your life. You've certainly already heard enough about mine."

"So now it looks as if Mom's planning for Catherine and Griff to get married next month, at the same time she and Dad renew their vows. Wild, huh?" Abby said, sitting back and patting the corners of her mouth with her napkin after taking a last bite of apple pie. "I think Catherine's dragging her heels until Mom agrees *no* Elvis wedding chapel."

Pete's laugh was low and musical and very, very sexy, and Abby smiled as she watched him, thinking she was probably the luckiest person in all of Las Vegas today. Because Dr. Peter Shaw was a very nice man. A very, very nice man. Not that she was looking for a very nice man. Not that she was looking for a man at all.

The waitress returned to their table with Pete's change and he picked up all but five dollars, then stood up, walking around to Abby and pulling out her chair for her.

Oh, yeah. A very, very, *very* nice man.

"Did you want to take me home now, go home yourself and get some sleep?" she asked, once they were back in the car again and driving away from the restaurant. "I mean, it was great that you followed me home this morning and charmed the parental units and all of that, but you really don't have to spend your whole day off with me.''

''I want to spend my day off with you, Abby Parrish,'' he told her as he put on the turn signal and turned onto a street that looked vaguely familiar.

''This is your street, isn't it?'' she asked, looking at the the suburban sprawl that resembled her parents' neighborhood in some ways, but that seemed a notch or three above the houses in that area. She'd already wondered how a surgical resident could afford a house as large and well furnished as Pete's, but since it wasn't any of her business, she hadn't asked. She would eventually, of course, because Abby always asked whatever question was on her mind, made any comment that happened to pop into her head. She'd just wait a while, that's all, until she and Pete got to know each other better.

If they got to know each other better.

''Do you mind?'' he asked as he pulled into the driveway and cut the engine. ''It's just that my dad knows I have today off, and he'll be calling from Paris to check up on me in another twenty minutes or so. A man of schedules and order, my dad. He'll go into a major panic if I'm not here to pick up the phone. You're not the only one who's the baby in the family, Abby. And I'm thirty-two, not twenty-five.''

She sat patiently as he walked around the car to open her door for her, then looked up at him in open interest. ''Paris? Your father is calling you all the way from Paris, just to check up on you? That is *très hystérique,* you poor thing,'' she ended, giggling as she extended her hand to him so that he could help her out of the car.

''*Oui, mademoiselle,*'' Pete agreed, exaggeratedly

bowing over her hand before pressing a smacking kiss against her flesh. "Eet is quite, as you say, hysterical. However, if you ever dare to tell a soul, eet shall go badly for you, *comprenez-vous?* And your accent is atrocious, by the way. Where did you learn French?"

"In Allentown, Pennsylvania. In Miss Schantz's conversational French class in high school, and I've forgotten more than I ever learned. And, although I've been told I can turn a phrase at least tolerably well, I've also been told I speak French with a decided Pennsylvania Dutch accent, thanks to Miss Schantz's somewhat less than Gallic inflections. Was I really that bad?"

Pete laughed all the way into the house, which was nice, because Abby was beginning to be just the least bit nervous around him. It was silly of her, of course—or *naturellement,* she should say—but she really was liking this man. Probably much more than she should. After all, she was only twenty-five, and she'd never even seen Paris.

"I'd like to see Paris," she told him as she followed him through the foyer and down the hallway leading to the kitchen. "Paris, Rome, Katmandu. I plan to travel at least until I'm thirty, see as much of the world as I can. I can do that, you know, with my job. Have laptop, will travel, and all of that," she trailed off, knowing she sounded like an idiot. Why was she trying so hard? Who was she trying to convince?

"Really?" Pete said, pulling his head back out of the refrigerator. "How's ice water suit you, Abby? It's either that or we go shopping, and I don't have time for that before Dad calls." He closed the door, leaned against it. "I think I'm growing some mutant penicillin in there. That'll teach me to tell Dad I don't need a housekeeper cluttering up his place, huh?''

"*His* place?'' Abby climbed onto one of the high stools at the breakfast bar, wrapping her legs around the rungs. She watched as Pete filled two glasses with ice and water from the serving compartment built into the front of the freezer door.

"Yeah, *his* place,'' Pete told her, sitting one glass in front of her, then leaning his elbows on the breakfast bar. "My car, but his house, his everything else. Dad's in Paris for a year, doing something very top secret—or very boring, as Dad likes to say—for the government, and I'm taking advantage of his offer to move back in here, rent free, for the duration. If I water the plants, that is, and don't throw more than one wild party a month.''

"And do you?'' Abby asked, sipping at the ice water.

"Do I what? Throw more than one wild party a month?''

"No, silly, do you water his plants? You're a resident, Pete, you don't have either the time or the energy for more than one wild party a month.'' She looked around the room, saw a very sad-looking aloe plant sitting on the windowsill over the sink. "And never mind. I think I already have my answer. Murderer. Shame on you, Pete.''

Still holding her glass, she disengaged her legs from the stool and walked over to the sink, poured some of her ice water into the bone-dry soil around the aloe plant. "There you go, you poor baby. That's what you need. That, and probably a good plant fertilizer, huh? Maybe a bigger pot, so that your little roots can stretch themselves out, wiggle their little root toes?''

"Don't be too nice, Abby," Pete warned. "We wouldn't want to spoil the poor baby, would we? Ah," he said as the phone rang beside him. "My master's voice. Excuse me, Abby, I'm going to answer this in the living room, okay? Then we'll take a ride or something."

She waved him on his way, already looking toward the refrigerator, her head tipped to one side as she wondered if he had an open box of baking soda sitting on one of the inside shelves. He really should, especially if he was growing mutant penicillin in there.

"Where are you going now?" Elly asked as she sat on the living room couch, her legs drawn up under her light cotton bathrobe as she drank her morning orange juice. "It's only ten o'clock, for goodness sake. This isn't anything like you, you know. I can remember the Abby who slept until at least noon when she was on vacation. Mom once made me creep into your room with a mirror, as a matter of fact, to hold it in front of your nose to see if your breath clouded it up or you were dead."

Abby grinned at the memories. "Yeah, I was a real slug, wasn't I? And I probably would still be sleeping, except that I'm not on vacation anymore, you know. I'm a working girl, and I'm working."

"At what?" Elly persisted with a wave of her hand, indicating the paper grocery bags Abby had in both arms. "What's in those bags, anyway? And, not to repeat myself, but where are you going? Surely not to Pete's again. You've been there every day this week, and he's hardly there himself."

Abby almost said, "Keeping count, are you? Don't you have anything more interesting to do?" But she bit her tongue, held back. Poor Elly. Nearly a month now, and still she wouldn't talk to anyone about her marriage, about Rob. And poor Rob, calling her mother and father late at night, after Elly was asleep—or crying herself to sleep—asking their advice, demanding that he be allowed to come to Summerlin and see his wife.

Abby sighed, then slid the two large paper bags onto a chair before sitting down on the edge of the large, square coffee table. She looked at her beautiful, talented sister. Her so unhappy sister. "You want to come along, El?" she asked hopefully. "Pete won't mind. I'm lining his dad's kitchen cabinets today. A really sweet lady from—" she reached into the small breast pocket of her Spiderman T-shirt and pulled out a envelope, looked at it "—from Diboll Texas wrote me this great letter on how to measure shelf paper without putting yourself into a tizzy. She said that, El. She said *tizzy*. I didn't know anybody said *tizzy* anymore. Anyway, I'm going to check it out, see if it works, then repaper all of Pete's dad's cabinets."

"Gee, Abby, that sounds fascinating, but I think I'll give it a pass," Elly said, pulling her legs up even more, as if trying to fold all five feet and nine inches of herself into a cocoon, where she could hide from the big, bad world. "Besides, I promised Mom I'd go grocery shopping with her. I need to pick up a few things myself, so I said I would. Maybe some other time? I mean, you're probably going to be testing a way to turn king-size mattresses in one easy flip of the wrist, or restringing Pete's dad's tennis racket or something any day now, and I wouldn't want to miss it."

Abby held her temper in check, but it wasn't easy. Elly had been having her private pity party far too long, and it was about time somebody told her so. But she'd promised her mom and Catherine that she'd keep her mouth shut, and she would.

"Pete's been great about this, Elly," was all she said, retrieving her bags and heading for the front door, balancing both in one arm as she dug in her purse for the keys to the car Griff had loaned them to replace the rental car for the length of their visit. "Just think about it—a whole series of articles on how to organize the bachelor or bachelorette household and then keep it organized. I've gotten three good columns out of this already, and I've barely left the kitchen. I don't even want to talk about the amount of powdered detergent the man had, gunked around the edges of the washing machine. I've already bought him a box of premeasured detergent packets, which solved that problem."

"Yeah, okay," Elly said, her voice quiet, already sounding far away, as far away as Elly was herself, lost in her own thoughts, as usual. "You have fun, Abby, and say hi to Pete when you see him."

"Oh, Pete's not going to be home. He's on duty until at least—oh, forget it," she said, then wrestled the front door open with one hand and headed for the driveway.

Old Blue Eyes belted out lyrics from the state-of-the-art stereo in the living room as Abby worked in the kitchen. Toiled in the kitchen. *Slaved* in the kitchen.

Odd bits of shelf paper littered the room, some of it with its sticky back exposed, so that yellow-and-white-plaid pieces were now stuck to the floor, the cabinets doors, the soles of Abby's size six sneakers, the seat of her black short-shorts. There was even one triangle-shaped piece stuck to the overhead light, but it remained a mystery to Abby as to just how it had gotten there.

There were a grand total of twenty-two cabinets and drawers in the kitchen, and the contents of each and every one of them were now scattered around the room, piled on top of countertops, stacked on the kitchen table, loaded into the sink. But she'd done it! It had taken four hours and more than a couple of curse words, but she'd done it.

"So much for Diboll, Texas," she said, tilting her head to one side as she admired her work. Four hours, two wasted rolls of self-sticking shelf paper, and more than one innovation of her own later, but she'd done it. She lifted a plastic bottle of ketchup to her mouth, using it like a microphone, threw out her other arm, bent her spine backward, and belted out in tune with Frank Sinatra's closing words: "and did it *my* wa…ay!"

As the notes from the stereo faded away Abby heard the sound of a single pair of hands clapping, so that she nearly fell flat on her backside as she whirled around to see Pete standing at the entrance to the kitchen, dressed in his green hospital scrubs. The grin on his face was unholy, at the very least.

"Pete! Hi…um…*hi!*" she stammered, looking at the ketchup bottle in her hand, then quickly tossing it in the general direction of the counter. It landed on the floor with a thunk, and she winced. "You're home early...no!...you're not supposed to be home at all. Is something wrong?''

"Nope. There was to be an afternoon seminar after surgery this morning, but the guy canceled," he said easily, walking past her to the refrigerator. He pulled out a can of iced tea, then automatically checked it off, just as she'd taught him.

She'd stocked his refrigerator earlier in the week, then attached a magnetic, reusable "inventory list" to the outside of the door. It was a simple enough invention. All "staples," and she considered iced tea a staple where Pete was concerned, were written down on the board with the attached felt-tip marker, and then checked off when they were used.

Right now the iced tea line read "twelve cans iced tea," followed by four slashes like the one Pete had just made, so that he knew at a glance that he only had eight cans left before it was time to add iced tea to the shopping list that was held by a magnet to the side of the refrigerator.

Abby considered the whole thing rather brilliant, as she'd typed up a list of staples as well as leaving space for "yeah, I want this, too," and then printed out a dozen copies. If Pete remembered to make his check marks and wrote down stuff he wanted to buy, all he had to do before he went grocery shopping would be to count check marks, complete the list, then take it with him when he went to the store.

"You really should eat more fresh fruit," she said now, thinking of the list and the lack of check marks next to the "produce section" of the thing. And then she grimaced again, inwardly, as she realized that wasn't at all what she wanted to say.

What she wanted to say was, ''Well, in that case,

big boy, since you have nothing else to do this afternoon, why don't you take me away from all this?'' No, that wouldn't work.

So, as Pete leaned against the counter—staring a hole through her, for crying out crumbs!—she picked up the scissors and quickly began cutting off another section of shelf liner, somehow getting the scissors caught between the liner and its paper backing, so that the whole dumb thing got stuck to the scissors. She tried to fix it, very nonchalantly, as if this happened all the time and was no problem to her at all—and within thirty seconds the shelf liner was neatly stuck to the front of her Spiderman shirt.

''Rats!'' she said, ripping it loose, then crushing it into a fat, sticky ball that now stuck to her hands.

''Having fun?''

She shot Pete a look meant to melt him where he stood. ''Yeah. Heaps,'' she snapped angrily.

He laughed, and that laugh warmed her insides. ''Doesn't look like it.''

''Well,'' she said, finally ridding herself of the sticky, wadded-up mess, ''looks can be deceiving, can't they? I haven't had this much fun since I tested a do-it-yourself home-improvement project that included using an electric sander. I was supposed to be able to make this cute wooden Santa Claus, and—'' She shook her head, made a deliberate funny face. ''Trust me, Pete. You wouldn't have wanted to be there.''

''Actually, Abby,'' he told her, walking over to toss the empty can into one of the plastic recycling bins she'd installed in the cabinet under the sink, ''I probably, as my grandpa Shaw used to say, would have paid down real cash money to see you working with an electric sander.'' Then he rubbed his hands together, looked around the kitchen, looked at the mess in his kitchen. "Need help?"

She needed a can of iced tea of her own. She needed another two hours to cut and place shelf paper, now that she'd finally figured out how to do it right— with no thanks to Diboll, Texas. She needed to put everything back in the cabinets now that she'd figured out the most efficient arrangement of food, pots and pans, dishes, glasses and utensils.

But mostly she needed to be with Pete. They'd seen each other every day since he'd agreed to her plan to organize his house and then write about it in her column, but theirs had to be the most platonic friendship in the history of the world. They ate pizza together, watched TV together, talked politics, world events, his patients and her columns together, but that was about as "together" as they had gotten.

Abby knew she wanted more, more than just this easy friendship. Pete, on the other hand, obviously did not.

Maybe she was sending the wrong signals, if she was sending signals at all. Maybe it was time to let him know that she was willing, more than willing, to take their relationship to the next level.

"Well, actually," she began, not quite sure what she'd say next, and then she stopped, watching as a tall, long-legged brunette dressed in pale blue culottes and a white knit shirt walked into the kitchen area. "Pete?" she asked, pointing to the woman. The absolutely gorgeous woman.

But Pete was looking at her, his expression strange, unreadable. "What?"

"You've got company," Abby whispered, feeling

like she'd swallowed a sticky ball of shelf paper and it had lodged somewhere in her throat.

He turned away from her, looked at the woman. "Oh. Oh, yeah," he said, turning back to Abby, his expression caught somewhere between sheepish and frustrated. "Sheila? I'd like you to meet my friend Abby. Sheila's a doctor who works with me, Abby. At the hospital," he said quickly, holding out his hand so that the woman took it even as she smiled down at Abby.

"Hello, Abby," Sheila said as she wrapped her arm through Pete's. "We just stopped here so Peter can change and pick up his golf clubs."

Sheila smiled at Abby again. People were always smiling down at her, damn it—why did she have to be so short? Why did the rest of the world have to be so tall? Why did Sheila have to be so drop-dead gorgeous? "Hi, Sheila," she said, smiling until her teeth ached. "Nice to meet you."

"Peter?" Sheila said, no, *purred*. "Don't you think you should go get changed? Your maid seems to have a lot of work to do, and I already called my club and made arrangements to have you as my guest. Our tee-off time is in less than an hour."

"Oh, no, Abby isn't my...that is, she's only here to..."

Abby watched as Pete's tongue stumbled over itself, then rescued him, the rat. "Yes, you really should run along, *Peter,* so I can get back to work. I wouldn't want to have to charge you overtime, now would I?"

"Abby..." he said threateningly, then rolled his eyes at her and let Sheila steer him out of the room. "We'll talk...later!" He said this over his shoulder

as he went, and Abby didn't know if she should take
his words as a threat or a promise.

She only knew that her heart was breaking, which
surprised her, because until that moment she hadn't
realized her heart was so deeply involved in her feel-
ings for Dr. Peter Shaw.

Chapter 9

"Abby? Abby, where are you?" Peter called out as he stood in the middle of the spotlessly clean kitchen. There was no answer, not that he'd expected one, because her car hadn't been in the driveway. Worse, with the kitchen put back together again, it didn't look like she had any reason to ever come back. "Damn it!" he exploded, punching the wall, then turned and ran for his bedroom, already stripping off his shirt.

Twenty minutes later, his hair still wet from his shower, he was on his way to Summerlin, still mad at himself. He'd hurt Abby, really hurt her. How could he have been so stupid? Next thing he knew, he'd be kicking puppies.

He'd kept it light with Abby, purposely light, because he didn't have time for a serious relationship right now. He wouldn't have time for a serious relationship for the next five years, at the least. Besides,

Abby had made it clear to him that she had plans of her own for the next five years, and they didn't include anything close to settling down, staying in one place, making any more serious commitment than keeping an appointment for her next manicure.

Why did everything have to be so complicated? Why did he have to be so attracted to her, so amused by her, so intrigued by her, so delighted with her? And why now? Man, his timing had never been this far off before.

They'd been having fun these past days.

They'd gone food shopping together, with Abby explaining the finer points of squeezing fruit until the produce manager had asked her if she was going to buy that cantaloupe or make love to it.

She'd stood on the bar above the front wheels of the cart, leaning forward as she held on to the edge of the basket, one hand raised over her eyes as she "scouted" out the canned goods aisle, calling out, "Creamed corn to starboard, cap'n, three for a dou-bloon!" as he'd laughed so hard he could barely steer the cart.

She'd squinted at prices, explained the meaning of those little price-versus-amount-of-contents stickers on each shelf. She'd told him that, no, he was not getting the best bang for his buck by buying the su-per-giant-economy size of Italian salad dressing if he couldn't possibly eat that many salads before the dressing's expiration date. Hell, he hadn't even known salad dressings *had* an expiration date.

She'd told him things about egg-packing standards and "sell by" dates that he probably could have gone through the rest of his life, quite happily, without ever hearing. He hadn't eaten a single egg since, without first testing its freshness by slipping it, shell and all, into a glass of water and waiting to see if it floated point up.

She even had been stopped, in the frozen food section, by an openly gushing woman who'd recognized her from the photograph published on top of her column, and asked to autograph a half-gallon container of double-chocolate-chip ice cream.

Oh, yeah, Peter had to agree with his smiling self as he waited for a red light to turn green, grocery shopping with Abby Parrish had certainly been an adventure.

As a matter of fact, everything he did with Abby was like an adventure. How she had gotten him to agree to spend a couple of hours at the local water-slide park, he would never understand—but he wouldn't trade his memories of those hours for a new convertible.

Abby was a child, a woman, a clown, a seductress. She was bright and funny and she seemed to instinctively know when he wanted to talk and when he was content just to sit on the couch in his living room, her head resting on his shoulder as they shared a bowl of popcorn and watched a ''Gilligan's Island'' rerun.

In less than a week, they had become buddies. Pals. Maybe even best friends. With the chance, just the chance, of something more.

Peter slammed the flat of his hand against the steering wheel. ''And now I've gone and blown it! Good going, Shaw—you jerk!''

''Abby should be home soon,'' Jim Parrish said as he led the way to the patio and waved Peter into a chair. ''She and Susie are out shopping for a sixpence

for Catherine to put in her shoe on her wedding day.''
He raised his hands to Peter before he could politely
inquire just where in hell Abby thought she could find
a sixpence, then said, ''Don't ask. With both Abby
and my wife, I've found it safer to be comfortable in
my ignorance. But they'll come back with one. I'd
bet my last dollar on it.''

''So Abby and her mother are alike in more than
their looks?'' Peter asked instead, smiling. ''They really could be taken for sisters, you know, and I'm not
talking about their height or their blond hair. It's their
great bone structure. And that's a professional assess-
ment, in case you're wondering, and not just a casual
observation. All of the Parrish women have really
classic bone structure.''

''Catherine and Elly take more after my side of the
family,'' Jim said, beaming with pride, ''while Abby
is Susie all over again. In looks, in temperament, in
her loving heart, in her sometimes off-the-wall ways.
Totally captivating to the right man, as I learned to
my amazement and gratitude thirty years ago. You
could take that as a warning, I suppose, but it's probably already too late for that. Isn't it, Pete?''

''I'm that transparent?'' Peter asked, frowning into
his glass of lemonade. ''That's not good.''

''No?'' Jim inquired, looking at him closely. ''Why
not? No—forget I asked that. I'm living with Susie
too long. That's her sort of question, not mine.''

''It's all right, Jim,'' Peter answered, putting down
his glass and standing up to pace the bricked patio.
''I wanted to keep it light, you know? Have some
fun, a few laughs, get to know Abby a little better.
Because she is unique, Jim, with the best of both you

and Susie inside her. Beautiful, smart, a real free spirit…''

''And a bit of a space cadet?'' Jim offered when Peter seemed to run out of words.

''Yeah, that, too,'' he admitted, grinning. ''Those clothes of hers, that mop of blond hair she doesn't seem to realize is as sexy as hell, the things she does.'' He stopped pacing, looked at Jim. ''Did I tell you what she did yesterday? Well, let me tell you. I came home to find her in her bathing suit—and sitting in the whirlpool tub in the bedroom.''

''She was taking a bath in her bathing suit?'' Jim shook his head. ''Well, that's a new one.''

''She wasn't taking a bath, Jim, she was cleaning the tub. She explained, very reasonably, that she was too short to reach all the way into the tub without falling into it headfirst. There had to be, she said, an easier way for shorter people to do it, and she was trying out her own idea. It didn't matter if she got her old bathing suit full of cleanser and, besides, she'd just clean up by taking a shower with it on once she'd tried out some new antimildew product on the shower stall tiles. And you know what? It made sense…in an Abby sort of way, you understand.''

''I can just imagine how this is going to sound in her column,'' Jim said, shaking his head. ''God bless her, she doesn't have any idea how hilarious that column of hers can be at times. I'd tell her, but then she'd probably try to be more serious, and that would take the fun out of a lot of people's lives as they search the newspaper every Tuesday and Friday morning, hoping for a good laugh instead of reading about another murder or international incident.''

Peter returned to his chair and sat down. ''I was

wrong, you know. She's not really a space cadet," he said honestly. "She's just an original thinker." He picked up his glass, then put it back down without taking another drink from it. "And I'm crazy about her, Jim, for all the good that's going to do me."

"Why? What did you—no, never mind. I'm not going to ask. I'm safer if I don't ask, because then Susie can't worm it out of me. Besides," he said, pushing himself out of the chair, "I think I just heard two car doors closing out front. Do you want me to get Susie out of the way? I'll grab her before she gets into the house and ask her if she wants to go get ice cream. That always works with Susie. And Catherine and Elly probably won't be home for hours, as they were meeting Griff at the dealership for some reason or another. Am I overstepping? I mean, you do seem to have a look on your face that says you're figuring out a way to apologize for something, right?"

"Right. Thanks, Jim," Peter said as the older man headed toward the doors to the house. Then he stood up once more and began to pace.

"Hi," Abby said a few moments later as she opened the sliding door a few inches and stuck her head outside the opening. "Dad said you were here. Let me grab a glass of lemonade and I'll be right out, okay?"

"Okay," Peter said cautiously, then waited for her to join him. Funny, she didn't sound angry. Or look it, for that matter. What Abby looked, as usual, was beautiful. Okay, and a little wacky, considering she was wearing a bright yellow sundress with a foot-wide daisy sewn smack in the middle of the front of it.

As she walked out of the house, he noticed that she

was also wearing sandals with a big, drooping daisy on each one, and she even had a silk daisy stuck over her left ear. God, she was cute. Eat-her-up adorable, actually.

So why wasn't she mad? She ought to be mad.

Peter's heart sank. Maybe she didn't care enough to be mad.

Well, that was depressing!

"Did you have a nice game?" she asked as she sat herself down on a chaise longue and levered her feet out of her sandals, sending them sailing across the patio one after the other. "You're playing again tomorrow, remember—with Dad and Griff."

Peter pointed a finger at her. "Exactly!" he said, jumping on her words before she could say anything else. "That's exactly what I'm doing tomorrow, Abby. I'm playing golf. With your dad. With Griff."

"And you needed a little practice," Abby then supplied for him, before he could say so himself.

"Yes, yes I did. Definitely did." Okay. So maybe this wasn't going to be as hard as he thought.

"And Sheila, being a member of one of the local country clubs, was nice enough to invite you on the course as her guest," Abby went on. "Just so you could practice. It wasn't a date, it was just a friend doing a favor for a friend. You're just sick that you had to leave me knee-deep in sticky shelf paper and with your kitchen looking like it had just exploded, but you didn't have any other choice. After all, your hospital co-worker Sheila had made a tee-off time for you both and all that."

Peter spread his arms wide, smiled at her. Relaxed. "You've got it, Abby. That's exactly how it happened, exactly how it was. Sheila was doing me a favor.''

Abby lifted up her left leg, aimed it toward him. ''Sure. Now pull this one, Pete, it's got bells on it.''

Peter stepped back, frowned in confusion. ''I thought you said you understood.''

''Understood what, *Peter?*'' Abby asked, sliding her legs over so that she could put her bare feet on the ground and stand up. ''You're afraid to tell me the truth. That hurts, you know. I thought we were friends.''

Pete pressed his hands to his head, closed his eyes. ''Now wait a minute. Let me figure this out, okay? Hey—stop that,'' he warned as she began to slip the large white buttons on the shoulder and running down one side of the dress out of their moorings. ''What are you doing?''

Her hands stilled on the third button from the top, which meant that nothing but one yellow strap of her bra was exposed. ''I'm not angry that you had a date, Pete,'' she told him, beginning to work on the buttons once more, rather ruthlessly. ''I haven't made any claims on you, have I? Why, we haven't even kissed or anything.''

''Define *anything*,'' Peter said, watching Abby, finding himself to be somewhere between fear and hope as she bent over to unbutton the last few buttons. Then she undid the last button, straightened up, and allowed the sundress to fall off her other shoulder, so that it puddled at her feet.

''Oh, Pete, close your mouth. You couldn't possibly have thought I was going to go skinny-dipping. Why, I haven't done that since, since...hmm, never mind,'' she told him as he looked at her, saw the yellow-and-white-striped bikini that skimmed her rather fantastic curves.

"You're wearing a bikini? Abby, you actually had a bikini on underneath that silly dress? You could have told me, you know," he complained, now caught between anger and disappointment. He'd think about the disappointment later, when he felt more sane, more in control. For now he would settle for anger. Because she really was going to drive him crazy. There was no doubt about it anymore.

She picked up a white bathing cap and pulled it over her curls, ruthlessly tucking in errant locks as she glared at him. "I'm angry, Pete, in case you haven't guessed yet, because you came here prepared to *lie* to me. You did, didn't you? Because you and Sheila did have a date. Because, if you didn't, Sheila sure had to be the last to know it. Why did you do that, Pete? Why did you think it was necessary to lie to me?"

"You look as cute as a bug in that cap, Abby, do you know that?" he said instead, taking hold of her arm as she turned, ready to dive into the pool.

"And I'll bet you look cute wet," she countered.

The next thing Peter knew, he was sticking his head out of the water and shaking his sopping wet hair out of his eyes while Abby stood above him on the patio, the bathing cap no longer on her head, and wiping her hands together as if satisfied with a job well done.

"There are towels inside that bench over there," she told him kindly. "Just lift the lid. Oh," she said, having turned away from him, heading for the house. "Two more things, okay? One, you may pick me up tomorrow night at seven-thirty and take me out to dinner, to apologize. I like lobster, and have been told

watching me eat it is very much like an occasion of
sin. And two—this isn't a bikini, Peter Dumb Bunny
Shaw. Think about *that,* why don't you!'' she ended,
then picked up her dress, draped it over one shoulder
and left him to find his own way out of the pool.

Not a bikini? Damn. He watched as she walked
away, noticed a certain hitch to her walk that would
have made a lesser man weep. Still, it was good the
pool was only five feet deep where he'd entered it,
because otherwise, Peter thought as he slowly made
his way to the ladder, it was a pretty sure bet he would
have drowned.

Abby had been right. Watching her eat lobster was
an occasion of sin. Watching her lick melted butter
off her fingers had probably earned him a special
place in Hell.

He leaned an elbow on the table, having pushed
away his plate after downing one of the best steaks
he'd ever eaten, and propped his chin in his hand.
''You're doing that on purpose, aren't you?'' he
asked her. ''Oh, you're pretending you don't know
what you're doing to me, but you do. Shame on you,
Abby Parrish. And shame on me for wanting to ask
you if you want something with whipped cream on it
for dessert.''

Abby laughed, as he'd hoped she would, then
looked at him carefully. ''Do you want to talk about
it now? We've talked about your golf game and the
one you chipped in on eighteen to break one hundred.
We've talked about the boy who fell off his bike and
how you stitched up his chin so that he won't have a
scar. We've talked about the heart surgery patient
whose chest wound wouldn't heal until you'd worked

on it—I think I could have done without that explanation, to tell you the truth, especially over dinner. We talked about types of shelf paper—the good, the bad and the truly ugly. So, do we talk about Sheila now?''

''She's a resident,'' he told her, still leaning his jaw on his hand. ''Orthopedic surgery, second year. And she really did ask me to go play golf with her, and not the other way around.''

Abby nodded, then smiled up at the waiter who removed her plate and replaced it with a bowl of warm water with lemon and a small towel. ''Thank you, Harry, that's really sweet of you,'' she said, as she and Harry had been on a first-name basis ever since he'd held out her chair for her.

Pete watched the waiter as he lingered for a moment—hovered, actually—then finally walked away. ''I think Harry wants you to have his babies, Abby,'' he said, smiling.

''Don't be silly,'' she told him, looking shocked. ''I was only being polite. I mean, what does it cost to be polite?''

''Fifteen percent, usually. Now, back to Sheila.''

''Oh, must we?'' She dried her fingers with the warm towel, then leaned forward, putting her own elbows on the table. ''She's mad about you. That's obvious. And you wanted to see if you might be even slightly mad about her. So, Pete. Were you?''

''I couldn't wait to get rid of her,'' he admitted honestly, knowing Abby was right on all counts. He had wanted to be with Sheila, just to see if he could enjoy her company, enjoy any other woman's company. And he'd spent the whole afternoon thinking about how cute Abby would look in golf shoes. He was a sick, sick man, and he knew it. "She talked shop for the whole round. Compound fractures, knee replacements, bursitis treatments, did I want to fly up to Reno with her for the weekend...."

Abby sat up, made little shooing motions with her hands. "Back up, okay? She actually invited you to go to Reno with her? For the weekend?"

Peter took off his glasses, began to polish them with his napkin. "Thought that might get your attention. Besides, I still owed you one for that trick you played on me out at the pool."

She laughed, and he relaxed at last, feeling that they were back where they belonged, feeling free and easy with each other. "That was mean of me, wasn't it? Will you ever forgive me? Is there anything I can do to make it up to you?"

"Don't ask loaded questions, Abby. We're in a public place, remember?"

She looked at him levelly. "We don't have to be," she said quietly. "Do we?"

"Abby, are you sure? I want to—God, *want* is such an understatement. But are you sure? Neither of us is ready for any sort of serious commitment. We both know that, we've both said as much."

"I agree," she told him, lifting her chin a fraction. Her so adorable, kissable chin. "You've got to establish your practice. I've got at least a half dozen more countries to visit before I'm thirty. So, if we both go into this with our eyes wide-open, nobody can get hurt, right? That is, of course," she said rather shyly, "if I'm not wrong, and you really don't want to—"

"What are you wearing under that dress, Abby?" Pete asked tightly, looking at the electric blue strapless sundress she'd told him she'd picked up in Mexico the previous summer. The dress was relatively subdued—for Abby—it was simply cut and ankle length, with only a medium-size burro painted onto the skirt.

She grinned at him. Half sinner, half saint. "Let's just say, Pete, that I'm not wearing a bikini. But how sweet of you to ask."

Peter tipped back his chair and raised his hand even as he was reaching in his pocket for his wallet. "Harry! Check please!"

There was a trail of clothing from the front door to the hallway, to the floor of the bedroom at the end of the hallway. A shoe here, a shirt there, a pair of ridiculous lace panties caught on the doorknob of the bedroom.

Inside that bedroom, tangled in the sheets of his king-size bed, Abby and Peter lay close together, her head on his shoulder as he slowly stroked her bare arm and tried to catch his breath.

"That was…incredible," he said slowly, looking up at the ceiling. He recognized the crack in it, the one vaguely shaped like the profile of his old anatomy professor, Doctor Cassels, so he knew it must be his ceiling, his room, his house. But, if he lived for another five hundred years, he knew he'd never remember exactly how he'd gotten there.

Abby stirred in his arms, looked up at him. "Only incredible? Gee, I was sort of thinking fantastic, myself. Only incredible for you, you say?" She slid her hand underneath the sheets. "Maybe if we tried again…?"

"That's it, Abby, kill me," he said, catching her hand in his, then bringing it to his lips. "Well," he said then, moving away from her, reluctantly moving away from her, to sit on the edge of the bed and pull on the khaki slacks he'd left there, "much as I hate to say this, it's probably time for the post mortem. I'll go get us each a can of iced tea, okay? You do agree that we need one, right?"

"A can of iced tea?" Abby asked teasingly as she sat up in the huge bed, the sheet drawn up over her breasts, the tips of her toes poking up the sheet a ridiculously short way down the length of the mattress.

"No, Abby," he said, trying to be serious, because he damn full well knew it was time to be serious. "We have to talk about what happened here tonight. And, before you say anything else—I can see you're dying to—I do *not* mean I want to hear a critique of my performance."

Her smile faded; her fantastic green eyes clouded. "I know, Pete. You go get the iced tea. I'll meet you in the living room."

He leaned over the bed, kissed the tip of her nose. "It's easy to find, Abby. Just follow the trail."

She'd done just that, he learned two minutes later as he walked into the living room carrying two cans of iced tea. She was sitting on the couch, wearing the white dress shirt he'd discarded somewhere in the hall and looking small and as fragile as a fine crystal vase. Her bare legs were tucked up under her, and she'd wrapped her hands tightly around her arms, as if she were cold. Only her tumble of blond curls still looked warm, touchable.

"Having second thoughts?" he asked as he held out one of the cans and she shook her head, motioning that he should just put the can on the coffee table. "I checked off two cans on the list,'' he offered, knowing he sounded close to pathetic, even as if he was begging for some sign of approval.

''On the coaster, please,'' she said, pointing to the stack of cork coasters that had appeared on the coffee table two days earlier. ''I now know how to get water rings out of wood, thanks to your bad bachelor habits, but now that I've proven I can do it, I don't think I want to do it again.''

He did as she asked, uncomfortably aware that there was some new gulf between them, which was pretty remarkable, considering how close they'd been only a little while ago. ''You're thinking we've made a mistake, aren't you?''

She looked at him with tears in her eyes. ''Aren't you? We were friends, Pete, really good friends. And then I went and blew it.''

He put down his own can, suddenly not at all thirsty. ''*You* blew it? How so?''

She shrugged her shoulders. ''I was jealous,'' she said quietly, so quietly he had to bend closer to her to hear the words. ''Jealous of Sheila and her sleek black hair, her long, killer legs. I wanted to prove to you that I'm just as much of a female as she is. Which is stupid, because I know who I am. Abby Parrish. Sweet, cuddly Abby Parrish. Every man's friend.''

He put a finger under her chin, turned her head so that she had to face him. ''Excuse me, but aren't you the same woman who was just in my bedroom, in my bed? Because there was a lot going on in there a while ago, and none of it had a damn thing to do with *friendship.*''

She leaned forward, kissed his cheek. ''You're so sweet, Pete. Thank you.'' She reached down, took his hand in hers, laid them both in her lap as she rested her head against the back of the couch. "I am going to go to Paris, you know. And London. And Katmandu. I promised myself, Pete, while I was still in college. I promised I'd travel until I was thirty, then maybe settle down."

He knew where this was heading. He stretched out his legs on the coffee table, laid his own head on the back of the couch. "I'm going straight into practice with a group in Las Vegas once my residency is completed. I accepted an offer from them last month. It's a hell of a lot cheaper than trying to set myself up alone, but I'll still be working my rear end off for the next couple of years, taking on all the scut jobs, most of the weekend on-call hours. And I'll probably be paying off my student loans for the next ten years, minimum. Dad wanted to help, but I told him he'd done enough." He turned his head to find Abby looking at him. "You won't be thirty for another five years, will you? By then I'll be thirty-seven. Wow. That's a long time."

She squeezed his hand. "I've heard that timing is everything," she said, her smile rather watery, but sincere. "Do you still want me to come here every day? I'd wanted to do a little work on your garden, try to make it more maintenance-free, and repot some of your dad's indoor plants for another column I'm thinking about writing, but—"

"I still want you to come here, Abby," he said, interrupting her. "I meant that—I really enjoy having you here. More than I ever thought I would... probably more than I should."

She nodded, not saying anything, and suddenly he couldn't take it anymore. He let go of her hand, slid his arm around her shoulders, pulled her close. "It's nearly midnight, Abby. Do you want me to take you home now?"

"Home?" she said questioningly, as if he might be speaking in some foreign language. "Oh, yes, yes," she said, moving away from him, getting to her feet. "Just let me go find my clothes and...and comb my hair, I suppose, and then we'll be on our way. I'll be right back, promise."

"Yeah. Sure," Peter said, then watched as she padded barefoot down the hallway, leaving him feeling more alone than he'd ever felt before.

Chapter 10

Abby stood in front of the mirror over the bathroom sink and watched as ridiculously huge tears ran down her cheeks. What a jerk she was! What an idiot! Or, as Bugs Bunny always said, "What a mar*oon!*"

"I'm going to Paris…and Rome…and Katmandu," she said, quoting herself as she glared at her reflection. "Yeah, right. You don't even know where Katmandu *is*, Abigail Parrish," she told herself. "Besides, you'll probably hate it. There couldn't possibly be a pair of golden arches within a thousand miles of the place."

She turned on the spigots with more force than necessary, then began splashing her tear-wet face with cold water, hoping her eyes wouldn't get all red and puffy, the way they usually did when she cried.

Then she slid open the mirrored medicine cabinet and pulled out one of the disposable toothbrushes she'd stocked inside, believing that every bachelor or bachelorette household should definitely be supplied with extra toothbrushes, travel-size containers of deodorant, a few disposable razors. For guests. Guests like her.

"Oh, good, Abby," she told herself, "be even more helpful, why don't you? Tell him he ought to get an extra bathrobe while he's at it. For all the women who could end up being overnight guests while you're off searching for Katmandu."

She pressed her hands to her forehead, began to rub at her skin. "Damn it, damn it, *damn it,*" she repeated over and over as the tears she thought had retreated rallied themselves for one more attack on her tear ducts. "Get it together, woman," she scolded herself. "You've got to go back out there, act all happy and carefree and like you're more than agreeable to a nice, civilized little affair, no strings attached."

A knock at the door had her all but jumping out of her skin. "Abby? Is everything all right in there? You've been gone for twenty minutes."

"I...I was just coming out," she called to him, forcing some semblance of cheer into her voice. Abby straightened her shoulders, shook back her hair and then opened the door, belatedly remembering that she wasn't wearing any lipstick.

Or any clothes.

"Oh, hell," she said, watching as Pete's eyes nearly popped out of his head. "Guess I forgot something, didn't I?" she said quickly, then tried to shut the door once more.

"Yeah, Abby, you did," Pete said rather huskily as he pushed the door open and stepped into the large bathroom, making it suddenly seem so small. He began opening the buttons on the fresh white shirt he'd put on—she'd washed it for him, with a new kind of fabric softener sheet from a company that swore it made clothes smell like the clean outdoors, and it did, darn it. It was bad enough he had to look so good. Did he have to smell so good, too?

"What—what are you doing?" she asked, backing up slightly as he opened his belt, slid down his zipper, stepped out of his dress slacks. "Pete? Why are you smiling like that? I don't think I like that smile."

"There's nothing to worry about, Abby," he said cheerfully, reaching past her to open the shower door to turn on the water. "I just remembered something, that's all. I owe you a dunking, don't I?"

"A dunking?" She looked back over her shoulder, watched the first hint of steam rising from the floor of the large shower stall, the one she'd cleaned yesterday, amazed to see that it held six shower heads, so that the water hit a person from a half dozen angles at a time. She'd thought it decadent, if interesting. Now she wet her lips, looked back at Pete, who had just squeezed liquid soap onto a dark-green mesh bath puff she'd told him would cut his showering time in half. "You're kidding, right?"

"Uh-uh," he said, then pointed to her. "You," he said, then took off his glasses, laid them on the sink, pointed to himself. "Me." He pointed the bath puff at the shower stall. "In there. Now."

"And they say I'm crazy," Abby said, laughing. Then she sobered. "You're serious, aren't you? You can't be serious, Pete. I mean, I've *never*—"

"Neither have I, Abby, although I've heard that millions have. And, much as I don't think you're going to get a column out of this on new, efficient ways of bathing, I also don't think either one of us wants to pass up this chance to see what all the shouting is about, do we?''

''You're a nut,'' Abby told him as she opened the shower door wider, stepped inside, felt the warm water hit her calves, her thighs, her stomach, her back, her breasts. She was instantly drenched, her hair plastered against her head, and she had to wipe water out of her eyes in order to see Pete as he joined her. He closed the door behind him, narrowed the world to include only him, only her...only that silly, soapy bath puff.

She'd already believed he had talented hands, the hands of an artist, and now she knew she'd been right. He did have talented hands, a talented mouth, a remarkable body. She could only imagine what the man could do with a soapy bath puff.

She didn't have to imagine for long....

He maneuvered her out of the direct spray of the water, then began soaping her body, from the small dip at the base of her throat to her ankles—and everywhere in between. She looked down at herself, at the swirls of thick bubbles encircling her breasts, drawn across her stomach, slathered down her thighs.

She held on to the safety rail with one hand. Otherwise she'd simply slide to the floor of the stall, for Pete knelt before her now, the bath puff discarded as he moved his hands over her soapy body. Smoothing her. Soothing her. Finding her, moving her. Making her realize that science was wrong—combustion was always possible, even when wet.

And then it was her turn. The bath puff was gone, not that it mattered. She merely rubbed herself against Pete, sliding her soapy body down his length, moving back up slowly, tracing his muscles with her hands, feeling those muscles quiver and jerk under her touch.

She slid her hands around his waist, cupped him low on his body, and threw back her head as she urged him back into the dizzying sprays of water. The look in his eyes brought fresh tears to hers, but they mixed with the water from the shower, so that she didn't think he'd notice.

All she wanted to do was stand here, be close to him, hold him, let him hold her. That's all. It wasn't so much to ask, was it?

And then Pete became the aggressor once more, a sure-but-gentle assault on her senses changing her mind for her, making her realize that she'd been wrong. She did want more. She wanted a lot more. And Pete knew just how to give it to her.

Her feet left the floor—had they floated upward on their own, to clasp themselves around his waist? She was hanging on to him, her hands wrapped around his shoulders, her head thrown back against the safe cradle of his arms as he kissed her throat, her breasts.

The shower stall was lost in steam, as if they were floating inside a cloud. The warm sprays caressed her body, pulsating against her lower spine, wakening nerve endings she didn't know she had.

There was no gravity. No sense of time or place possible. Just Pete. Only Pete. Always and forever, Pete.

She buried her face against his shoulder and whimpered in ecstasy as he took her with him, took her higher and higher. Took her to the edge of the universe and beyond.

"We have to talk."

"Again?" Abby turned onto her stomach, pulled

the pillow over her head. "Don't wanna," she mumbled, then smiled as she felt Pete trailing his fingers down the length of her spine, drawing small circles at the very base of it. "Now who's trying to kill whom?" she asked, giggling, as she turned onto her back once more and looked up at him as he hovered over her, his damp hair still too long and faintly shaggy, but now she wouldn't want to see it any other way.

She reached up a hand, smoothed a thick lock of hair away from his forehead. "You're insatiable."

"And this would be a complaint?" he teased, raising his eyebrows as he grinned down at her.

"It would have been a compliment, but you're looking entirely too smug, Peter Shaw." Abby retrieved the pillow she'd tossed aside, shoved it up against the headboard, then sat up. "And it's a good thing I phoned Catherine earlier, telling her I probably wouldn't be home tonight, because the idea of getting up, getting dressed, doing something with this mop of hair—well, I just don't see it happening."

"Which means we have time to talk," Pete persisted, and Abby sighed, knowing she'd just opened her mouth and inserted the proverbial foot. "Good. Because I think we went a little nuts a while ago, Abby. More than a little nuts."

She heard the worry in his voice. "Meaning?"

"Meaning, I somehow managed to be careful the first time. But in the shower...?"

Abby lowered her eyelids, inspected her fingertips as she brought her hands together in her lap. "Oh," she said, her voice barely a whisper. "And now you want to know if I'm on the pill, or something like that?"

"Yeah. Or something like that," he said, taking her hand in his, raising it to his lips.

"Or nothing like that, which is what I'm on, Pete. Nothing. I'm sorry, I guess we both got a little carried away, didn't we?"

"In that case, Abby," he said, looking at her intently as he stroked her cheek with the back of his hand, "will you marry me?"

Catherine was just walking out of the kitchen with a glass of water and two aspirin as Abby removed her key from the front door lock, then quietly closed the door. "Hey? I thought you said you weren't coming home tonight? Is something wrong? You look sort of—ah, baby, come here," she said sympathetically, holding out her arms as Abby stumbled into them, sobbing.

A half hour and a lot of tears later, Abby and Catherine sat on the patio under an inky black sky and a million stars, not that Abby noticed. She'd cried, been comforted, taken the two aspirin Catherine had handed her, and now she felt a little silly. But no better than she had after she'd demanded that Pete drive her home, then escaped the car almost before he'd put the gearshift in Park.

Catherine pulled another tissue from the box on the table beside her and handed it to Abby, who was still sniffling. "Now, let's get this straight, okay?" she said, then looked up as Elly walked outside, running a hand through her sleep-mussed hair as she squinted into the darkness.

"I thought I heard voices out here. Do you guys know it's almost five in the morning?" she asked, hugging her arms as she stood in her shortie nightgown and matching robe, her long legs exposed to the night air. "Well, I'll never get back to sleep now, that's for sure. Is this a private party, or can anyone join in?"

Abby wiped at her eyes once more, then silently waved her sister to a chair. Would her mom and dad be far behind? Gee, maybe they could invite the neighbors, put some hot dogs on the grill.

"Pete asked Abby to marry him," Catherine said as Elly looked at her questioningly. "So, being Abby, she called him a jerk and demanded he bring her straight home."

Elly nodded. "Okay, that sounds like Abby. Is there anything more, or should I just go inside, crawl back into bed and pretend this has all been a dream?"

"Ha-ha, Eleanor Anne," Abby grumbled, raising her head to glare at her sister. "You had to pick now to get your sense of humor back, right?"

"Sorry, babe," Elly said, going over to give her sister a hug. "But you've got to admit it, most people don't call other people jerks when they've just proposed marriage."

"He didn't want to," Abby muttered. "He was just being polite."

Catherine and Elly exchanged looks over Abby's head, then said in unison, "Polite?"

"I guess I wasn't listening too closely while she was blubbering, Elly," Catherine apologized, "because that's a new one to me. Abby, do you think you could *enlarge* on this 'polite' business. Just a little, as I'm not sure we're old enough for the unabridged version. Not when I consider that your hair is damp and you look like you must have gotten dressed in a dark telephone booth."

"We made love," Abby said quietly, then sighed. Oh, they most certainly had made love. Made love, not spoken of love. There hadn't been a single, solitary word about love.

"And then he asked you to marry him? If memory serves, that's how it happened with Rob and me. In fact, I imagine it happens all the time. Except this time, huh?" Elly sat down once more. "Well, Catherine, I'm stumped. You want to ask another question?"

Abby stood up now, began to pace. "We made love, okay? I damn near seduced the man, and we made love. Twice. Only...only the second time we sort of...we sort of *forgot* to...to..." She trailed off, shaking her head, wishing she was dead. Or at least alone. What had made her think she wanted to share any of this with her sisters?

"Forgot to? Forgot to what?" Catherine prompted, then winced. "Oh, okay, I get it. You get it, Elly?"

"No," Elly said facetiously. "Draw me a diagram, will ya, Teach? Of course I get it. But, Abby, he can't really have proposed to you because he thinks you might be pregnant, can he? I mean—one time? That only happens in novels. Besides, I'm living proof that it can take years before...never mind. That's another subject. Let's stick with this one, okay?"

"He doesn't want to get married now, Elly," Abby told her, sighing. "He has to establish his career, pay off student loans, feel free to work long hours. All that stuff. Five years, he told me. He's got five more years before his life is his own."

"Five years, huh?" Catherine said, once more looking at Elly, who was nodding her head. "Yes, El, you're right, if you're thinking what I'm thinking.

Five years sounds very familiar. Abby, isn't that how long you plan to keep running around, seeing the world? Five more years?''

''You know,'' Abby said, lost in her own thoughts, ''I'd like a baby. I mean, nobody says I have to wait until I'm thirty, then go find some willing guy and marry him. It's the one thing that used to bother me about my plan. Sure, traveling makes me feel free and independent, but it's also somehow rigid—like I have to keep going, keep moving, even when I don't want to. All because I thought, at twenty-two, that that's what I wanted.''

She sat down again, put her hands on her stomach. ''But nothing's ever written in stone, right? Not even tax laws—maybe especially tax laws.''

''Here she goes, El, fasten your seat belt,'' Catherine warned, rolling her eyes, and Elly laughed.

''I was looking at those pamphlets you had, Catherine,'' Abby went on, noticing her sister's involuntary wince. ''No, no, they're a good idea. But then I threw them away, because I think I'd want my baby to know who his father is. Although, if a woman had a *friend,* a very good friend, they could have a child together, couldn't they? A baby with blond hair and green eyes…''

''If you're wondering why she looks so mushy all of a sudden, Catherine,'' Elly put in, ''just remember that Pete Shaw also has blond hair and green eyes.''

But Abby wasn't listening. All the restlessness she'd been feeling for the past year or more, all the hours she'd sat and stared at mothers playing in the park with their children, all the times she'd found herself in the infant department in stores, smiling over tiny dresses and little sailor suits—the memories all came together at once.

Just like Catherine, just like Elly, she wanted a baby. She'd always seen her life with children in it— lots of children. Someday. She had a full, satisfying life, but there was a hole in that life that could only be filled by a small, warm bundle snuggled in her arms. Not that she'd ever met anyone she'd wanted to marry, have babies with, grow old with.

That's why her bedside table in Miami was filled with brochures from adoption agencies. She thought she'd been collecting them for a column she'd write one day, but people don't keep that sort of brochure in their nightstands if they're writing columns at the desk in the kitchen.

She wanted a baby. That's why she'd taken the brochures from Catherine. That's why she still remembered the article she'd read about a woman having a baby with a good, trusted friend, someone who would stay in the picture only as much as he wanted to, but who would be there if their child ever really needed him.

Pete would be there if his child needed him.

And that's when Abby shook her wandering brain back to attention. Yes, she'd been fantasizing again. She'd played "what if" mind games ever since she was a child, making up scenarios, building fantastic castles in the air.

But she wasn't a child anymore. That's why the adoption brochures had stayed in the drawer for over a year. That's why she'd thrown out the pamphlets she'd taken from Catherine, thrown them out over a week ago. That's why, although the woman who'd written the article about having a baby with her friend seemed very happy, Abby had instinctively known she couldn't handle that sort of arrangement.

Yes, she wanted a baby. But she wasn't obsessed with the idea, the way Elly seemed to be obsessed—so that it had caused a rift between her and Rob, caused Elly to come running home to hide, to spend her nights crying herself to sleep.

"Earth to Abby, come in Abby," Catherine said, waving a hand in front of her sister's face.

Abby looked up at Catherine, looked over at Elly, who was looking back at her worriedly. "I don't want a baby," she said, slowly beginning to smile as a weight lifted from her mind, her conscience. "Oh, I do, I do. Eventually. And I still want Paris and Rome. Eventually. Although I've decided to give Katmandu a miss. What I really want, what I really, really want, is for Pete to tell me he loves me. He doesn't have to marry me. Just tell me he loves me. The rest of it—that will happen or not, but it will happen naturally. That's all I want. Is that too much to ask?"

"I think you're asking the wrong person, Abby," Elly said, shrugging. "And I also think Catherine said something important, not that you were listening, were you, Abby? Catherine, do you want to repeat it?"

"Repeat what?" Catherine looked blank for a moment, then nodded. "Oh, I remember. I think, Abby, what Elly means is that I get the feeling that both you and Pete keep hitting each other over the head about the next five years. What you're going to do for the next five years, all about the plans you both have for the next five years. And I can't help but wonder—don't you think maybe you're both protesting too much? Is it possible that you keep telling each other what you *think* the other guy wants to hear?''

Abby sat back, stared at Catherine, tipped her head, looked at Elly, who was nodding her agreement with her sister's sentiments.

They both stood up, both of her sisters. Two women, united, with a mission.

''I'll turn on the shower,'' Elly said.

''I'll see if I can find something in her closet that doesn't have a Mickey Mouse face on it,'' Catherine said, following Elly into the house. She stopped just at the door, turned around, looked at Abby, who was still sitting very still, her jaw still dropped in amazement. ''Are you coming or not, Abby?'' Catherine asked. ''Pete's probably due at the hospital in a little more than an hour. Maybe you can cut him off before he gets there.''

Abby stood up, then sat back down again. ''But what if you're wrong? What if Pete wasn't doing what I was doing—saying everything I thought he wanted to hear? What if he really does have no intention of entering into any serious arrangement for another five years? Even worse—what if he does love me, but still thinks the timing is all off, and that he wishes he'd met me in five years, but that right now all I'm doing is screwing up all his plans? I love him too much to make him choose between me and his plans for his career.''

''Oh, great,'' Catherine said, rolling her eyes. ''Miss Impulsive, the gal who'd hop a jet to D.C. for the weekend with nothing but a toothbrush and a credit card, just because she's always wanted to see the cherry blossoms in bloom. Where is that girl when we need her? Oh, no. *Now* she decides to think. *Now* she decides to reason, to—Lord help us all—apply logic to the one area of any woman's life where logic is about the *last* thing she wants to think about.''

''Hey, what's the holdup, ladies? The shower's already running. Besides, I think I heard Dad's alarm going off,'' Elly said, sticking her head back out the door. ''Abby, unless you want Mom in on this discussion, I'd suggest you start moving. Chop, chop, girl!''

Abby stood up, smiled, felt her chin wobble just a little. ''All he can say is no, right?'' she asked nervously, right before Catherine and Elly took hold of her arms and marched her down the hall toward her bedroom.

She saw him just as she pulled into the hospital parking lot. He was walking across the macadam, his head down, his steps slow, tired, as if he hadn't slept all night. He looked wonderful. He looked miserable. Her heart did a small, hopeful flip.

She double parked behind a delivery truck, hopped out of the car and began to run. A part of her brain realized that she'd left the keys in the ignition. Griff probably wouldn't be too excited about how carelessly she was treating the car he'd loaned them, but if she stopped, went back, Pete would be inside the hospital, on duty and out of her reach for the next thirty-six hours.

''Pete!'' she called out as she ran, her hair flying, her skirts tangling around her legs. ''Peter Shaw, you just wait one darn minute!'' She was rapidly running out of energy. Catherine and Elly had all but killed her, throwing her into the shower, getting her dressed. Within fifteen minutes they had pushed her out the front door as their father, holding a coffee cup and wearing a faintly bemused expression, had called out directions to the hospital. She'd just put the car in gear and was backing out of the driveway when her mother appeared at the front door to throw her a kiss and wave her on her way.

"Pete!"

Pete stopped, shook his head as if he thought he might be hearing things, then started walking again. Then he stopped once more, slowly turned around, saw her. His initial, baffled look gave her hope. The slow smile that spread on his face made her blood sing in her veins.

"Hi, sailor," she gasped out breathlessly as she finally reached him, skidded to a halt. "New in town, are you?"

"Sailor, Abby?" he asked, looking at her as if he still couldn't quite believe she was standing in front of him. "Nevada is landlocked, in case you haven't noticed." Then he took her arm, steered her down a narrow path and into a small space between two tall buildings. "I'm on duty in the O.R. in twenty minutes. I have to relieve Mrs. O'Farrell of a really king-size nevus. What are you doing here, Abby? I thought you said you never wanted to see me again."

"And you believed me?" she asked, still trying to control her breathing. "Well, Pete," she said, looking up at him, "if you're going to *believe* everything that comes out of my mouth, I can see we still have a lot of work ahead of us."

His eyes narrowed behind his glasses. Funny, she hadn't known a man in glasses could be so sexy, not until she'd met Pete. "What do you mean?"

"Well," she began, then took a deep breath.

"When I called you a jerk. You didn't believe me then, did you?"

His smile broke her heart. "I don't know, Abby. I'm trying not to think about that, actually. What else? There's more, isn't there? More I shouldn't have believed? Wait a minute," he added, looking past her, toward the parking lot. "Is that Griff's car being towed away, Abby?"

She turned around, saw the front of the green sedan being lifted up by a large tow truck. Yup, that's what it was all right. Griff's car, being towed away. "Oh, well," she said, smiling at Pete. "Everyone has days like this, don't they?"

"I have a feeling you might have more of them than most of us, Abby," he said, then threw back his head and laughed out loud. "It's a good thing I know Griff thinks you're adorable." Then he looked at her again, his eyes growing dark and unreadable. "You are adorable, you know. But I shouldn't say things like that, should I? What else do you want to tell me, Abby? What else shouldn't I believe?"

She lowered her eyes, took a deep breath. Now they were coming to the heart of it all, the moment when she'd know, once and for all, if she was the biggest fool in the world, or the luckiest one. "It...it's about that five years," she said quietly. "I'm...well, I'm really not all that set on them, you know. Paris, Rome. I want to see them both someday if I get the chance. But I could have seen them last year, or headed there this summer, if I'd really wanted to that badly. Obviously, I didn't."

"You didn't? And you forgot the third one. Katmandu, wasn't it?"

"Do you write down everything I say, that you

remember it all?'' she asked as she looked up at him, loving him, but longing to stuff a hankie in his mouth so he'd shut up and let her talk.

Then she shook her head, wishing away the tears that seemed determined to fall. She always cried such *huge* tears; they were embarrassing. ''I've had a lot of fun, Pete, traveling where I want to, doing what I want, when I want. I had my twenties all planned out, ever since college. But the whole thing started to lose its appeal over a year ago. I…I haven't told Mom and Dad yet, but I'd already planned to look around while I'm here, buy a house near them.''

''Buy a house. Here. Near your parents.'' Pete spoke quietly, repeating her words slowly, as if trying to assimilate them.

She nodded. ''You know how it is, Pete. You're the baby in your family, too. I had more bosses while I was growing up than a private does in the army. I wanted to get away, try my wings, be independent. And I did that. I've done that. I was ready for something else. And then you said that you needed at least another five years before you could think about anything but your work, and—''

''And you told me you needed at least another five years on your own before you'd ever think about settling down,'' he finished for her. He took hold of her shoulders, gave her a small shake. ''I only said that stuff about five years because *you* were so adamant that you weren't thinking about settling down. I didn't want you to worry that I might get too serious about you. I didn't want to scare you away. Why do you think I let you screw up my father's house, for crying out loud. I wanted as much of you as I could, for as long as you'd agree to stay.''

She nodded furiously now. "That's what Catherine said," she told him, grinning. "Well, not that business about having me screw up your father's house, but we'll let that go for now, all right? We've both been busy telling each other lies so that neither one of us felt like we were getting too serious, even while we were falling in love with each other. We are falling in love with each other, aren't we, Pete?"

"Oh, Abby, I'm already way past the falling in love stage. I was already halfway there by the time we were rid of those wonderful handcuffs. I'm so in love with you, Abby, I can't think straight."

"You are?" Abby closed her eyes, felt her bones going soft inside her. "I've been in love with you ever since we talked over coffee that first morning, and you offered to come home with me to explain everything to my family. Only I didn't know it until Sheila showed up and I wanted to climb her, claw her eyes out," she said, wrinkling her nose at him.

"Poor Sheila. She never stood a chance, did she? And you'll marry me?"

"Because you think I could be pregnant?"

"Absolutely not. Because I can't live without you, Abby," he said, wiping away the last of her tears with the back of his fingers. "Please, Abby. Please marry me. And hurry up, okay, because now I'm on duty in ten minutes, and I want to spend at least five of them kissing you."

"What a busy morning you're having, Doctor Shaw—a proposal and Mrs. O'Farrell's mole, both in the next twenty minutes." She wet her lips with the tip of her tongue, smiled at him. "Marry you? Hmmm," she said, laughing as he squeezed her closer, gave out a warning growl. "I believe that would be *très magnifique, monsieur.*"

"God, Abby," Pete said, laughing. "You're going to slay them in Paris when I take you there on our honeymoon. Your accent is atrocious."

She snuggled closer in his arms. "But you like it," she said, slipping her hands under the hem of his shirt to feel the heat of his body against her palms.

"Yeah, Abby," he told her, breathing the words against her mouth. "I like it. And I adore you. Now come here...."

BOOK III
ELLY

Chapter 11

Rob eased closer, his hand snaking out slowly beneath the thin sheet, sliding across her belly, skimming her lightly as he moved his hand upward, toward her breasts.

Elly sighed, relaxed, melted closer to him in the bed. Sought his warmth. Anticipated his next move. Smiled as she lazily roused from sleep.

"Eleanor? You do know that the membership committee is meeting with us tomorrow to interview you? This isn't just an ordinary ladies' luncheon at the Plaza. This is important. Vitally important to Robert, to his career. Now, don't you agree that you should rethink your decision to wear the blue dress? To be frank, Eleanor, is it truly necessary for you to show that much leg?"

Go away. Go away. Get out of our bedroom!

Elly kept her eyes closed, turned onto her side, snuggled more closely to Rob, let her hand drift

across his waist. He kissed her throat, her shoulder.
He murmured love words to her, his warm breath
tickling her ear.

"Eleanor? Do you see that man over there, the one
talking with Robert? That's Barnes, of Barnes and
Black, and one of our most important clients. Now,
I'll be taking you over to meet him, my dear, and if
I know Jake Barnes, the first thing he's going to do
is ask you to tell him all about yourself. Nosy bastard,
vetting everyone to see if they measure up to his standards. But business is business and makes for strange
bedfellows. Now, Robert's mother has suggested that
you not mention that dancing you did in Las Vegas.
In fact, she thought it a good idea not to mention
anything about Las Vegas at all, all right? Humor her,
Eleanor, please? It's, well, it's just easier that way."

*You, too? Get out! Can't you leave us alone, even
here?*

Elly squeezed her eyelids shut so tightly that she
began to see stars behind the lids. Rob was kissing
her. Rob was holding her. Rob was loving her.

But the voices wouldn't stop. They kept droning
on, and on, and on. Censuring her. Instructing her.
Warning her. Pointing out her every flaw.

And then the stars behind her eyes rearranged
themselves, lined themselves up on a grid marked
with the days of the month. She knew this grid, knew
what this paper meant. It was her ovulation chart.
That damn ovulation chart. How had it gotten into
bed with them?

The stars trailed after one another in a row along
one line of the grid, then one star dipped before the
next star jumped high onto the grid and began flash-

ing, flashing, flashing. Another star lined up beside it.
And then another. Four. Six.

This time. This month. This one time, the stars
would stay on the line. One after another they'd stay
and stay and stay. Temperatures rising, feel the heat,
feel the heat...

And then the next one dropped. Dropped all the
way down the grid.

No, no! Don't fall! Don't fall! Not again!

All of the stars began to dance. They sprouted legs
and arms, and their centers suddenly had eyes, laughing mouths. They came together in a kick-line, arms
joined, legs dancing in unison, and began to sing.
"Too late, baby, it's too late..."

Elly felt herself grow cold, felt her limbs stiffen
even while they had been melting under Rob's touch.
She knew she was withdrawing, growing distant. And
he knew it, too. He collapsed onto the mattress, one
hand flung up over his head.

"No sense, huh? Totally wasted effort. That's how
you see it, don't you, Elly? Why bother? But stay by
the phone, Rob, be ready to rush home next month
again at noon, when that old temperature goes up.
Hell, it's almost six. I might as well get up, get an
early start on the day. At least at work I know I'm
appreciated, can get the job done."

Elly felt the sheet fold back onto her body. Felt the
cool air of separation. Felt the mattress shift under
Rob's weight as he sat up at the side of the bed,
prepared to rise. To leave. To leave her all alone.

"No," she said, reaching out, finding nothing.
"No, Rob. I'm so sorry. Don't go. Don't go!"

"Elly? Elly, sweetheart, wake up. You're having a

nightmare. Come on, love, open your eyes for your
old Dad. Ah, that's a good girl.''

"Dad?" Elly reached out, her eyes still closed, and
felt her hand being swallowed up by her father's. She
opened her eyes, looked up at his kind, loving, worried face through the tears that clouded her vision.
Then she sat up, launched herself into Jim Parrish's
loving arms. *"Oh, Dad."*

"Elly—phone!"

Elly put down the book she'd been pretending to
read, slid her long, dancer's legs over the side of the
chaise longue, stood up. She walked to the sliding
door that led into the house and slid it open a few
inches. "Who's on the phone, Mrs. Williams?" she
asked the housekeeper her dad had hired for two days
a week four months ago, when he'd come home to
find his wife balancing on a kitchen chair as she held
a broomstick topped with a dust rag—trying to clean
one of the huge overhead fans.

Elly stepped inside the house, looked to the kitchen
bar, saw the phone resting on it, waiting. Leering at
her. "Mrs. Williams?"

The sound of the vacuum running somewhere in
the house once more was Elly's only answer. Well,
damn. Her parents were out, her sisters were gone.
Mrs. Williams was definitely busy, too busy to be
asked to stop what she was doing and take a message
because Elly had developed a phobia about answering
phones.

"Probably somebody selling something," she said
aloud, taking a step backward, out of the house. "But
it could be Mom, or Dad. It could be Catherine, asking me to meet her at the mall to look at more gowns.

It could be Abby, asking me where a person might put car keys if a person was going to lose them. If I don't answer, if I don't pick up the phone, then I'll have to answer eight million questions as to why I didn't pick up the phone. Oh, hell, now I'm talking to myself!''

Taking a deep, steadying breath, she walked across the room and slid her fingers around the receiver. It felt cool, impersonal. Dangerous. She'd rather pet a snake.

''Hello?'' she said hesitantly as she lifted the thing to her ear. ''Parrish residence. I'm sorry to keep you waiting.''

''Elly? Elly—is that you?''

She collapsed onto the kitchen stool next to her. Her stomach had done a back flip. Her arms and legs were going numb. A million buzzing bees invaded her skull. ''Rob?''

''Yeah, sweetheart. Rob. My God, I thought you'd never— Never mind that. Are you all right?''

She rested an elbow on the countertop, dropped her head into her hand. She couldn't believe it. Rob. She'd answered one damn phone in a month, and Rob was on the other end of the line. She stared across the room, at the clock over the stove. Noon here, four o'clock in New York. He was still at work. ''Yeah. Yeah, I'm all right, Rob. You?''

She winced as she heard his short laugh. ''Me? Oh, hell, Elly, I'm fine. Just great. Missing an arm and a leg and half my damn mind, but I'm fine.''

''Don't do that, Rob. Please.''

There was a pause, a sigh. ''I'm sorry, Elly. I've played it cool, did what you wanted, stayed away, kept my mouth shut. And then I finally get a chance to talk to you, and I royally screw it up. I've been listening to Susie, being patient, giving you space or whatever. But, honey, I love you. Isn't it time we talk? Really talk?''

She wanted to. Oh, Lord, how she wanted to. The sound of his voice, the words he'd said…she felt the same way. As if half of her had been ripped away. The most important half. ''Rob, I—''

''Damn it! I don't believe this! Of all the rotten timing…''

''Rob?'' She heard another voice, a female voice. Mechanical-sounding, as if his secretary was speaking to him over the intercom. ''Rob, are you still there?''

''Elly? Forgive me, Elly. I have to take this call. There's a million calls I don't have to take, could care less about—but I have to take this one call. Sweetheart, let me call you back. Ten minutes. An hour, tops. You will answer the phone when I call back, won't you? I love you, Elly. I'm going crazy without you. Elly? Elly?''

She hung up the phone. Found her shoes. Took a long walk in the hot Nevada sun. Anything, anything, to be away from the phone when it rang.

Elly paged through the oversize book of wedding invitations as she sat on the living room couch, trying not to think about her own wedding, her own invitations, the ones she'd dreamed of for years, but never actually had. Gold script on ivory vellum. Simple. Elegant. Even Althea would have approved. *Doctor and Mrs. James Parrish request the honour of your presence for the ceremony uniting their daughter, Eleanor Anne…* And then there was that other gold script on ivory vellum. A note card. A very formal note card. The one she had placed on the bed before she'd left New York....

"Louise? Your middle name is *Louise?*" Pete grinned as he lounged against the wall between the dining room and kitchen.

Abby stripped the ripe banana she'd snatched up from the bowl of fruit resting on the dining room table, then glared at her fiancé as he trailed after her, heading back into the living room. "Yes," she said, rolling her eyes. "My middle name is *Louise.* Louise was my great-grandmother's name. And it's traditional to put our middle names on the invitations. Elly says so. Do you have a problem with that, Peter *Aloysius* Shaw?"

Pete held up his hands, shook his head. And then winked at Elly. "None, honey. Absolutely none. But you do realize that your new initials are going to be A.L.P.S., don't you? Alps. Are you sure you don't want to rethink this, and go to Geneva on our honeymoon, instead of Paris?"

Abby stopped peeling the banana, looked at Pete as if considering his words. "Well, I've always wanted to learn how to yodel..."

"You wouldn't dare," he said, playfully grabbing her, sliding his arms around her waist as he pulled her back against his stomach. "Switzerland's been neutral for a lot of years, Abby, but they'd be declaring war on the U.S. within the week if you started yodeling."

She leaned her head back against his chest, smiled up into his face. "Really? Well, how about if I just buy one of those cute little outfits? You know. Green velvet shorts, with suspenders and everything?"

"For you?"

"No, Pete—for *you*." She turned in his arms, slid her hands behind his neck, pulled him down for a kiss. "I mean, anyone can wear a tuxedo for their wedding. This would be new, bold, different. Besides, you've got the cutest knees. Elly? Don't you think Pete's got the cutest knees?"

"They're adorable," Elly agreed. Then she put down the invitation book, stood up and left the room. She doubted she'd be missed.

They were sitting out on the patio, relaxing, sipping iced tea, waiting for Catherine to join them.

"Are you sure, Elly? You don't want to rush into anything."

Elly nodded her head. "I'm going to stay in Las Vegas, Griff. I'm sure of that. And I don't feel right driving one of your cars, as considerate as you've been about the thing. So I've decided. I want to buy the red one we saw on your lot, when Catherine and I visited you at the dealership. Or would it be better to lease it?" She smiled, just a little. "You know, I haven't owned a car, have barely driven, since Rob and I were married. There's just no reason to have a car in Manhattan, not unless you're a huge fan of dents and ridiculous parking fees. Oh, Rob has a car, but that's for business, so I take special radio cabs wherever I go. I'd take the subway, but Rob's mother explained to me that Lyndons don't *do* public transportation."

She lowered her head, bit her lips together. "Sorry, Griff. I'm rambling, aren't I? But I really do want a car of my own. I want to be…independent."

"And having a car will do that? Is that what you think, Elly?"

She lifted her head, stared at her older sister's fiancé. "Sell a lot of cars this way, Griff, do you? By trying to talk the customer *out* of the purchase?"

He grinned, and Elly saw again what had first attracted Catherine to Griff Edwards, car dealer extraordinaire. He was just so darn *human*. She'd buy a used car from this man. She'd vote for him for Congress. And she was happy to see Catherine so happy.

And her parents, of course, were just about over the moon. Catherine and Griff were going to marry, live in Henderson. Abby and her Pete were going to marry and live somewhere in the Las Vegas suburbs. So why had her parents, first her mother, then her father—doubtless sent to her by her mother—both told her that she shouldn't rush into renting an apartment two miles from this house? Why was Griff talking her out of buying her own car, taking yet another step toward permanence, toward being back in Nevada? To stay.

"Oh, wait a minute. It's my mother, isn't it? She got to you, told you to humor me but not let me make any commitments. What did she promise you, Griff? No sky-diving Elvises at the reception? I know Catherine already got her to agree that a double ceremony was bad enough, but a triple one was just too far over the top. As a matter of fact, I think I heard Mom say something only this morning about this wedding chapel thing being back to just the two of them renewing the vows, and you guys being allowed to have your own, separate ceremonies." She rolled her eyes. "Bribery. Works every time, and Susie Parrish could give lessons in how it's done."

Griff rubbed at the back of his head. "It wasn't bribery, Elly. Well, not exactly. But you're right

about the ceremonies. Catherine wants her own ceremony, and so does Abby. I think it has a lot to do
with Catherine and me wanting a large church wedding and Abby thinking about tying the knot in the
hospital chapel. Your mother, however, is still hanging tough with Jim about the Elvis theme. You do
know the whole renewal of vows thing has been re-
scheduled at last? Next Tuesday, in a chapel along
the Strip.''

Elly shook her head, felt stupid tears threatening
again. ''No, I didn't know that, although I'm sure
somebody told me,'' she said, sighing. ''I'm not surprised, as I really don't pay much attention to anything, do I? But I have gotten very good at moping
and feeling sorry for myself. This is not a great house
to be in right now, Griff, not if you're ending your
marriage just as your sisters are starting theirs. Oh,
I'm sorry. I'm sorry I'm being such a slug.''

''The red one, huh?'' Griff said as Catherine slid
back the sliding door, stepped onto the patio. ''A
three-year lease, all right? I'll bring the car and the
papers tomorrow.''

Elly smiled her thanks, then stood up, gave her
older sister a hug. ''You've got a real winner there,
Catherine,'' she said sincerely. ''Hold on to him.
Hold on tight.''

''Elly?'' Catherine called after her as Elly dropped
a quick kiss on Griff's cheek, then turned to go into
the house. ''Elly, are you all right?''

''Fine,'' she bit out, suppressing a sob as she ran
for the safety of her bedroom. ''I'm just fine, honest.''

Elly heard the door to her room open, then close. The
sound of the button lock being depressed followed.

She remained on her bed, lying with her back to the door, her hands cradled beneath her cheek. She didn't have to turn over, didn't have to look. She'd been waiting for this for at least two weeks. "Hi, Mom. Guess my pity party's over, huh?"

She felt her mother sit down beside her on the mattress. "As I'm growing weary of tuning up the violin for you every day, yes," Susie Parrish said, softening her words by the simple application of her hand on Elly's back. She moved her hand rhythmically, stroking her daughter's ramrod-stiff spine. Elly closed her eyes, shocked at how badly she needed to feel human touch. Her mother's touch.

Elly used the wadded tissue in her hand to wipe at her eyes, then sat up, pushed herself back against the headboard. She smiled, made a weak joke. "I'm sorry I've been such a crybaby, Mom. I never was, you know. I can't believe how much I've been crying, ever since I got home. Do you think I'm trying to regress to my childhood?"

"You didn't cry as a child," Susie reminded her, patting her knee. "Not my dearest middle child. You were so busy trying to keep up to Catherine and out-distance Abby, you didn't have time to cry. Dancing lessons, voice lessons, captain of the cheerleading squad, editor of the high school newspaper, lead in the senior class play. You volunteered at Dad's hospital every weekend and every summer. I don't think you ever sat down long enough to even think about crying. You moved out here on your own, got your job on your own, built yourself a life, a career. You and Rob married, you moved to New York, you began a whole new life as his wife. You never gave your father or me a moment's trouble, Elly, not in twenty-seven years. Which is why we've allowed you to wallow—yes, *wallow*—here for a month. You've earned some downtime, some time to sit back, reflect, consider what you're going to do next."

"Thanks, Mom," Elly said, summoning the ghost of a smile. "But…?"

"But time's up, sweetheart," Susie said firmly. "It isn't easy for you to watch while Catherine and Abby fall in love, plan their weddings. In fact, it has to hurt like hell. And, much as I know you're trying not to rain on their parades, it's getting a little difficult tip-toeing around your moods."

"I know," Elly agreed, sighing. "I'm like a wet blanket at a love-in or whatever you guys called that stuff in the sixties. I'm sorry."

"Nope, not good enough, darling," Susie said, standing up, wiping her hands together. "No more 'I'm sorrys.' No more long, blank stares or deep sighs or 'I don't want to talk about it.' Starting today, young lady, you're going to talk to me. Talk to your father. Talk to the guy at the delicatessen, I don't care. But you're going to talk to somebody. Is that understood? Because we can't help, honey, if we don't know what's wrong."

Elly looked up at her mother, all five feet two inches of her. At her bouncy blond curls, her younger-than-springtime face, her petite body set in a posture that tried to be bullying and ended up looking like a cuddly bunny asking for someone to please, please give her a carrot.

Elly stood up, rested her hands on her mother's shoulders. "I'm bigger than you now, you know," she said, dredging up an old ploy she'd teasingly used on her mother in high school.

"And I'm still older than you," Susie answered now as she had then, gathering Elly into her motherly embrace. "And don't you ever forget it."

"Yes, ma'am," Elly said, trying to look sheepish. Which wasn't easy. Abby could look sheepish. She excelled at being cute and cuddly and easily forgiven. But Elly was five feet nine inches tall in her stocking feet, and she hadn't been able to play the cute, cuddly little girl since the fifth grade. Except when Rob held her....

"So, we'll talk now?"

"Yeah, Mom," Elly said, pulling her mother back down beside her on the edge of the bed. "We'll talk now. Would it be too snarky of me to start off by saying that Althea Lyndon is a great big pain in the—what?"

Susie had hopped to her feet, pressed her hands to her cheeks. "Oh! I forgot!"

"Forgot? You forgot what?" Elly asked, also rising.

"I *forgot* that Althea Lyndon called here a half hour ago," Susie said, taking Elly's hand in her own. "That's how she identified herself, you know. 'Hello, this is Althea Lyndon speaking.'" Susie shivered. "I shouldn't say this, but that woman frightens the very dickens out of me. I always feel as if I should come to attention, even on the phone, when she can't see that I'm wearing a pink bathing suit and standing in my own kitchen in my bare feet, and making tuna fish salad for Mrs. Williams's lunch. Can you imagine Althea Lyndon making lunch for her housekeeper? I don't think so, Elly. I really don't."

"Mo-*om*," Elly cautioned, feeling like shivering herself. "Could we leave the tuna salad for now, and get back to Mrs. Lyndon? You said she called. What did she want?"

"What did she want? Besides to make me feel as if my family arrived in America on entirely the wrong boat? Oh, I'm sorry again, Elly. That woman has rubbed me wrong ever since she let me know that she believed it entirely my fault that you and Rob eloped, then told us about the marriage."

"I know, Mom, I know," Elly said, sighing. Did more than two days ever go by without Althea Lyndon reminding her of how she'd "cheated" her out of planning her only son's wedding. "But what did she want *now?* I can't believe she'd want to talk to me, ask me to come back to New York. She's probably already hired two divorce lawyers so that Rob can take his pick. And then thrown a party at the club to celebrate Rob's lucky escape from 'that flashy Vegas showgirl who sank her greedy teeth into my dear boy.' She never wanted to understand that I was dancing in a very upscale production, professional enough for Broadway."

Elly realized that she'd lost track of the important part of the matter at hand in her short, unhappy stroll down the mine-filled memory lane of her relationship, or lack of it, with her mother-in-law. "The call, Mom. Why did she call?"

"Because she thinks we kidnapped her Robert, of course," Susie said, pulling a face. "It seems he disappeared yesterday afternoon. Just up and left the office."

"Yesterday afternoon?" Elly repeated hollowly,

remembering the phone call Rob had made to her yesterday afternoon.

"Yes, Elly, and he isn't at home, in your apartment, because Althea went over herself and checked. Her Robert, it seems, has been kidnapped. By us. Although how she thinks we could kidnap the boy, considering that he bought his own plane ticket to Vegas, escapes me."

"Here?" Elly said, backing toward the bed, sitting down before she fell down. "Rob's coming here?"

"He is, according to Althea," Susie told her, folding her arms across her chest. "And we're to send him straight back, probably with a note attached to his jacket saying who he belongs to when he reaches JFK in New York. When is she going to see that Rob's all grown up now? And what makes me so mad is that I didn't hang up on the woman. Elly? Are you all right? I kept Rob away, you know, even though he called me at least three times a week, begging me to say it was all right to fly out here to see you. But I think he's right, you know. It's been a month now, sweetheart. It's time the two of you sat down, talked this all out."

"Here? He's coming here?" Elly repeated stupidly. She looked at the clock on her nightstand. It was twenty minutes past one o'clock. "He's here," she amended, feeling her stomach clench. "He's been here since noon, if he took our usual flight." She looked up at her mother, held out her hands so that Susie gripped them, squeezed them. "Oh, Mom, what am I going to say to him?"

"That you're pregnant? I'm only a man, but as a conversation starter, it seems to me that ought to do for openers."

Both Elly and Susie looked toward the bedroom door. "Jim!" Susie exclaimed. "I distinctly remember locking that door. How did you get in here?"

Jim smiled, held up the screwdriver-shaped key, one of which was stashed on the jamb above each doorway in the house. "You keep forgetting, Susie, because you can't reach them," he said, smiling. "So, baby," he asked, walking over to sit down beside Elly, so that she had a parental unit, as Abby called them, to her left, another to her right. "You are going to tell him, aren't you?"

"But," Elly began, putting a hand protectively to her lower belly. "But, Dad, I'm not pregnant."

"Aren't you, sweetheart?" he countered, smiling. "You're crying, you're moping, you've been sick in the mornings, more than once. And you're either saying you don't feel like eating or you're consuming three bowls of double chocolate-chip mint ice cream in one sitting. Now, taking all of this into consideration, and balancing it against my many years of schooling and many more years of clinical experience…well, I'd say you're pregnant. Wouldn't you, Susie?"

Elly looked to her mother, who was nodding, smiling, and then back to her father. "But…but I took one of those home pregnancy tests two weeks ago, and I wasn't pregnant. I figured it's just my nerves keeping…keeping everything away."

Susie patted her arm. "Those tests are not infallible, honey, and it was probably a little too early, anyway. But," she said, hopping up, heading toward the hallway linen closet, "I happened to pick up a test kit myself yesterday, when I was out shopping. One that can be used any time of the day, not just in the morning. Shall we give it another try?''

Jim leaned close to his daughter, whispered into her ear. ''She bought three of them, Elly. I think she's hoping for a bumper crop.'' He stood up, bent to kiss her cheek. ''Now, humor your mother, all right, while I go get my bag and draw some blood. That way you can humor me, too, and I'll have the lab results back by dinnertime tonight. I want you to be seen by one of my colleagues as soon as possible, start with vitamins and all of that.''

Elly's head was spinning. ''But, Dad—''

''Don't argue with me, Elly. I've had a devil of a time keeping your mother from dancing onto the roof and announcing your pregnancy to the entire neighborhood. Are your breasts sore, honey, a little tender, sensitive? I'll bet they are.''

''Dad!'' Elly exclaimed, quickly crossing her arms across her breasts as her mother skipped back into the room, holding a bag with the name of a pharmacy on it.

''They are, aren't they? Thought so. Go ahead, Susie, give her the test. But I don't need a test. I don't think I've been wrong in twenty-five years.''

''Smug, isn't he?'' Susie said as she closed the door behind her husband. Smiling at Elly, she pointed to the door leading to the Jack-and-Jill bathroom Elly and Catherine shared. Abby had been given the bedroom with its own bathroom, as nobody else wanted to live with her mess. ''Now, are you ready, Mommy?''

Elly's bottom lip began to tremble. ''I'm not pregnant, Mom. I can't be pregnant. Not now.''

* * *

"Nobody can tell him I'm pregnant," Elly told her assembled family an hour later as they all sat in the living room, the width of their grins showing enough teeth for an Osmond Family reunion. "Nobody. You got that, Abby?"

"I resent that, Elly," Abby said, pouting as Pete slid his arm around the back of the couch to pull her close against his shoulder. "Why are you singling me out? You act as if I can't keep a secret."

"You can't!" This chorus of voices included those of Elly, Catherine, Jim and Susie.

"She was only two when she came to me and told me about the new twirling baton Mom had bought me for Christmas," Elly said, looking at Pete. "Mom didn't know she could even speak in complete sentences, for crying out loud, and figured it was all right to buy the thing with Abby along. Then Mom called her 'gifted.' Oh, yeah, she was gifted, all right. Gifted with the biggest mouth on either side of the Continental Divide."

"She told Bobby Brewster that I liked him," Catherine told Griff, who was trying very hard not to laugh as he took a sip of lemonade. "I was still upstairs, getting dressed for our first date, and Little Miss MaryJane Shoes and Anklet Socks was downstairs telling him how I'd written 'Catherine loves Bobby' all over my mirror in Tangee lipstick. I wanted to die…right after I choked her."

Griff gave up trying to sip his lemonade and just sat back and howled.

"She told Mrs. Warmkessel that I wasn't home the day she called to ask me to be on the Hospitality Committee, and then added that I was hiding in the kitchen but it wasn't really a fib because mommies don't fib. Can you imagine what it was like, meeting Mrs. Warmkessel at the PTA after that?''

''Mothers shouldn't have their children fib for them,'' Abby said, jutting out her lower jaw. ''It's dishonest.''

''She's got you there, Susie,'' Jim said as he sat down on the arm of the chair beside his wife. ''However, she can't keep a secret. Can you, Abby?''

''Abby?'' Pete questioned her, twirling one of her blond ringlets around his fingertips. ''You want to tell this one, or do you want your father to do the honors?''

Abby sighed theatrically. ''Oh, all right, Pete, so I told a few people that I once caught Mom and Dad necking in the living room. Big deal.''

''Big deal?'' Jim repeated, laughing. ''And you didn't *tell* a few people, Abby. You wrote it up as your fourth-grade essay on families. Martha Warmkessel may have gotten over your mother's fib, but I think seeing that essay tacked up for Parents' Night is what prompted her retirement to Florida.''

''If we've proven my point?'' Elly asked and Abby, who had appeared about to protest yet again, sat back, crossed her arms, shut her mouth with a snap. ''Rob's in Las Vegas. Dad called the airlines and found out that he landed at McCarran around noon. It's six o'clock. If he's not here tonight, he will be tomorrow. And he can't know. He absolutely, positively cannot know.''

''Why?''

Elly turned to look at Catherine, who'd asked the question. ''Because he can't, that's all. He's probably coming here to ask me to come home, and I'm not going back to New York. I can't, Catherine. I was smothering there. And he can't come here. It's hopeless, and I don't want him using my pregnancy to get me to do something I know I can't do.''

"Do you still love him, Elly?" Catherine asked, sounding part loving sister, part teacher asking the bonus question on an oral exam.

"Yeah," Elly said, rubbing at her forehead, trying not to cry. "Yeah, I still love him."

"And you want this baby?"

Elly raised her head, looked at Catherine levelly. "More than anything in this world. Except for Rob."

"Then we'll stay out of it," Catherine declared, looking at the other occupants of the room in turn. "Completely and absolutely out of it. Understood?"

"I love it when she plays teacher, don't you? So damned sexy," Griff said as he stood up and pulled Catherine to her feet. "And now, ladies and gentlemen, I believe Elly might like to step outside and see her new car."

"You brought it? Oh, Griff, that's wonderful," Elly said, happy to have the subject changed. Her father would want to test-drive the thing, and the men could talk cars while the women talked babies, and maybe she'd forget that Rob was in Las Vegas, that Rob was probably going to show up at their front door early tomorrow morning.

She walked across the room, smiling only a little too brightly, the rest of the family in tow, and threw open the door...and looked straight at Rob Lyndon, who had his hand poised an inch away from the doorbell.

Chapter 12

Rob Lyndon had come home one night about six weeks earlier, thrown his briefcase on the hall table, and called out his wife's name. He'd left abruptly that morning, neither of them speaking after the argument they'd had the previous evening, neither of them happy, neither of them feeling anything close to content.

She'd answered him immediately, saying that she was in the living room and he should change into comfortable clothes, then join her. She'd called him "darling." She sounded all right, maybe even happy.

Okay. They would forget the quarrel, wouldn't mention it again. That worked for him. And making up had its merits.

"You got it, hon," he'd agreed, already stripping off his tie as he turned to his right, headed down the hallway to their bedroom. He whistled as he shrugged out of his suit coat, unbuttoned his shirt.

The bed was already turned down, he noticed as he stepped out of his dress slacks, headed for the closet and a wooden hanger.

Encouraging sign. Definitely.

Rob would only admit it to himself, but he really did love their bed. King-size, with heavy brass head and footboard. And a flowered comforter over something Elly had called a dust ruffle. Lace-bordered pillows, dozens of them, all different shapes and sizes. Flowered sheets. Huge, pink cabbage roses.

The rest of the room was furnished in cherry wood, with deep rose paper on the walls, creamy white paint on the ornate old woodwork, an assortment of white carpets scattered on the century-old hardwood floors. Lace curtains hung in the tall, thin windows stretched almost from the floor to the ceiling. And Elly had this dressing table thing set in between the two windows, all lacy skirt and mysterious crystal bottles arranged on top.

It was a woman's bedroom, and he had been invited in. Welcomed. At least that's how it felt. He liked the feeling.

Still whistling a tune he couldn't quite remember, Rob had hung up his suit, pulled off his socks, and stuffed both shirt and socks into the hamper inside the closet. The closet was his, and it was totally masculine. Built-in drawers, specially positioned racks for his suits, his slacks, his shirts. A floor-to-ceiling shoe rack. Even a mirror, so that he could check the adjustment of his tie.

Feminine bedroom, adjacent manly haven. It worked. It really worked.

He'd grabbed a pair of khaki shorts and dived into a pullover shirt, checked his reflection in the mirror.

He ran his fingers through his dark brown hair, only slightly mussed when he'd pulled the shirt over his head, and then winked at himself. "Admit the truth, man. For all you complain about it, you know you love it when Elly's ovulating," he'd told himself as he headed back through the bedroom, then down the hallway once more.

Their's was a big apartment, especially for New York. A big apartment with a good address, the most prestigious zip code. They had seven rooms plus a small room attached to the large kitchen, a room for a housekeeper, not that Elly wanted one.

His mother had found the apartment for them, but he and Elly had decorated it, much to his mother's chagrin. His mother, he knew, saw the apartment as a status symbol, an indication of success, a fitting backdrop for elegant dinner parties. Elly saw a home, his home and hers, and she'd decorated it as such. Just one more bone of contention between his mother and his wife. One he did his best to stay out of, ignore.

He'd stopped off at the kitchen, but Elly wasn't there, wasn't busily putting the final touches on some romantic dinner for two. He'd cut through the dining room, a large room also furnished in cherry wood, along with a china cabinet that had been in his mother's family for three generations. The table wasn't set.

He'd opened the double glass doors that divided the living room and dining room and stepped inside. "Wow," was all he'd said as he looked at the small table set in the middle of the room. The lit candles on that table, the lit candles scattered all around the room.

And there, in the middle of it all, was Elly. His Elly. Dressed in the black lace peignoir set he'd bought her last Christmas, the one that showed off her long legs as she walked, the one that gave tantalizing glimpses of her high, firm breasts. The one that set off her bottomless green eyes and flawless ivory skin.

She'd smiled at him, gotten up from the overstuffed floral couch and walked toward him.

He'd felt his tongue cleave to the roof of his mouth. Three years. They'd been married for three years. But she still got to him. Lord, did she get to him.

"Hello, darling," she said quietly, sliding her fingers into the waistband of his shorts, tugging his shirt free. "I think you're overdressed for dinner."

"You expect me to eat?" he'd asked teasingly as she stood on tiptoe, lifted her mouth to his. She was tall, his Elly, but he stood six foot five himself, and she always said she loved that he made her feel petite, feminine. He looked over her shoulder to the two place settings on the table, to the silver covers on two plates. "I hope you didn't go to too much trouble, hon, because there's no way in hell I'm going over there to do anything so mundane as eating dinner."

She'd nuzzled at his neck, laughed softly. "I was hoping you'd say that, darling, because the only thing under the cover over your plate is a piece of paper with the take-out number for the pizzeria around the corner. You can call it now," she said as he lifted her high in his arms, headed for the overstuffed couch that was one of the most brilliant purchases Elly had made, "or I suppose we could wait until later?"

"Yeah, hon," he'd growled even as he lowered her onto the cushions, joined her. "Later." He kissed her hair, her cheeks, grinned down at her. "So, how do you feel about pizza for breakfast? I'm game if you are."

She'd laughed and drawn him down to her, and Rob had been lost, as he loved to be lost, in her arms....

He'd gone into work late the next morning, sneaking into his office in time to see his mother sitting in the chair in front of his desk, her legs crossed, her right foot jiggling, jiggling, jiggling. "Hello, Mother, how are you?" he'd said as cheerfully as he could as he kissed Althea Lyndon's taut cheek. Cosmetic surgery, what a marvel.

She didn't return his greeting. But, then, she rarely did. Instead, she immediately launched into the reason for her presence in his office. "She did it again, Robert," she said in her clear, clipped accents. "And this time her actions are unforgivable. Completely unforgivable."

"Yes, I'm fine, too, thanks," Rob said as he took off his suit jacket, hung it on the wooden hanger he'd pulled from the clothes tree in the corner of the room. "And Dad? Isn't he due back from Brussels this morning?"

"Robert, don't be flip, it doesn't suit you," his mother said, standing up, smoothing down the skirt of her navy blue suit. "Eleanor did not appear at the Plaza yesterday, for our luncheon with the committee."

"Committee?" Rob asked, even as he began sorting through the mail his secretary had opened, then left on his desk. "What committee would that be, Mother?"

Althea Lyndon began to pace, stopping only to use her long, manicured fingernails to snip a wilting leaf off the plant standing in front of one of the windows in Rob's corner office. "That isn't really germane, Robert," she told him, dropping the offending leaf into the wastebasket. "She phoned the chairperson with some ridiculous excuse, and she didn't attend. Do you know how embarrassing that was for me? Your wife, Robert, has no sense of what is proper, what is expected from her as wife to the scion of this firm. Oh, I know she volunteers in that children's ward at the hospital, but that isn't what Lyndons do. She needs to be on committees, planning charity balls. Your wife needs to be more *visibly* involved, Rob, do the sort of charitable work that keeps your names in the columns. Surely even your wife can understand that."

Rob had felt his hackles rising. He was very close to being very angry. Angry with his mother, who lived her life according to how best that life would reflect on her, her husband, and the almighty family firm. Angry with his wife, who seemed to go out of her way to upset his mother. It was just a damn lunch. Why couldn't she have attended? "My wife, Mother, has a name. Elly."

"Yes, yes, Eleanor. I know. Now," she said, picking up her purse, her gloves, "I've arranged for another luncheon next week—I cannot tell you how I had to beg and wheedle—and I expect your—that is, I expect Eleanor to attend. And, Robert, I expect you to make it clear to Eleanor that she does."

Rob stood, came around the desk, kissed his mother goodbye. "Only if she wants to, Mother. Only if she wants to."

He'd watched as his mother swept out of the room, the society matron at her most intimidating, and then leaned back against the desk, pinched the bridge of his nose between his fingertips. "Dad, I don't know how you stand it," he'd grumbled as he headed back to the letter he'd been reading. "And I definitely don't know why."

"I decided to go to a matinee," Elly had told Rob later that night, when he'd finally decided he had to at least tell her about his mother's plans for her. "*Cats*. There's this half-price booth in Times Square, and I—"

"I know about the booth, Elly," he'd said, cutting her off. "But *Cats?* That show's been running forever, and will probably be running for another ten years, at the least. So why did you have to go yesterday?"

"Because I wanted to," she'd told him as she opened a cabinet in the kitchen, took down two dinner plates—slammed down two dinner plates. She turned away from the counter, pressing her hands back onto the lip of it as she glared at him. "I needed to calm down, relax, after my audition."

Rob had been nibbling on a carrot stick, but pulled it out of his mouth as he said, "Your *what?*"

"I said, after my audition. That's *a-u-d*—"

"I know how to spell it, Elly," Rob had bit out, tossing the carrot stick into the sink. "Now tell me what in hell you're talking about, okay?"

She'd moved away from the counter, reluctantly letting go of it, and walked across the room to pull a small rump roast out of the wall oven. "I auditioned

for a new show. Off-off-Broadway. Nothing big, just
one of the chorus. But I've got it, if I want it.''

Rob had felt a pounding begin in his temples.
''And? Do you want it?''

''What would you say if I did? Lord knows I have
nothing to do around here.''

''Oh, right, and that's my fault, isn't it?'' Rob had
pulled out a kitchen chair, flung himself into it. ''Elly,
we've been round and round about this sort of thing.
You're in New York, for crying out loud. If you can't
find something to amuse you in New York, you won't
find it anywhere.''

''Amuse me? *Amuse* me? What am I, Rob? A child
to be amused? Entertained? I thought we'd be pregnant by now, but we're not. I thought—''

Rob had held up his hands, knowing he was about
to venture into very dangerous territory, but somehow
unable to stop himself. ''And that's another thing,''
he'd said, glaring at her. ''What's this *we* aren't pregnant yet? I can't tell you how much I hate that touchy-
feely kind of garbage. You get pregnant, Elly. I'm
just the sperm donor, remember? And obviously not
a very good one.''

''That's not true! You were checked, Rob, I was
checked. There's nothing wrong with either of us.
Doctor Rosen says there's nothing keeping us—me—
from getting pregnant except the fact that maybe
we're too uptight about it, too worried about it. So I
thought that if I were to take this job, get busy with
rehearsals, get my mind off it, well, then maybe I'd
conceive.''

Rob had shaken his head, sighed. ''Well, that's a
new one. And when were you going to do this con-
ceiving, Elly? Even off-off-Broadway, we're talking

daily rehearsals, eight shows a week. We make enough appointments for sex as it is.''

''You hate that, don't you?'' she'd asked, sinking into the facing chair. ''Oh, Rob, it's falling apart. It's all falling apart. We married too soon, you know. We didn't talk about our futures, what we both wanted. I hate New York, and you can't leave. I can't be the daughter-in-law your mother wants, I'm no good at luncheons and card parties. I want kids, a house in the country, a husband who coaches Little League. But it's not going to happen, is it? You're going to follow in your father's footsteps, just the way your mother and dad always planned, and I'm going to keep holding you back, wanting something else. Maybe it's good that I haven't been able to conceive. Maybe it's best all around.''

He'd let her go—let her go to run into the bedroom and lock the door after her. Not that she would cry, because Elly never cried. She just drew in on herself, closing him out. Always closing him out.

Rob had come home the next night, thrown his briefcase on the hall table, and called out his wife's name. He'd left abruptly that morning, neither of them speaking after the argument they'd had the previous evening, neither of them happy, neither of them feeling anything close to content.

When she didn't answer, he'd gone into the living room, calling out her name once more. ''Elly?'' he repeated, making his way through the dining room, into the kitchen.

Nothing. No food simmering on the stove or in the oven. No note on the refrigerator. No nothing. Okay, so they'd go out to dinner. Make it a real celebration.

That'd work. Because, when she heard his news, heard what he'd been investigating, what else he'd begun in the hope of pleasing her...well, yeah. They'd have something to celebrate all right. He was sure of it. Pretty sure of it. Really needed to talk to Elly about it...

He'd checked the laundry room off the kitchen, but she wasn't there, unable to hear him above the whir of the washer and dryer, both of which stood silent.

And then he'd smiled. The bedroom. Damn, he hadn't checked the bedroom. Love among the cabbage roses. That was perfect. With the news he had for her, he couldn't think of a better, more convenient place for them to be when he told her. After all, people could always eat.

"Elly?" he'd called out, loping down the hallway, back to the foyer, then turning left, heading down the hallway to the master bedroom. "Elly, I've done something, a couple of things, and I know we really should talk about them together before they go any—Elly?"

She hadn't been in the bedroom, either. Not in the bedroom, not in the bathroom. He looked at the clock over the fireplace in the bedroom. Seven o'clock. Where in hell could she be at seven o'clock?

"Rehearsal?" he'd asked himself, then shook his head. No, Elly wouldn't have done that. She might have talked about this show she could be in, but she wouldn't really do it. Not without the two of them discussing it more, at least. Would she? After all, he might have been doing some planning, some feeling-out of options, but he wouldn't really go any further with either idea if Elly didn't agree. That's what they did. They planned, they discussed, they agreed.

At least that's what they used to do.

And then he'd seen it. He'd seen the note propped against the mound of pillows on the bed. She'd put it in an envelope, then written his name on the front.

"No," he'd said, shaking his head. "No. I don't want to read that. Elly!" He turned on his heels, sprinted across the room to look in her closet, then stopped as he noticed her dressing table. Her empty dressing table. All the mysterious bottles were gone.

He opened the doors to the closet, although he knew he didn't have to, although he knew what he'd see. Gone. All of her clothes were gone.

And then he couldn't stop. He returned to the bedroom, opened every last drawer in Elly's bureau, finding them all empty. He walked into the bathroom, saw his toothbrush hanging there by itself. All by itself. The lingering scent of Elly's bath powder was in the air, but the container holding that powder was gone.

She'd left him.

One too many arguments. One too many disappointments. One too many dreams lost.

He'd picked up the envelope, loosened his tie as he walked back to the living room, his steps dragging. Falling into the overstuffed couch, he lifted the flap of the envelope, pulled out the small, folded note.

She'd used the stationery she'd received as one of their wedding presents three years ago, at the elaborate reception his mother had insisted upon throwing for them a full month after their marriage. Elly had been excited about the party, up until the moment she'd realized that Althea hadn't been celebrating the marriage, she'd taken an opportunity for yet another clever business party, another social event that had a lot to do with Althea Lyndon, and not a damn thing

to do with celebrating the marriage of her only son
to a Las Vegas ''showgirl.''

''Mr. and Mrs. Robert W. Lyndon.'' The flowing
script was small, neatly centered on the front of the
card. He flipped it open, began to read.

> Rob, forgive me. I should have told you, but I
> didn't think you could get away from the city
> right now. Mom and Dad are celebrating their
> thirtieth wedding anniversary by renewing their
> vows. They've asked Catherine and Abby and
> me to come out to Nevada for the ceremony.
>
> That's where I am, Rob. Las Vegas. Mom said
> I could stay as long as I liked, and I'm going to
> take her up on it. I've got a lot of thinking to
> do, Rob, and so do you. Please, don't call me,
> don't come out. We're not working, darling, not
> together. I don't know if we can work better
> apart, but anything's better than the way it is.
>
> I love you, Rob. I love you with all my heart.
> But I don't know anymore if love is enough.
>
> Elly.

He'd called Summerlin immediately, talked to Jim,
talked to Susie. Yes, Elly was there. Yes, she was all
right. No, she didn't want to talk to him.

Give her time, they'd both told him. Time to think,
time to miss him, time to realize that running away
never solved a problem, and never would.

And he'd agreed. It had half killed him, but he'd
agreed. For four long weeks, he'd communicated with
Susie and Jim on the phone, always hoping Elly
would pick it up when it rang, always disappointed
when she hadn't.

He'd waited, he'd bided his time. He'd even flown to Lake Tahoe one weekend, to work on that surprise he'd been ready to share with Elly the day he'd come home to find her gone.

He'd talked with his dad, explained everything to his dad. And he'd broken his mother's heart. It was a lot to do in four weeks.

But on none of the long, long nights of those four weeks did he sleep in Elly's bedroom, Elly's bed. The marriage bed, he'd decided, was his By Invitation Only, For Couples Only.

He no longer qualified.

Rob drove the rental car off the lot near the airport, driving down the Strip in the early-afternoon traffic. He never tired of the scenery, the ever-changing scenery. He smiled in spite of himself as he drove past the Luxor casino and hotel, shaking his head at the incongruous sight of the Las Vegas version of the sphinx, of the glass pyramid behind it.

He tipped an imaginary hat to the MGM Grand lion as he stopped in traffic near the impressive entrance, where casino gamblers and guests could enter the building through the gaping mouth of the gilt lion. Too impressive, as a matter of fact, because that gaping lion mouth had bothered enough prospective patrons that a new, more conventional entrance had to be constructed at the back of the huge building. A fascinating world, the world of casinos and hotels and catering to guests from every country, every continent, every culture.

Elly had been working at the MGM Grand when he'd met her, dancing in the chorus of a lavish production that had been part fairy tale, part Broadway

show, part technical masterpiece. But he hadn't seen
the show when he'd met her. He hadn't even stepped
inside the MGM Grand.

He'd been in Vegas on business, spending three
months there helping a client arrange financing for a
new hotel and casino. Interesting work. Fascinating
work. And a wonderful city. He'd fallen in love with
Las Vegas the moment he'd stepped off the plane.
And he'd fallen in love with Elly the first moment
he'd seen her standing on Freemont Street, holding a
young child's hand as they watched a bunch of sen-
ior-citizen square dancers going through their paces
as one of the free shows the city seemed to put on
daily.

She'd been surrounded by kids. Kids on crutches,
kids in wheelchairs, kids who might only be able to
dream of one day dancing like the men and women
they watched whirl around in circles, bow to their
partners.

Elly hadn't been the only adult in the group of
about a dozen children, but she had been the one
who'd seen him, thanked him when he stopped,
helped a fallen child to his feet. It was then that he'd
noticed that all the kids were wearing identical
T-shirts with the name of a local hospital on them,
that Elly and three other young women were wearing
the same T-shirts.

That had been the beginning. She'd thanked him,
he'd lingered, they'd talked. And it had been impossible to say goodbye.

He'd learned a lot about Elly that day. She humbled
him. It wasn't enough for her to dance. She had to
bring music and dancing into the lives of these children. She and a few other dancers from her troupe

volunteered their time every week, taking the children on small excursions, putting on shows for them at the hospital.

Elly loved kids. She'd always loved kids. And she'd make a damn fine mother.

Rob looked to his left as he eased his foot onto the gas pedal, urged the car forward once more. The New York, New York Resort stood on the corner of the wide intersection. It hadn't been quite completed the last time he and Elly had visited her parents, the Statue of Liberty still missing her head and torch arm, the building facades depicting the city of New York not quite ready for occupancy. But it was all there now, and fascinating to look at. The world's greatest metropolis, miniaturized and plunked down inside the world's greatest playground.

It was about as much of New York as Rob ever wanted to see again, at least on a day-to-day basis.

His secretary had made hotel reservations for him at a suites-only hotel closer to Summerlin, and Rob gave one last look down the Strip before heading for the highway, heading for Summerlin, heading for Elly's parents' house.

He was sure of his welcome at the hotel.

He wasn't sure of his welcome at Elly's parents' home.

Rob stood there, just stood there. Looking at her.

"Elly? *Beep-beep.* We can't get outside to see this new car of yours if you're going to admire it from the doorway, now are we?" Abby said.

Pete leaned down, whispered in Abby's ear. "I know you can't see over her head, sweetheart, but there's somebody on the porch."

"Somebody on the—Rob?" Rob had already recognized Abby's voice, and wasn't surprised when she brushed past Elly and pushed open the screen door, then launched herself at him. "Ah, my favorite brother-in-law," she said, giving him a smacking kiss on the cheek as he caught her easily, all one hundred pounds of her. He wondered if it was cowardly to hold on to his bubbly sister-in-law, hide behind her as he kept his eyes on his wife.

Elly looked wonderful. She looked terrible. She looked surprised. She looked terrified.

Damn. Maybe he should have listened to Susie and stayed away. But he couldn't. Not after he'd talked with Elly, heard her voice. Not after he'd taken that other phone call, at last heard the words he'd needed to hear.

"Elly?" he said as he let Abby slowly slide down him, until her feet met the cement slab of the porch.

"Rob," she said shortly, then turned and walked away from the door.

"She hates me, right?" Rob asked Abby, knowing she'd tell him the truth. "She hates me, she wants me staked out spread-eagle in the desert with pancake syrup poured on me and two buckets of ants at the ready. Am I at least close?"

"Well, actually," Abby began slowly, grinning, then frowned when she heard her father's voice.

"Abby! Does the name Martha Warmkessel mean anything to you?"

"Sorry, Rob, but my lips are sealed, and all of that," Abby said, shrugging.

Jim Parrish held open the screen door, suggested that Rob and Abby come back inside so that everyone could be introduced to everyone else, and so that Susie Parrish could hug her son-in-law.

He kissed Susie, then shook hands with Griff Edwards, asking him if they'd ever met before, as he looked vaguely familiar. He knew pretty much about both Griff Edwards and Pete Shaw, thanks to his talks with Susie, but he hadn't recognized either name. And yet he was sure he'd seen Griff somewhere before, and recently, too.

"Did you take a drive down the Strip before heading out here?" Catherine asked, and Rob said that he had. "That explains it, then," she told him, grinning up at her fiancé. "Now, here's Pete Shaw, Doctor Peter Shaw, the poor deluded fool who's actually willing to take on Abby, although why is anybody's guess."

"Pete," Rob said, shaking the man's hand, and liking Pete's firm grip, his clear-eyed expression. "My condolences."

"Rat," Abby said, then giggled. She and Rob had a long-standing history of teasing each other, and he'd often told Elly that he'd married her just so he could have Abby as his baby sister.

"You're a tall one, aren't you, Rob?" Pete asked as the three men headed toward the kitchen and the iced tea Susie had already promised them. "You and Elly ever consider raising your own basketball team?"

"Pe-ter," Abby ground out, poking her fiancé in the ribs. She rolled her eyes. "Brother, and they say I'm bad. Rob, ignore this idiot, he's got sports on the brain. As a matter of fact, he's probably going to ask you if you want to join Griff and him for a pickup basketball game down at the schoolyard later. But, then, boys will be boys, won't they? Now excuse me, okay, and I'll go check on Elly, make sure Catherine has everything under control.''

Rob looked at Jim and sighed. ''I thought she might yell at me, tell me to go home, tell me to go to hell. But I didn't think she'd run away from me. Not again. I guess I should have listened to you and Susie and stayed in New York.''

Jim laid a companionable hand on Rob's shoulder, directing him back through the living room toward the front door. ''She'll be fine, son,'' he told him bracingly. ''And I think your timing is excellent. Of course, Elly's opinion on that is probably another matter entirely. What do you say we take a walk, have ourselves a little talk? I've got some information for you.''

Chapter 13

"Are you all right, Elly? Maybe you ought to sit down, take a couple of deep breaths. You went white as a sheet out there."

Elly continued to pace as Catherine sat on the edge of the bed, watching her. "I'm fine. Fine." She raised her hands in front of her, clenched her fingers into fists. "Just peachy. Oh, Lord. Why did I have to think of peaches?" She put a hand to her mouth and ran into the bathroom.

By the time she reemerged from the bathroom after brushing her teeth and washing her face, the whole lineup was there. Catherine on the bed. Abby sitting cross-legged on the floor. Susie in the chair in the corner.

"Poor baby," Susie commiserated. "I remember morning sickness so well. Not fondly, by the way."

"Man, what a thing to look forward to," Abby

said, wrinkling her nose. "If they can put a man on the moon, why can't they—well, you know."

"It was just the power of suggestion," Catherine pronounced calmly, patting the mattress beside her. "Now, what are we going to do? Back off, help, throw him to the wolves—what? He's already out there, bonding with Griff and Pete, and you can't blame them for that because, one, they're both friendly guys and, two, Rob is a nice guy. Although I've seen him looking happier. And Dad, well, we all know he's always been crazy about Rob."

Elly dropped her head into her hands. "Maybe we should just go back to New York. I never thought I'd say this, but it's less crowded there."

"No!"

Elly looked from sister to sister, then to her mother, for all of them had spoken in unison. "I take it there's been some kind of vote while I was in the bathroom?"

"Darling," Susie said, joining Catherine and Elly on the bed. "I know you feel pressured here, with all of us around. And I know you'd feel just as pressured in New York, with…well, you'd be pressured there, as well. And that's why we packed a bag for you while you were in the bathroom."

Elly blinked twice, looked at her sisters and mother again. Why were they beginning to look like co-conspirators? "You did what? You couldn't have. I wasn't gone that long."

"It was only one bag, Elly, and a smaller bag with cosmetics and shoes and stuff," Abby said, grinning. "Besides, an airline attendant—they don't call themselves stewardesses anymore, you know—sent me her helpful hints on how to pack for a week in less than ten minutes. I did a couple of columns on Hyper-pack last year, as a matter of fact. I don't think I missed anything. And if I did, you can always pick it up at the Nugget. Which reminds me. I still have to get your stuff from the bathroom. Be right back. Don't say anything too interesting while I'm gone, okay?''

Elly's knees were going weak, so that she was glad she was sitting down. ''Nugget? As in the Golden Nugget?''

Catherine nodded. ''It's Griff's favorite place, right on Freemont Street and very elegant without being stuffy. You'll love the hot-fudge sundaes, El, once your stomach goes from Empty All to Eat At Will. Griff called a friend there and got you a room.''

Elly found herself playing the part of someone who could only react and not act. ''Got *me* a room?''

Susie began lightly rubbing her daughter's back. ''Only you, Elly. Rob's staying in some hotel out here. Dad asked him, and he told him the name, although it escapes me at the moment. But, be that as it may, we all concluded that it's just too crowded with well-meaning family here at the house right now, and that you need to be alone. Well, as alone as you can be with Rob here, as well. But with you staying at the Nugget, you and Rob can meet, talk. Date?''

''Date?'' Elly winced, realizing she was still doing it. Echoing. Parroting. ''I don't want to *date* my own husband. That's ridiculous.''

''Oh, I don't know, El,'' Abby said, grinning as she stuffed toilet articles into Elly's carry-on bag. ''I think it's kind of romantic, myself. And with nobody else around to interrupt, or get in your way, or confuse you with advice—well, maybe you two guys can start talking to each other. *Really* talking to each other. Mom says that's what you need.''

Elly stood up, walked to the window that faced the front of the house. Outside, parked at the curb, was her brand-new car. She could drive herself to Vegas, check in at the Nugget, order herself some room service. Take a bubble bath. She'd like a bubble bath.

And then later, if she wanted to—and only if she wanted to—Rob could meet her and they could take a walk around town, or go to a show, or maybe just sit and talk. No family. No sympathetic looks. No advice.

She turned away from the window. ''Catherine? Griff has some papers for me to sign....''

''Got 'em right here, El,'' Catherine said, pulling a thin sheaf of papers out from under her, as she'd been sitting on them all along. ''Sign at the *X*s. Griff's already arranged for insurance, tags, stuff like that.''

As Elly took a pen from her mother, who was looking quite wonderfully misty-eyed, Abby opened the bedroom door, stuck her head out into the hallway, then turned to say, ''All clear, babe. Dad's got Rob out on the patio with Griff and Pete. Your suitcases are already in the car. Oh, I forgot something!''

Abby met Elly at the car, throwing open the passenger door and tossing in a full box of soda crackers. ''Here you go, babe. Mom says you're to munch on a couple of these every morning, even before you lift your head from the pillow. She also said you're being sick because you're pregnant, but also because you now *know* you're pregnant. She says your stomach will settle down pretty soon. Now be good, have fun, take care of yourself and my little niece or nephew. And for crying out crumbs, Elly, call Mom every night so that she doesn't put on a trench coat and mustache and sneak into town to check up on you. That could be embarrassing, especially since Catherine and I would probably come with her.''

Elly felt tears prickling behind her eyes as she smiled at her baby sister. ''I've got the best, most understanding family in the whole world. And I love you all, so very much,'' she said, feeling unaccustomedly sloppy and sentimental.

''Yeah, all the emotional, pregnant ladies say stuff like that,'' Abby said teasingly, then leaned further into the car so that she could give her sister a kiss. ''Now get out of here before we both start blubbering, okay?''

''Okay,'' Elly said quietly, slipping on her sunglasses. ''But don't expect any miracles, all right?''

''We don't need any miracles, El,'' her sister told her as she held on to the passenger door. ''Between you, you and Rob have already created one. Now all you have to do is remember how much you love each other. Everything else will fall into place, I promise.''

Elly sniffled and grinned, cried and smiled, all the way to the valet parking driveway at the Golden Nugget. And, as she watched her suitcase and carry-on being wheeled away by one of the hotel employees, she actually found herself wondering if Abby had packed her black peignoir set. And then she shook her head. What was she thinking? Abby had packed the suitcases. Of course she'd packed the peignoir set.

Elly walked back into the living room of the suite Griff had reserved for her, still brushing her straight, shoulder-length brown hair. Catherine and Abby had the same curls as their mother. She had her dad's straight hair and long legs.

She smiled as she looked at the huge basket of fresh fruit that had been delivered an hour earlier. The basket had been her dad's contribution, of course, and the enclosed note had been adorably Dadlike: "Plenty of fruit, plenty of milk, and at least eight hours sleep a night. All my love, Doctor Dad."

She was still getting used to the idea that she was at the Nugget, that her clothes were already hanging in the closet in her bedroom and that she was here all alone, on her own. She loved her family, but she certainly hadn't had much privacy this past month. And they were all so gosh-darn *happy*. Catherine in love. Abby in love. Her mom and dad so obviously still in love. Talk of wedding gowns and reception menus and honeymoon destinations. No, her parents' house had definitely not been the refuge of choice for a woman contemplating ending her own marriage.

She walked back into her bedroom, then into the large bathroom that had been fitted out with a huge tub, a separate shower, a makeup mirror. Even a hair dryer and a telephone. A person could put a bed in the corner and move into the bathroom for a few days, that's how huge it was. She turned her head from side to side, checked her newly washed hair one last time, then put down the brush.

It was funny, her hair. Thick, straight as sticks, it had always tended to be just the least bit oily, so that she'd long ago begun shampooing every day. But lately her hair seemed to have more body of its own, even a richer texture.

She leaned forward over the sink, touching a hand to her cheek. And her skin. Smoother, clearer, almost brighter. And, like her hair, less oily, although not dry, either. Just sort of "Blooming," Elly said, then smiled.

That was it. She was *blooming*. Glowing, as if lit from within. Even with all the morning sickness, all the tears she'd shed this past month, she looked almost disgustingly healthy.

Amazing.

She turned to her side, looking at herself as she stood there in strapless bra and bikini panties. She ran her hands down over her fairly sensitive breasts— Lord, she still couldn't believe her father had asked her that question!—then pressed them against her still-flat stomach. This was going to take some getting used to, that was for sure.

Elly had always kept her body in condition, both during her professional dancing days and since. She'd done aerobics twice a week, maintained her regimen of stretching and toning exercises. She was well-muscled, without looking like she pumped iron. Her legs were strong, her stomach muscles were tight, her posture had always been important to her.

"You'll probably be waddling like a duck before this is over," she told her reflection, then grinned as she headed back into the bedroom. "And I'm going to love every waddling, quacking minute of it."

She caught a glimpse of the digital clock on the nightstand and decided it was time she got dressed. Rob hadn't called her, but a huge basket of white roses had been delivered before she'd taken her bubble bath, and the enclosed card had informed her that Rob would come to her suite at seven, to take her downstairs for dinner.

She didn't know how her family had done it, but

obviously they'd convinced Rob to "court" his
wife—to go slow, to take his time, to get reacquainted
with the woman he'd married.

So, how did you tell your husband that you're in
love with him but that you really don't think you can
coexist in New York with his mother? That you don't
think you can coexist in this *universe* with his
mother? That you think New York is a nice place to
visit, but that you now know you can't possibly live
there, breathe there, exist there?

And that was just for starters....

Elly removed an ivory silk pantsuit from the closet
and slipped the slacks on over her pantyhose, vaguely
disappointed when the zipper closed without the
slightest problem. She'd actually lost three pounds
since coming to Nevada, and she knew that wasn't
the way it was supposed to work. But that would
change, now that she knew she was pregnant. If she
had to choke down the food, she'd eat balanced meals
three times a day.

She pulled an almost electric green silk, spaghetti-
strapped chemise that matched her eyes over her
head, then shrugged into the hip-length jacket. The
suit was good, with a superb cut. The jacket nipped
her waist. The slacks were boot length and had just
the right "kick" to them when she zipped up ivory
leather heeled boots and walked over to the dresser
to retrieve her scarf.

Yes, the suit was good. Acceptable. But the scarf
was not, at least not to Althea Lyndon. She'd wanted
Elly to wear a simple strand of pearls, not a long,
trailing silk scarf decorated with colorful peacocks.
"Too flamboyant and flashy," Althea had decreed the

night the four of them had met for dinner at the top of the World Trade Center.

"Cut it out, Eleanor Anne," Elly told herself as she slid the scarf around her throat, threw one long end of it back over her shoulder. "Stop blaming Althea for walking all over you when you've been her uncomplaining doormat for three years. If you'd had more confidence in yourself you could have either ignored her or politely told her to go hell."

She smiled, picturing a scene where she would actually tell Althea Lyndon to take a hike to hell. Oh, yeah, that'd work. No, it wouldn't. Because then Althea would have definite proof that Eleanor Parrish Lyndon was *not* their "sort of people." And she'd drive poor Rob crazy, not that she didn't do that anyway, poor thing. It can't be fun, constantly apologizing for his bear of a mother.

Which didn't mean she hadn't been waiting three years for Rob to defend her, stand up for her, tell his mother to back off, leave his wife alone. Was that fair? Was it fair to want him to fight her battle?

She also couldn't understand how Richard Lyndon had survived forty years of marriage to the woman. But then, she didn't understand much of the Lyndon family dynamics and wasn't sure she wanted to. Her parents had raised her, raised all three sisters, to be their own persons, not carbon copies of their parents. Rob, on the other hand, had known his future since he'd been in diapers. He was the son, the only child, and he was raised to take over from his father in the family business—educated accordingly, programmed from birth to think like a Lyndon, dress like a Lyndon, walk and talk and marry like a Lyndon.

Althea must have blown at least three discrete gas-

kets when Rob had called home to tell her that he'd
married a Las Vegas dancer in a wedding chapel on
the Strip.

There had been nothing, nothing, Elly could do
from that point on that would have pleased Althea
Lyndon. And both women knew it, Elly thought now,
as she paced the plush carpet in her suite, waited for
Rob's knock on the door. The mother-in-law, daughter-in-law relationship had been doomed from the out-
set.

And she'd wondered. Had Rob married her because
he loved her, or because she was so different from
anyone he'd ever known? Had he married her because
he loved her laughing, normal yet sometimes wacky
family, or to shock his own, so-proper family?

She wondered now. Wondered why she'd never
asked him those questions. Wondered if she dared to
ask him now. Wondered if she could live with his
answers.

Elly nearly jumped out of her high-heeled boots
when the knock sounded against the door, and she
ran to the mirror over a credenza in the suite, checking her appearance one more time. Did she look all
right? Did she look pregnant? Did she have time to
crawl around on the floor of the suite, picking up all
the marbles that had fallen out of her brain?

She took a deep breath, smoothed down her jacket
with both hands, picked up the small ivory leather
purse with the long, skinny shoulder strap and headed
for the door.

"Rob," she said a moment later, as he stood in the
hallway, dressed in navy blue slacks and a blue-and-
cream-patterned golf shirt. She'd bought him that
shirt for his birthday last year, and it was one of her

favorites. One of his favorites. She stepped into the hallway, closed the door behind her. Otherwise, they'd be in the bedroom of the suite within five seconds, and that wouldn't solve anything. Although Rob probably had come here believing that they'd be in bed together within those first five seconds. Poor baby, he was about to be disappointed.

"Elly," he answered, and the sound of his voice was enough to bring quick tears to her eyes. "Are you ready for dinner?"

That was it? That was all he was going to say? He was going to be a good boy? He wasn't going to kiss her, hold her, tell her he loved her? He wasn't even going to try to get her into bed?

Well, that stank....

"How's work?"

"Work? Oh. Oh, fine. The usual."

"Uh-huh. Good. And your father?"

"Dad? Oh, he's okay. He left for Texas last night, to see one of our clients. Guy with more oil money than he knows what to do with. He's throwing some huge weekend party for about a thousand of his closest friends. Cookouts at the old corral, horseback rides, a tour of his estate, which Dad says is about roughly one and a half times the size of Rhode Island. He's even built a stream near his house, then imported rocks from Colorado because he didn't like the look of Texas rocks, if you can believe that. Oh, and there's to be a square dance or something—a hoedown, maybe?—the last night, with everyone asked to wear costumes. Dad said he thinks it's going to be a hoot. Mother didn't go."

Elly bit back a small smile. "And Althea didn't go? Wow, color me shocked."

"Be kind, Elly," Rob said. But he smiled when he said it.

The waiter put their salads in front of them, and Elly made a face at the raw spinach. But her dad would be proud of her.

"Griff and Pete seem like nice guys."

"Um, the best," Elly answered around a small forkful of assorted greens. "Griff is just the sort of guy Catherine needs, steady, dependable, and Pete actually thinks Abby is just about the most clever creature in God's creation. Mom's been smiling so much that Dad's threatening to have her rolled into the O.R., to surgically wipe that silly grin off her face."

"And Jim and Susie are as wonderful as ever."

Elly nodded.

"They've invited me to the renewal-of-vows ceremony. Is that all right with you?"

Elly dug through her salad, wishing there had been another cherry tomato. Wishing she could relax, at least look at Rob. "You're going to be here that long? I wouldn't have thought you could be away from the office that long, especially with Richard in Texas."

"There're seventy-five employees, Elly. The place isn't going to go under if Dad's away for a week."

There was something slightly wrong with that statement, but Elly couldn't put her finger on it. "Okay," was all she said, then she sat back as the waiter removed the salad plates.

This was worse than a blind date. At least then you could talk about the weather or movies you'd both seen or books you'd read. Tonight Elly had all the first-date nerves she hadn't felt in more than three years, but none of the anticipation of discovery. She and Rob knew everything about each other. They had a history. And yet she was going insane, trying to find something safe, something neutral, to talk about.

She looked around the large dining room, began playing the game she and Rob had played at times when they'd gone out to dinner together. Guess the married couples and how long they've been married. No points if they had kids with them, of course.

Newlyweds, they'd decided, barely touched their food, and spent the time myopically staring at each other, lost in their own private world. Young marrieds sipped white wine and talked incessantly, sometimes forgetting to eat as they filled each other in on their day, sharing every minute moment with each other. Those married more than, oh, six or seven years, traveled in packs of at least four, sometimes six or eight. The women talked to the women, and the men talked to the men, and everyone laughingly fought over the check.

And then there were the others. The ones who'd been married long enough that they'd run out of conversation. They sat at the same table, but on separate small islands. They discussed the menu, then lapsed into silence for the remainder of the meal. The wife watched the newlyweds and sighed. The husband ordered a third gin and tonic.

Yes, you could always tell the ones who'd run out of things to say. She and Rob had promised each other that they'd never be like that. Never.

Elly sighed, took a sip of ice water, thanked the waiter as he placed her broiled haddock in front of her. Broiled, not fried. Dad would be so proud. And Rob had been so right. *We* didn't get pregnant. Not unless *we* both had to drink four glasses of milk a day and spend way too much time looking at the insides of a toilet bowl.

"Not hungry?" Rob asked as Elly pushed small bits of haddock around her plate as he cut into his filet mignon. "You could order something else?"

"No, no, that's all right. It's delicious, really," she said, spearing a piece of fish and raising it to her mouth. And then she sank to the lowest of the low. "So, how's the weather in New York? Getting much rain?"

The casino lights flashed back on as the lights died on the canopy above Freemont Street. The crowd, which was considerable, began filtering away, leaving Rob and Elly standing outside the Golden Nugget. With no place to go. Nothing to do.

"Do you want to play a little roulette?" Rob asked, taking her hand as the doorman held open the door to the casino.

"Russian?" Elly answered automatically, for it had been a private joke between them, as neither considered gambling much more than a goodbye party for their money.

And then she saw the huge slot machine directly inside the door. "Oh. That must be the one Catherine and Griff won on," she said, walking toward the machine, pulling Rob after her. "Would you believe it? Catherine, *gambling.*"

"We all take gambles, Elly, at some time in our lives."

She looked up at Rob, saw the hard line of his jaw. He was a very imposing guy, when he was serious. At six foot five, he was physically imposing, at the least. But his eyes could resemble a warm summer sky or two chips of blue ice. When they'd first met she'd been immediately attracted to his unaffected smile, his shock of unruly dark brown hair, those laughing eyes.

But once they'd flown to New York he'd begun severely combing his hair back from his forehead à la Michael Douglas in most of his recent movies, and his Brooks Brother suits and power ties had seemed to drain the smile out of his eyes. There were times, uncomfortable times, when she wasn't quite sure she knew who he was, which Rob Lyndon she'd married.

He'd obviously just towel-dried his hair tonight, however, and it was the way she liked it. Faintly mussed, eminently touchable. He looked more relaxed in his knit shirt and slacks. But his eyes were still in winter, even if the rest of him was in sunny Las Vegas.

"Are we gambling now, Rob?" she asked at last, watching as the four spinning reels slowly ground to a halt, one after the other, and the woman who'd fed her coins into the machine sighed, then walked away. "Is that what we're doing?"

"Why not?" he said, deliberately misinterpreting her, she was sure. He pulled a twenty-dollar bill from his pocket, then led her over to a row of machines along the wall, each one featuring a different sign of the zodiac. "Scorpio, right?" he said, feeding the bill into the machine.

"Yes," Elly answered dully. "Do we sting our mates to death, or is that just black widow spiders?"

"I don't know, El," he said, smiling as he waved her over to the machine. "You're talking to a Gemini, remember? Half the time I don't know who *I* am."

"Gemini," she told herself quietly as she pushed the lit button marked Maximum Bet. Go big or stay home, isn't that what Catherine had crowed laughingly the night she'd come home with a purse stuffed with hundred-dollar bills? "The twins of the Zodiac, right? Well, that explains one thing, doesn't it? I'm married to two men. The not-in-New-York Rob, and the in-New-York Rob."

The three reels stopped, and the Insert Coin button lit up. Rob leaned over her shoulder, hit the Maximum Bet button again. "And I'm married to the happy-in-Nevada, unhappy-in-New-York Eleanor Lyndon," he said, his voice faintly gruff as he tried to whisper and still be heard over the sounds of people talking and coins dropping into metal trays. "Now, if we could only get the two of them together, work something out…"

The reels stopped, and thirty coins spat into the metal tray. "And we have a winner," Rob said, indicating that Elly should play again. "Unless you want to cash out, play it safe, not take another chance?"

Elly looked up at him, saw the question in his eyes, knew it had nothing to do with slot machines. She sat down on the chair in front of the machine and pushed the button.

Rob took the key from Elly and opened the door to the suite, pushed the door open, then stood back as she walked inside. And then he stood there, one arm holding the door open, and waited for her to invite him in or send him away.

The power she held at that moment shocked her.

The thrill that power gave her surprised her. And the thought of Rob leaving her here alone damn near destroyed her.

''There's an honor bar, if you'd like a soda or a drink?'' she asked, avoiding actually inviting him into the suite.

''Soda's fine,'' he answered, stepping inside, allowing the door to swing shut behind him and lock automatically. ''You?'' he asked, scanning the room quickly, just as quickly locating the small refrigerator.

''Me? Um, is there orange juice?'' Elly asked, dropping her purse on a chair, slipping out of her jacket.

Rob went down on his haunches, looked inside the refrigerator. ''One orange juice, coming up,'' he said, straightening, a can of soda in one hand, a small bottle of orange juice in the other. ''How about macadamia nuts, El? You've always liked those.''

She didn't know. Where macadamia nuts on a pregnant woman's list of nourishing foods? She'd have to ask her father, as she thought there was something about a lot of saturated fat in macadamia nuts. It would figure, as they tasted so good. ''I don't think so, Rob,'' she said, then walked into the bedroom to hang up her jacket, slide the scarf from her throat.

Rob was standing at the window when she returned to the living room, looking out over the miles of lights that marked residential areas that were nearly impossible to see from the hotel during the daytime. The view seemed to be one of a couple of city streets, then the railroad tracks, then the highway, and then nothing but desert until the mountains jutted up in the distance. But at night that empty-looking desert dazzled with lights, with homes, with families. It always amazed her.

"I love it here," Rob said as she stood beside him, looking out over the living desert, at the shadow of the mountains. "The land, the people, the raw energy, the entrepreneurial spirit. The land of optimists. You'd think the chamber of commerce would put that on their billboards, wouldn't you?"

"Maybe they have," Elly said, and then somehow found herself leaning against Rob's shoulder, sighing as he slid his arm around her waist, drew her closer. It felt good, this closeness. It felt so very good.

"We were happy here, El," he said quietly, looking down into her face. "What happened?"

She walked away from him, picked up the opened bottle of orange juice he'd left on the table. "We were falling in love, Rob," she told him reasonably. "We probably would have been happy in downtown Rangoon."

"That's true enough," he agreed as he walked over to the couch, sat down beside her. "But it was more than that, Elly. We were happy with each other, yes, but we were happy with life in general. I don't think we took that with us to New York. Or, if we did, it didn't last."

"Real life intruded, huh?" Elly said, slowly turning the cold bottle around in her hands. "Unless what we had wasn't enough to really last. Couple of speed bumps and, bang, everything blew up."

"Do you believe that, Elly? Do you truly believe that?"

She felt him take the bottle from her hands, replace it on the table in front of them. She looked at him, looked at those warm-summer-sky eyes, at the lock of hair that had fallen forward onto his forehead. "I don't want to believe that, Rob," she said quietly, then closed her eyes as he traced her cheek with his fingertips. "I don't want to."

"Susie said I'm to treat you gently, move slowly. And she's right. I don't think I've ever seen you look this fragile, Elly."

"Fragile? Me?" Elly tried to smile. "Well, that's a neat trick."

"It's more of a scary trick, El. You've been scaring me for weeks, for months. But I don't want to talk about that now, do you? So let me ask another question. Would I be breaking any of Susie's ground rules, do you think, if I were to kiss you? Because I really, really do want to kiss you."

"A kiss won't settle anything, Rob," she told him, avoiding his eyes.

"Truer words were never spoken, El," he said, obviously trying for a little levity. "I've been trying to pretend that kisses, that loving you, were enough to solve any problem. Your problems, my problems. I was wrong. You weren't happy, I wasn't happy."

"I know you weren't happy, Rob." Elly sank back against the cushions, her eyes stinging with tears. "Because of that damn ovulation chart and everything that went with it, right? I turned our lovemaking into a chore, an almost mechanical thing. And I'm very sorry for that."

"Oh, I don't know, Elly," he said, leaning over her, grinning at her. "It had its moments. Do you remember the night we were going to order in pizza?"

Elly certainly did remember. If the calculations her father had made earlier today meant anything, that had been the night she'd conceived. She longed to tell Rob that, tell him now. But something held her back. And that something was the fact that she knew something else. She knew she could never return to New York. She couldn't raise this child in the city.

She'd tried, she'd really tried. But she didn't fit in. Worse, she didn't *want* to fit in. It wasn't that she constantly disappointed Althea, it was that she didn't want to please her. She didn't want to fit in, be a corporate wife, spend her time shopping and going to parties and serving on committees.

Elly sighed, wiped a tear from her cheek. "We have so many problems, Rob. Sometimes they seem bigger than those mountains out there. I don't know how to climb them."

Rob moved even closer, tipped up her chin with his hand. "Together, El," he whispered as his mouth descended toward hers. "We climb them together."

Chapter 14

Go slow. Go slow. The words repeated themselves inside Rob's head as he slanted his mouth across Elly's, deepened the kiss as she sighed, melted against him.

Her skin was like warm satin as he caressed her bare shoulders, slid one thin green strap down over her upper arm. Fragile. She was so fragile, for all of her strengths. His sweetheart. His love. His life.

He kissed her again, and again, and again. Long, drugging kisses. Something empty inside him began to fill up, and when she braced her palms against his chest, then slid them up and over his shoulders, he knew he'd come home.

His mouth broke from hers, and he trailed kisses across her cheek, down the side of her throat. "Missed you...missed you...missed you."

She was kissing him. Pressing her lips against his hair, his neck, her arms fully around him now, holding him to her as if she were afraid he might vanish, disappear. "I know...I know...I know."

There was so much to say. Too much to say. So he'd say none of it. Not now. Now he would touch her, love her, cherish her. Now he would soothe her, relearn her, protect her from any pain.

He lifted her into his arms, and she leaned her head against his chest as he carried her into the bedroom. The covers had been turned down, there were two foil-wrapped mints on one of the pillows. Yeah, right. Like he was hungry for food.

Somehow they were on the king-size bed, lying together on the cool sheets. Somehow their clothing disappeared.

He loved her slowly, as if it were their first time. They lay front to front, so that he felt the fire of her skin against his chest, his thighs. Her long dancer's body was smooth, yet strong, and he traced his fingers along her hip, smiled into her mouth as he felt her skin shiver responsively under his touch.

Physically they were perfectly matched, perfectly mated. From the beginning they had come to each other as if they'd always known each other, always loved each other. Knew just how to please each other.

Rob kissed her breasts, ran his tongue over her nipples, molded their weight in his hands.

And Elly went wild. She threw back her head, made soft, mewling noises at the back of her throat as he suckled, teased. Worshiped.

He slid a hand lower, skimmed her rib cage, followed the path with his mouth. He kissed her belly, dipped his tongue into her navel, kneaded her strong thighs. Felt her open to him.

She was clawing at his back, begging him to come to her, to let her hold him. Hold him, hold him.

And she was right. They had all night, they had forever. But, for now, they needed each other. Quickly. Completely.

He eased her onto her back, levered himself over her, settled himself between her thighs. She smiled into his eyes, reached up her hands, pressed them against his cheeks, pulled him down to her.

"Love me, Rob," she whispered, half command, half plea. "Please love me."

He plunged into her, always careful with her, always surprised when she greeted him with such passion, such immediate response. "I always have, Elly...I always will."

"We shouldn't have done that."

Rob's hand paused halfway to his mouth, the can of soda held in midair. "Really?" he asked, trying to keep his tone light, teasing. "Would that be the first time or the second time? Because I'd be hard-pressed to say which one I could give back and not miss with everything that's in me."

"You know what I mean." Elly rolled her eyes, tucked her legs up under her bathrobe so that only her toes were visible. She was covered head to foot in white terry cloth and looked about as wanton as a novitiate. "We shouldn't have made love—either time. It just confuses the issue."

Rob sat down beside her on the couch, tried not to sigh. "Confuses the issue, El? I thought it might have cleared it up. At least part of it. We love each other. That wasn't any animal mating ritual, or even a medically approved fertility rite. That was two people who love each other loving each other. And, yes, I'll admit it—it's a damn sight better than making love on a time chart. Temperature up, come home, Rob. Temperature down, so what's the point, I think I'll read a book and come to bed later.''

''I apologized for that,'' Elly said stiffly, rolling up one end of the terry cloth sash snugly tied around her waist. ''I...I think I was becoming obsessed. I wanted your baby so much. Now, looking back, I can see that I turned our lovemaking into some sort of clinical trial.''

Rob wanted to hold her, comfort her. But this, he feared, was one of those times that no matter how he reacted it was going to be wrong. They still had a lot to settle before he dropped his bombshell on her, dropped both his bombshells on her.

Still, he decided that he'd speak from his heart, then duck if she decided to punch him. ''Elly, I want our baby, too. I want that very much. But at what cost, honey? When does wanting a baby evolve from something we want into...well, like you said, an obsession? We got married, El, to be together, to love each other, to love our children if we had them. But who says giving birth is the only way to welcome a child into our home, into our hearts?''

She cocked her head, looked at him closely. ''What are you saying?''

He took a deep breath and decided to let it all hang out, drop the first bomb. And he honestly, truly, did not know how she'd react. She'd either hate him or love him. But he had to find out, for this was one secret he couldn't keep, had to share with her, needed so much to share with her. ''I've been talking to a lawyer friend of mine, El. Mark Hagan. You remember him?''

She nodded, biting her bottom lip.

''Okay. Mark says private adoptions aren't the nightmare some isolated cases make them seem. We could have our baby, El, if we're prepared to wait a little, trust Mark to make the arrangements. Or we could have a baby now. There are so many kids with special needs, kids that are harder to place...''

''Adoption? I...I thought you were going to tell me you'd filed for divorce. But a baby? Adoption?'' Elly pressed a hand to her mouth, and a single tear rolled down her cheek. ''You did all this? You talked to Mark? You investigated adoption? Without first talking to me?''

Rob took another sip of soda, stared down at the top of the can. ''Yeah, I did. It's something I've thought about for a long time, nearly a year. But, frankly, I thought you'd bite my head off if I were to tell you about it, so I decided to do a little investigating first, see if it were even possible, plausible. I hadn't planned to do anything, *really* do anything, until we'd hashed it all out between us and you agreed. If you didn't agree, well then, I'd just tell Mark no dice, he should just forget I'd talked to him.''

He put down the soda can, looked at her, tried to read her expression. He couldn't. ''But then something happened, El. For one, you left, so that we couldn't talk about it. And then something else happened. Do you remember that call the other day? The one I had to take, even though I wanted nothing more than to talk to you, to hear your voice?''

''I remember,'' she said quietly, laying a hand in

his lap, rubbing at his thigh beneath his slacks. At least she seemed willing to listen, hadn't yelled at him, told him he was out of his mind. "Go on."

He scratched a spot at the back of his neck, took her hand in his, raised it to his lips. Clumsy. He felt so clumsy. But, then, his heart was very much involved. "There's...there's this baby. A little girl, El, about six weeks old. She was born with some sort of hole in her heart, and her mother left the hospital without her, doesn't want her. She's an inch away from signing private adoption papers with Mark. There's a lot of legal red tape, El, but Mark says that if the adoptive parents agree to take over complete financial responsibility, agree to some other stuff, well, then everything could move faster. The baby needs at least one surgery, maybe two, and then she'll be fine." He felt a small tic begin in his cheek. "If she makes it through the surgery."

"If...if she makes it through the surgery? She is going to make it, isn't she? She has to make it."

Rob held Elly's hand against his cheek, looked at her closely. "I saw her, El, the same afternoon I talked to you," he said quietly. "I called you back after Mark and I hung up, but there was no answer. And then, well, then I just walked out of the office, went to see her. She's never left the hospital, not when she has nowhere to go. She...she's got this absurd mop of red hair, and the biggest blue eyes..."

Elly's eyes were awash in tears, her bottom lip trembling so hard that she finally bit it between her teeth. At last Rob began to relax. This was Elly he was talking to, his Elly. She was probably already half in love with the baby, without even seeing her. "You saw her?"

"Yeah," Rob said, then stood up, unable to sit still any longer. "I talked to Jim before I flew out here, gave him the name of the baby's cardiologist. He called, talked to the man. Your dad says the baby has a chance, a good chance. She just has to gain some weight, get a little stronger, and then they can do the first operation."

He stopped pacing, turned to look at Elly, knowing he was pleading with her. "I watched her for a long time, through the window of the care unit. Her little forehead turns blue when she cries, El, because of that damn hole in her heart. Her little fingers turn blue. And all I could think was that she wouldn't cry so much if she had somebody to hold her, to love her."

Elly uncoiled her long legs, stood up. She went to Rob, wrapped her arms around his waist, laid her head against his chest. "And Dad knows? He knows all of this?"

"Your father's one hell of a man, Elly," Rob told her sincerely. "And he moves fast. He's already been in contact with a group of pediatric cardiologists out here, talked with a pediatric heart surgeon he swears is one of the tops in the country. There have been faxes and phone calls flying back and forth between here and New York almost nonstop since yesterday afternoon. That's what your dad and I talked about when we took our little walk this afternoon. We could have the surgeries here, the doctors agreed, once we have custody, because she has to gain some more weight before they can do the operation, anyway. But she doesn't have to stay in a hospital until then, not if she had a family to come home to, to watch over her. I thought it would be better out here, where you could be close to your mom and dad, where Susie could help. Lord knows she's wanted a grandchild long enough. Anyway, Jim wants you out here. He was very definite about that.''

''Yeah, he would be.'' He felt her raise her shoulders, heard her shuddering sob.

''Anybody can have babies, El,'' he said, holding her, rubbing her back. ''Not everybody has what it takes to be a good mother. I know you. I watched you with those kids from the hospital, watched how you cared, how you helped. Mark...Mark's done all the preliminary paperwork, and all we have to do is go back to New York, talk to some people. If you want to, El, only if you want to. The final decision is yours.''

He felt her head move as she nodded, held him tighter.

''She was sleeping when I left her,'' Rob said as he followed Jim Parrish out to the patio, sat down on one of the chairs beside the pool. ''She had a million questions, of course, but I thought she looked tired, so I made her go to bed. I'll pick her up later. We're going to have lunch, talk some more.''

''So she wants the adoption. I thought so. She wouldn't be our Elly if she didn't.'' Jim sat down, as well, looked at Rob levelly. ''Did she say anything else? Talk about anything else?''

Rob smiled, shook his head. ''Are you kidding? Once I told her about the baby, she was our only topic of conversation. When she could see her, when she could hold her, when we could have her. I'm telling you, Jim, that daughter of yours can be like a whirlwind. She wanted to pack, take the next flight to New York. But I don't want that, Jim. I don't want her to see the baby until Mark's got all the details nailed down. It's a private adoption, pretty straightforward, but there's still official stuff I don't understand.''

''I see,'' Jim said, looking out over the yard, the swimming pool. ''What did she say about bringing the baby here, to Nevada?''

Rob rubbed at his chin, frowned. ''That's the weird part, Jim. She didn't say anything about that. I think she believes I meant that we'd only come here for the surgeries.''

''Son,'' Jim said shaking his head, ''I think you'd better go talk to my daughter again. Between the two of you, you still have a lot of talking to do, and a lot of listening.''

''You mean about my second—''

''Well, if it isn't my favorite son-in-law,'' Susie said, pushing back the sliding door and stepping out onto the patio. ''But soon not to be my only son-in-law,'' she continued as Rob stood up, then bent down to kiss her cheek. ''Just remember that, Rob, and make sure you keep scoring points.''

''Fickle woman,'' Rob teased, sitting down once more only after Susie sat down. He looked to Jim, who was shaking his head slightly, warning him to keep silent on the subject they'd been about to discuss. ''And after meeting Griff and Pete, I'd say I have my work cut out for me. Are you open to bribes?''

Susie crossed her legs and sat back, looking adorable in her short denim skirt and bright yellow blouse. The woman could give flirting tips to the entire younger generation. ''Well, that depends, Rob. What are you offering? Griff is providing a limo for our renewal of vows, and Pete has already agreed to sing.

He has the most wonderful voice. Oh, and he's also agreed not to let Abby sing a note. We can only consider that a blessing, don't you think? So, if you're going to play Can You Top This—what are you going to do for your mother-in-law?''

Knowing he was opening himself up for a good hour of Susie's questions and probably a few hugs, he answered, ''Well, actually, I was thinking about providing another bride and groom for the ceremony. Elly and me.''

It all hit the fan at two o'clock.

That's when Rob, having cried off from his lunch date with Elly, met his mother at McCarran Airport, then drove her into town, checked her in at the Golden Nugget.

He'd gotten the news around ten, when he'd left the Parrish house and gone back to his hotel to check his phone messages. He'd hoped for a call from Mark. He had one waiting for him. But, just as a bonus, now that he was feeling so great, he also had to listen to four increasingly frantic voice-mail messages from his mother's social secretary, Ms. Hughes, informing him that Mrs. Lyndon was on her way to Las Vegas.

And arriving in full sail, Rob had decided as he watched Althea Lyndon enter the terminal, cutting through the waves of gaily dressed tourists like a man-of-war and taking dead aim at him. A woman with a mission, that was his mother.

She'd talked to his dad. Oh, yeah. No doubt about it.

She was a tall woman, his mother was. Both his parents were tall, which pretty much explained his own height. And she was still slim, kept herself in the finest shape diet foods, expensive spas and a few surgical nips and tucks could provide. She was handsome, rather than pretty, her designer clothes whispered of understated elegance, and her posture would have done a Marine drill sergeant proud.

There were times, Rob thought, smiling, when she scared the living hell out of him. Luckily this wasn't one of those times. In fact, he was almost looking forward to this meeting, as long as he could keep Elly out of the line of fire.

"Hello, Mother," he said, kissing her offered cheek. "Never thought I'd see you in Sin City. Have you come for the annual no-limit poker game at Binnian's?"

She looked at him blankly. "Do you know, Robert, there are times I absolutely do *not* know who you are. Now I suppose we'll have to wait somewhere for my luggage."

Rob scratched his head, watching his mother move forward once more, a living wall of self-confidence and downright pushiness. Oh, yeah. This was going to be fun.

"Your mother is *where?*"

"Here. In Vegas. In this hotel. Down the hall, actually," Rob ended, then waited for the explosion.

"I think I'm going to be sick."

"Now, El—"

"No, I mean it, Rob. I'm really going to be sick. Excuse me," she said, then bolted from the room.

He wanted to follow after her, but when he heard the slamming of the bathroom door he rethought that impulse. Instead, he paced the living room area of the suite, wondering how a nice guy like him had ended up in a mess like this.

"Because Dad never sat on her, that's how. He never said, 'No, Althea.' He never said 'Put a sock in it, Althea.'" he ruminated aloud, then cocked his head, thought about what he'd just said.

And then he picked up the phone. "Well, maybe it's about time."

Rob was just putting down the receiver when Elly walked back into the room. She looked lovely, but pale. "Orange juice?" he asked helpfully.

"Orange juice? Oh, God, no," Elly said, sighing. "I'm going to pack my suitcases, Rob. I'm going back to Summerlin, back to Mom and Dad. You understand, don't you? I don't want to sound melodramatic, but this town just ain't big enough for Althea and me."

"No, Elly," he said firmly, taking her hands, squeezing her fingers between his own. "You're not running away from this. We've got plans, remember?"

"The baby." She sighed, leaned her head against his chest. "I still don't believe it. I've wanted a baby for so long, and now..."

"And now it's going to happen," Rob finished for her, pretty sure that wasn't what she'd been about to say. But he didn't want her to tell him there was some problem with their new dream, their new hope. "Mark left me a message at my hotel. I called him back from the airport, while I was waiting for Mother's plane to land."

Elly pushed back against his arms, looked up at him searchingly. "And?"

"And if it's all right with you, I'd like us to name her Eleanor, after her mother."

"Name her after—oh, Rob! We've got her? We've actually got her? This fast?"

"Not all that fast, Elly, since I've been talking to Mark about adoption for nearly a year. Both the birth mother and father signed the papers this morning. They're just kids, Elly, the mother only sixteen, the father not much older. They couldn't handle a special-needs child like Eleanor and, thank God, they both know it. There's some sort of waiting period before everything is totally final, but Mark says he doesn't see any problems. We can see Eleanor anytime we want and make arrangements for her to be flown out here as soon as her doctors declare her able to travel. And, thanks to my own contacts, it looks like we'll have her on a special medical flight by the end of next week."

He held on to Elly's arms, rubbed at them nervously. "If you still want her, El. If you still want me. Because we're a package deal. Eleanor needs a mother, but she also needs a father."

"Everything's happening so fast, Rob," she told him, playing with the button on his shirt, avoiding his eyes. "There's still so much to work out, still so much to tell you. And if we were to bring Eleanor here, then I'd want to keep her here, near her doctors. It wouldn't be right to have her traveling back and forth to New—" She dug her fingers into the front of his shirt as they both heard the sharp knock on the door.

"Timing is everything, isn't it, El?" Rob asked, recognizing the imperious knock. "Look, Elly, I'm going to ask you a favor. A couple of favors. We don't talk about Eleanor, we don't talk about bringing her here for her surgery. Okay? We just make nice-nice with Mother until tonight, when Dad has promised to show up like the Mounties, and save the day. Or pick up the pieces," he added thoughtfully, sure his mother was going to explode when she learned the full extent of what she would only see as his insane defection.

The knock came again, and Rob didn't know whether to laugh or pretend he and Elly weren't in the room. Wasn't there a damn desert island somewhere? Anyplace he and Elly could go, be alone together? Someplace where he could tell her everything he'd come here to tell her?

"Your *father's* coming here? But...but I thought he was in Texas?"

"Yeah, well, he was. But within the hour he's going to be on his host's private jet, heading here. I figured somebody ought to be around when Mother goes ballistic."

Elly looked at him curiously. "She's going to go ballistic? I didn't think your mother could do that."

"Trust me, El. She's going to do it. And I don't want you here to watch the blastoff. Let's just get through the next couple of hours, and then you can come up here to wait for me, or go home to visit with your parents for a couple of hours."

She looked suddenly mulish. "No. I've had a lot of time to think about this, Rob, and it's time your mother and I came to some sort of agreement. Thinking about running away from here was just some leftover knee-jerk reaction. I'm not going anywhere, I'm not hiding, and I'm definitely not letting you fight any more of my battles for me. Understand?"

Rob gave her a quick hug. "I love you when you're fierce," he said quickly. "And I agree with you. You're staying right here, with me. And you're sleeping here, El, and so am I. I've already packed my bags and checked out of my hotel. I am never going to sleep anywhere but beside you for the rest of our lives. Oh, and one thing more," he said as the knock came a third time. "You know our couch at home?"

"Yes, Rob," Elly said carefully. "I do seem to recall it."

"Yeah, well it isn't all that damn comfortable after all. And it's about ten inches too short, too."

He was already walking toward the door when Elly caught up to him, pulled him around for her kiss. "You big dope. You slept on the couch the whole time I've been gone, didn't you? Oh, Rob, I do love you, I do. And I've got so much to tell you..."

"We still have so much to tell each other, it seems," he said, putting an arm around her shoulder as he laid his hand on the doorknob. "You haven't figured it out for yourself yet, but let me tell you, sweetheart, I'm full of surprises—hello, Mother," he said, opening the door. "Isn't this nice? I get to take my two best ladies to lunch."

Althea looked around the lobby as they walked out of the elevator on the ground floor of the hotel. "So, Eleanor, is this where you...danced?"

"No, Althea," Elly answered as Rob gave her hand a bracing squeeze. "I performed at the MGM Grand, out on the Strip. But there's a nice show here at the Nugget. I haven't seen it in a few years, but it was a country music revue at that time. I had a few friends who were in the show, but we've rather lost touch

since I moved to New York. Do you swim, Althea?''
she then asked, as they walked along the long, right-
angled hallway that was bordered on two sides by
plate-glass walls that gave onto a large patio and a
good-size pool. "If you do, I recommend early morning, before the sun gets too high in the sky. And
plenty of sunscreen.''

"I don't swim," Althea said, and Rob turned to
waggle his eyebrows at Elly, who bit back a smile.
No, of course Althea didn't swim. What could she
have been thinking?

"Mother used to be a hell of a skier, though, Elly,"
he told her as they were being led to their table in the
Carson Street Café. "An Olympic hopeful, to hear
Dad tell it. Isn't that right, Mother?''

To his complete surprise, his mother actually
blushed. "That was a long time ago, Robert," she
said, arranging her linen napkin in her lap. "I attended college near Stowe, and became enamored of
the sport. My mother convinced me that I should look
to other interests, something more suited to the life I
was being groomed to lead. That was forty years ago,
of course, when women's skiing didn't have quite the
cachet it has today.''

Elly leaned forward, clearly interested. "You're
kidding. She ordered you to stop? And you *listened*
to her?''

"It's a child's duty to listen to its parents, Elly,
obey its parents." And then she shocked Rob down
to his toes. "But I was good, Eleanor," she added,
leaning forward, as well. "I was very, very good.
Now I'd probably be relegated to the bunny slopes,
and even then fall and break my hip. Not a palatable
prospect.''

"I'll bet you wouldn't, Althea," Elly said, and Rob gave her a slight kick under the table, although he wasn't sure if he was warning her to change the subject or encouraging her to speak even more freely. "I'll bet you'd pick it up again in no time. There's some great skiing resorts here in Nevada. Up at Lake Tahoe, for one. You and Richard really should try it. Really. Nevada's a wonderful state."

Rob blew out a short breath. Warning her to silence. That's what the nudge should have meant. Definitely. This was no time to launch into a sales pitch for Nevada. He smiled, looked across the table at his mother.

"Yes, Nevada must be a *wonderful* state," Althea said shortly. "And I'm sure that's what you said to Robert when you convinced him to—"

"Hot bread, anyone?" Rob asked quickly, lifting the basket of rolls and all but shoving it into his mother's face. "Oh, and Mother? Did I tell you that Dad's flying out here later today? In fact, I think his plane will probably be landing in about three hours or so. Isn't that nice?"

Now it was Elly's foot that collided with Rob's shin, and she wasn't half as gentle in her warning as he had been.

"Your father's coming here?" Althea looked at him blankly. "But why on earth would he come here?" Then she narrowed her eyes, glared at Rob and Elly. Pinned them to their chairs like butterflies pinned to a board. "Oh, I see. You're going to gang up on me, aren't you? Tell me I'm wrong to worry about my son, to worry about the future. Wrong to believe that you're close to making the biggest mistake of your life."

She stood up, folded her napkin, laid it on the table. "I'll be lunching in my room, Robert," she said, her chin raised, the very picture of the Manhattan society matron. "And as for you, Eleanor, don't think you've won, because you haven't."

Elly watched Althea leave, regally threading her way through the tables on her way out of the café. Then she turned to Rob, looked at him curiously. "What was all that about? Won? What did I win?"

Rob pinned a smile on his face, rather glad they were in a public place. "Oh," he said as offhandedly as possible. "Didn't I tell you, El? Must have slipped my mind. I quit my job."

Chapter 15

The door to the suite slammed shut. Elly stomped into the living room area, threw down her purse, turned to glare at Rob. "Slipped your mind? Slipped your mind? How could quitting your job possibly *slip your mind?* And it's not a job, Rob. It's your family's firm. It's your career, your future. You can't just quit."

Rob walked over to the couch, sat down. "Yes, I can. I can, and I did. Sort of. So, are you still hungry, want to order something from room service? All I had downstairs was a glass of water and a couple of crackers. Best tip that guy ever got for not taking an order. I can't be sure, but I think I threw down a twenty when you bolted from the table and I had to go running after you."

Elly ran a hand through her hair, not realizing that it then slid back into place like a sleek brunette curtain. "I did not *bolt*. I left. And you're darn lucky I did, because otherwise I probably would have screamed at you. Not that you didn't deserve to be screamed at. Not that you still don't.''

She threw herself into the chair across from the couch, glared at him, stood up again. Began to pace. "Quit your job," she repeated, trying to get the words to sink into her own brain. "God, no wonder your mother flew out here. I'm only surprised she didn't land with a regiment. Two regiments. One to kidnap you, take you back to New York, and the other to surround me, keep me here. And the worst part of that, Rob, is that I don't blame her.''

She raked her fingers through her hair one more time. "God! I'm taking your mother's side. Can you believe that? I can't. But I am. Poor Althea. She must be devastated! And your poor father. Rob, how could you do this to them? And how can you look so damn *satisfied* with yourself while you're at it?''

"I'm not satisfied with myself, El," he told her, smiling. "But I am getting a rather large charge out of you. And, yes, I am enjoying myself. I don't remember the last time you got mad, really mad. I don't remember the last time you yelled at me. No, wait...I think that was the night I got tied up with a client and forgot to call home, and there was some gas main explosion near the office and you had me dead, or at least in several pieces, until I finally called. That's true love, you know, Elly. Loving someone so much you want to murder them for not being hurt. Or at least I hope it is.''

Elly faced him, jammed her fists on her hips. "Are you done now? There's nothing else you want to say? Good. Now, tell me the number of your mother's suite.''

Rob gave a sort of rueful chuckle, shook his head. "No way. No way, no how. At least, not until you tell me what you're planning to do."

"I don't *know* what I'm going to do, Rob," Elly flung back at him as she picked up her purse, slung it over her shoulder. "Maybe I need a few details first, don't I?"

"Details?" Rob was eyeing her as if she might be packing an uzi in the thing, and he wasn't sure if she was going to use it on his mother or on him.

"Yes, Rob. Details. You say you quit your job. Does your father know? How did your mother find out? What are you going to do now that you don't have a job? Were you just planning to follow me to Vegas and hope to find a job when you got here? And what about Eleanor? How can we adopt her if you have no income, no steady employment?"

He opened his mouth to speak, but she shut him down, shut him off. Elly didn't know why she was so angry. She didn't even know if she should really be happy. She just knew that things were moving fast. Too fast. *Way* too fast. And it was her fault, all her fault. That business about most marriages failing due to a lack of communication wasn't just something trendy to say. It was *real*. And right now, and for a long time, she and Rob were the poster children for Not Communicating.

Rob tried to stand up, but she waved him back onto the couch. She couldn't let him touch her. Not now. She was feeling so…so brittle. "Well? Are you going to tell me?"

Rob scratched at the side of his neck, a habit she was used to seeing when he was trying to collect his thoughts. "Yes, Elly. Dad knows. I imagine he told

Mother. And, before you accuse me of being some
sort of coward, running away from home—and, no, I
don't mean that *you* were a coward—let me tell you
that I didn't actually *quit* my job. I just *moved* it. Not
that you let me get more than one sentence out before
you bolted—sorry—left the restaurant. After that it
sort of got to be fun watching you blow up. You
should do it more, sweetheart. It's probably good for
the soul, or something."

"Yeah, well I cry more now, too. I'm doing lots
of things more lately." Elly cocked her head to one
side, saw the twinkle in her husband's eyes, and sat
down on the chair once more. Obviously there was
something here that she'd been missing. And somewhere in the back of her mind, she realized that she
didn't feel sick to her stomach. Maybe it hadn't all
been morning sickness. Maybe she'd been beating
herself up. Whatever it was, she could feel new
strength flowing into her. It felt good. "Go on."

Now Rob stood up, began to pace. It seemed like
they were playing "change places." She smiled inwardly, still feeling amazed with herself.

"You weren't happy, El. I wasn't happy. Oh, the
first year was okay. You were happy discovering New
York, seeing shows, going to museums, decorating
the apartment. You kept busy. Then we started this
baby business, and it wasn't working. We read the
books, we saw the doctors…" He spread his hands,
dropped them to his sides once more. "By the end of
the second year, you were pretty frustrated, we both
were pretty frustrated. And you were getting more and
more dissatisfied with what my mother believed to be
your *duty* as my wife, as a, God help us, Lyndon."

Elly sighed. "It…it wasn't the life I wanted," she

admitted, twisting her hands in her lap. She saw things more clearly now—her strengths, her weaknesses. "But I could have tried harder, bent a little."

"You bent yourself into a damn pretzel for her, El, for crying out loud," Rob told her, walking over to her chair, going down on one knee in front of her. "But you hated it. I hated watching it. And you refused to stand up to her. Don't get me wrong, Elly. I love my mother. But the woman can sense weakness like a shark smells blood underwater. In short, in long—if you ever want to be my mother's friend, be at all comfortable with her, the first thing you have to do is tell her to go to hell." He shook his head, grinned. "You never did. And now, it seems, you're about to go to her room and tell her you feel sorry for her. Bad move, El. Bad move."

"You think so, huh?" Elly considered it all for a minute, decided to shelve thoughts of her mother-in-law and get back to Rob's announcement. "Tell me how you didn't quit but just moved, okay?"

Now Rob smiled, and she thought how adorable he looked. "I was beginning to think you'd never ask. You haven't made the connection yet, have you, El? There were two projects I've been working on for the past year. Both of which I should have told you about, and I'm more sorry than I can say that I didn't, but I also didn't want to get your hopes up if neither of them worked out. The baby—well, that worked out. Unexpectedly, a lot faster than I could have believed. I was going to tell you the other news the day I came home to find you gone. At which point, no, we did not tell Mother. Not until you knew. She found out yesterday, through one of the secretaries or something, and that's why she's here. I'm only surprised she didn't stop off in Texas, to murder Dad.''

Elly held up her hands, silently asking him to stop, desist. ''If you were going to tell me this—whatever it is—can I safely assume that you *did* tell my parents? That they know all about your *move,* as well as all about Eleanor? Mom and Dad were much too happy with you, in my opinion, considering the fact that I'd left you, and that I was suffering. So, did they know?''

Rob pulled a face. ''That depends, Elly. If I say yes, are you going to take a swing at me? Suffice it to say that your parents said you had a few problems of your own to work out and that I should wait awhile before springing two very large surprises on you. Susie also said that if we just sat down together, *talked* to each other for five minutes, we'd realize that we're both idiots who love each other and have gone so far out of our ways to not hurt each other that we've made a huge mess out of our lives.''

''Yeah,'' Elly said, smiling wanly. ''I was beginning to think she was going to have that all embroidered on a throw pillow, except that it's too long. Now, one more time—tell me about your job.''

She watched as he stood up once more, took her hand, led her to the couch. ''You do remember how we met, don't you? Why I was out here, in Vegas, in the first place?''

She nodded. ''You were putting together financing, venture capital for a new casino.''

''Exactly. I was doing what our firm does, except I was doing it out here for the first time. And I liked it. I liked the town, the state, the climate, excitement, the people—and I loved you. That's most important, El, then and now. I love you.''

She reached out a hand, stroked his cheek. "Keep going, big boy. I think we're making progress here.''

He grinned, and she watched as he turned from Rob the husband to Rob the businessman—sans the slicked-back New York hair, thank goodness. "This city is growing by leaps and bounds. Every time we come out here, there's another casino going up, another office building, another…whatever. Our firm arranges financing, El. We get the right people and their money together, and we help build businesses, empires. We've done it in New York for three generations. Now, with Dad's blessing, we're going to do it in Nevada. Set up a permanent office here in Las Vegas. And I'm in charge.''

Elly narrowed her eyes, looked at Rob suspiciously. "And Richard just agreed to this? Said, wow, Robert, what a grand idea, now why hadn't I thought of that? I don't believe you.''

Rob grinned, raked a hand through his hair. "And you shouldn't, sweetheart. But when presented with the fact that either I got my own end of the business or I walked—well, it took a long time, but Dad came around. Especially when I told him I'd begun talks with a firm out here and they wanted me. I told Dad, Dad told Mother yesterday that she could either be good about the thing or lose her son forever, and then took off for Texas—not that I blame him—and I came here to, damn it, collect my wife. Oh, and to look at office buildings, maybe build our own, get things rolling.''

"Blackmail? That's what it was, you know. You

with your dad, your dad with your mother. You Lyndons can be ruthless, can't you?''

He chuckled low in his throat. "I'm a teddy bear, El. Not at all ruthless. Except when it comes to my wife's happiness," he told her, drawing her into his arms. "And to mine, by the way. I'm not making any huge sacrifice here, you know. I owe you an apology, Elly. Lots of apologies. I kept secrets, I worked behind your back. I had the best intentions, not wanting to give you hope if I couldn't work everything out, but I should have told you. But I promise, sweetheart. From here on out—no more secrets. Not ever."

He kissed her forehead, her nose, her mouth. She melted against him, smiling, sighing contentedly. And then her eyes flew open wide and she sat up, looked at him in a panic. "I've got to go see your mother now, Rob," she said quickly. "Because there is no way I'm going to allow our children to grow up without both grandmothers. She's either going to be happy for us on her own, or I'm going to *make* her happy for us."

"You're still going to do this? Elly, I'm warning you, this isn't a good idea. Let her settle down, let Dad show up like the calvary. You've known my mother for three years. I've known her a lot longer. She's not a good loser."

"Room number, Rob. Now," Elly said, already walking toward the door.

He gave it to her, still shaking his head, still obviously believing she was about to go off to fight a losing battle. But then, he didn't know what she knew, did he? After all, if blackmail worked once…

"We'll be back in a half hour or so, Rob," she told him as she opened the door. "In the meantime, I suggest you order a bottle of champagne for Althea and yourself, and a glass of milk for me. A big one. Because you're right. We've been keeping secrets from each other, and we're not going to do that anymore. Not ever.''

Rob stood up, started toward the door. ''A glass of—*what?*'' And then, because he wasn't a stupid man, his eyes opened wide as he looked at her. She smiled, put a hand to her belly. Nodded. And he sat back down on the couch. Dropped back down on the couch. ''Sonofagun,'' she heard him say as she closed the door behind her. ''Sonofagun...''

''Eleanor,'' Althea said shortly, as she walked away from the open door, leaving Elly to follow after her. ''If you've come to apologize...'' Althea had let her words die away, the implied ending being ''I'm not going to accept your apology.''

''That's not why I'm here, Althea,'' Elly said quickly.

''Really,'' the older woman said, sitting down regally, motioning Elly to a chair. ''In that case, I'll admit to being totally at sea, as Robert has never needed anyone to fight his battles for him.''

''Is that how you see this, Althea? As a battle? One winner, one loser? I don't see it that way.'' Elly even smiled as she said the words, looked directly into her mother-in-law's eyes. The smile wasn't for Althea, it was for herself. Because she knew, at last, that you can't have a war unless both parties agree to pick up weapons.

''No, of course you don't,'' Althea said, smoothing down her skirt. ''Why should you? You've got my son, and I don't. You've already won.''

"Oh, Althea, is that how you've been seeing me? As the enemy?"

Althea raised her chin, almost physically took hold of herself, commanded herself to be civilized, regal and damn imposing. That's how Elly had always seen the woman. Now she saw behind the facade, saw the real woman. The frightened woman. Why hadn't she, Elly, seen all of this before? Had she been too busy trying to be someone she wasn't, someone she knew she couldn't be, didn't want to be?

"Althea," Elly began slowly, "we don't have a lot in common. But we have the most important thing in common. We both love Rob, want him to be happy. I think that's a pretty good foundation to build on, don't you?"

"He was happy, until he met you," Althea snapped. "I thought he'd realized his mistake at last, when you left him, but he hasn't. He's even willing to turn his back on his parents, his future, and all because of you."

"No, that's not true," Elly said firmly. "And, if you'd looked, you would have seen that it's not true. He loves you, Althea, you and Richard both, and that's why he hung on as long as he did. Trying to please you, juggle that with his happiness, my happiness. Juggle other things," she ended, remembering the two-year struggle with fertility specialists, ovulation charts, lovemaking by appointment. "Part of that was Rob's fault, and he knows it. And I'm not blameless in any of this, or you, Althea. We both thought we knew what would make Rob happy, and both of us were wrong. We made mistakes. But only because we love him."

Althea looked at her for a long time, finally spoke.

"I thought it wouldn't last a year," she said finally. "A showgirl? I'd decided you were cheap, trashy, and that you'd tricked Robert into marrying you. A gold digger, as we used to call those who married for money. Perhaps we still do."

She lifted her shoulders, let them drop. "But you weren't a gold digger. I kept trying to believe you were, but you weren't. And that's when I knew I'd really lost him. But this—" She spread her arms, as if to indicate all of Las Vegas, all of Nevada, all of the world that wasn't Manhattan. "I can't believe he wants this, too. But he does. I know that now. He really does."

Another time, another Elly, and she would have shut her mouth, drawn in on herself, hidden herself away. But not this time. And she wasn't angry. That surprised her. She really wasn't angry, insulted. This pregnancy stuff must be pretty potent, making her understand, empathize, with another mother.

"We can share him, Althea," she said, walking over to sit down beside her mother-in-law. "There doesn't have to be a winner, a loser. Rob loves you very much. But I'm his wife, and we're going to live our own lives, how we want, where we want. You can't live that life for us, but we both want you and Richard to share it."

"No, it's too late for that," Althea said, and Elly could hear tears in the woman's voice. "I've done everything wrong. Richard tried to warn me, but I wouldn't listen. He called me a few minutes ago, you know, from the airplane. He's says I'm the punch line for a bad mother-in-law joke, showing up here, making a fool of myself here, where I'm not wanted."

Elly couldn't help herself. She laughed. "Oh, Althea, you're not a joke, and I'm really glad you're here," she protested, taking the woman's hands in hers. "You see, Rob sprung a surprise on me, a lovely surprise, and now I've just sprung one on him. We're going to have a very busy year, Althea, with the move here to Vegas, with Rob's surprise, with mine. I'm going to need your help, both in New York and here. And I'd really, really appreciate that help... Grandma."

Althea looked at her. Her eyes began to fill. Her bottom lip trembled. And she looked so very, very human as she whispered, "Grandma?"

"And that's the way it's going to be, Richard," Althea said firmly, sitting down beside her husband on the couch in Elly's suite. "Eleanor and I have discussed the entire thing, and we're in perfect agreement. Aren't we, Eleanor?"

Elly felt Rob squeeze her hand as he sat on the arm of the chair, smiled down at her. "Perfect agreement, Althea," she said, returning Rob's smile. "We're all going back to New York, together, after my parents' renewal of vows. We'll all go to see baby Eleanor in the hospital, make arrangements to take her home, fatten her up for her trip out here for her first surgery."

"And we'll keep the apartment in New York, sign it over to the company and use it whenever we come to visit, which will be often, we promise," Rob continued as Elly took a sip of cold milk. She really did hate milk, which was a pity, because now she had three more people to nag at her, make sure she did everything possible to take good care of her unborn baby.

"And we'll be setting up a company apartment here, possibly a condo, where we'll visit—often," Richard Lyndon added, grinning. "Why, I might even take up golf."

"It's going to be a boy," Althea said, taking recourse to her linen handkerchief as she dabbed at her eyes, not for the first time. "I've not a doubt in my mind. Our own little boy, our own little girl. I'd always wanted a little girl, you know. With long ringlet curls and pretty smocked dresses. Rob, I believe I saw a Neiman-Marcus sign as we drove to the hotel? It's never too soon to start shopping, you know."

Rob took Elly's hand, had her walk with him to the windows overlooking the street below, the desert beyond. "You're a miracle worker, do you know that, a miracle worker, or a magician," he said softly, and she melted against him, felt his arms go around her. "Now snap your fingers, El, and make them disappear, okay? Because if I don't have you and our second-born to myself in the next ten minutes I might just go crazy."

Elly lifted her head for his kiss, putting her fingers to his lips at the last moment to say, "I'm sorry I kept our baby a secret, Rob. But I didn't want you to think you had to make any decisions regarding our marriage on the fact that I'm pregnant."

"*We're* pregnant, El," he said, kissing her fingertips. "Trust me, I've got the queasy stomach to prove it, or at least I did, the moment I realized why you wanted me to order you a glass of milk. I love you, Eleanor Parrish Lyndon. Mommy Lyndon."

"And I love you, Daddy Lyndon," she told him, vaguely hearing her father-in-law pointedly suggest to his wife that they probably should be getting back to their own suite. She adored her father-in-law. Such a perceptive man. "I love you very, very much."

"...and do you, James, take Susan as your lawfully wedded wife. To love her, to cherish her..."

Elly held tightly to Rob's hand as they all stood as witnesses to her parents' renewal-of-vows ceremony inside the small white wedding chapel.

She snuggled closer to him, then looked at her sisters, one after the other. Catherine was smiling as she stood beside Griff. They weren't going to be married for another month, not with the preparations needed for a guest list as large as Griff wanted. Elly was hopeful that she and Rob could be there for the wedding, that Eleanor would be strong enough to accompany them by that time. Because it was going to be a wonderful wedding. Catherine was going to be a beautiful bride.

Abby was standing beside Pete and sniffling into a handkerchief, smiling and crying and being good old sentimental Abby. Pete had his arm around her as he stood in his green scrubs, having had to race straight to the ceremony after an emergency surgery earlier in the morning. Catherine had worried that Pete might not arrive in time, but Abby hadn't turned a hair. She was going to make a great doctor's wife. And Pete was perfect for Abby, as he'd only laughed, then gone along with the joke when Abby had produced a black silk bow tie from her purse, then tied it around his neck so that he was dressed more as a member of the wedding party.

He'd sung "Evergreen" before the ceremony had begun, and Elly had bit her lip so that she wouldn't blubber like a baby. She hadn't known a Las Vegas Strip wedding could be so beautiful, so touching.

Elly turned to her right and smiled at her in-laws, who had been asked to step forward with the rest of the family, to serve as witnesses.

Richard looked comfortable and at ease in his dark business suit, his face and neck not quite as uncomfortably red as they had been after his first round of golf with Jim Parrish the previous day. And Althea looked positively radiant. She had her hand tucked in her husband's, and she was listening to every word of the ceremony, a rather speculative gleam in her eyes. Elly had a feeling it wouldn't be long until Richard found himself back at the altar, repeating his own vows.

Althea leaned forward slightly, to smile at Elly, and Elly smiled back. This was going to take some getting used to, being Althea's friend, Althea's equal. But Elly was certainly up for it. She'd said a definite *no* to Althea's suggestion that she hire a nurse for Eleanor, and Althea had backed down. But then, Elly had said yes when Althea picked out a lovely white crib with an eyelet canopy top for the baby, agreeing that, yes, a princess definitely did need a bed fit for royalty.

Elly sighed, squeezed Rob's hand again. There was still so much ahead of them. Seeing Eleanor. Getting the last papers signed, so that she was really theirs. Getting her fattened up, getting her through that first, most important surgery. They might have a lot of tears ahead of them, but a lot of joy, as well. And they'd face it all, as a couple, as a family.

"…I now pronounce that you are still man and wife!"

Elly snapped out of her reverie, to applaud along with everyone else, and the next minutes were full of hugs and kisses and a few hearty back slaps among the men.

And then Rob found her and pulled her forward, to where her parents had stood only a few minutes earlier. "What?" she asked blankly as Catherine produced a short, white wedding veil and stuck it on Elly's head, kissed her cheek.

"Here you go, El," Abby said, shoving a small bouquet of pink rosebuds and baby's breath into her hands. "I've wrapped a couple of tissues around the stems, in case you need them. It's a helpful hint from...well, never mind." Then Abby kissed her, stepped back.

"Mom?" Elly asked, as her mother slipped off her shoe, shook out a sixpence.

"Lift your heel a moment, darling," her mother instructed her, then dropped the sixpence into her daughter's shoe. "For luck, not that you need it. It's also your 'something borrowed.' And, since you're wearing that blue dress I wanted you to buy, you're all set with the 'something new' and the 'something blue.' We'll count Rob here as your 'something old,' since you've already had him around for a long time. Right, Rob?"

Elly looked at her husband, who was looking entirely too smug and happy with himself. "You had this all planned, didn't you? All of you. I thought we weren't going to have any more secrets between us?"

He bent down, whispered in her ear. "I lied," he confided happily, then kissed her cheek. "Will you still remarry me?"

She purposely hesitated, then said, sighing, ''I suppose I should, if only for the sake of our children.''

Rob lifted one eyebrow. ''It's not too late, you know. I could still ask the guy dressed like Elvis to read us our vows.''

''You wouldn't dare,'' Elly squeaked as Rob smiled a truly evil smile. ''Oh, all right, all right. I forgive you, really.''

''And you love me?''

''And I love you,'' she breathed, standing on tiptoe, pressing her lips against his.

''Hey, that's for *after*,'' the guy in the Elvis suit complained as he stood in a corner. He'd been in that corner for a while, sulking because he hadn't been allowed to sing and some guy in wrinkled greens and a bow tie had taken his place.

''Here's another fifty, son, and we'll want a chorus of 'Love Me Tender' right about now, okay?'' Richard Lyndon said as Elly smiled against Rob's mouth and he drew her closer into his arms.

Epilogue

Jim Parrish sat in his favorite deck chair and watched the scene around him. Ah, the differences a year can make. Almost unbelievable. All of it wonderful.

The Lyndons—the *senior* Lyndons—were back in Nevada, having arrived for little Robbie's christening a week ago, and Richard and Jim had played golf that morning before the family picnic, scheduled for this afternoon. Poor Richard. His drives were getting better, but the man couldn't sink a five-foot putt to save his life. Jim smiled, patted his pocket and the twenty dollars he'd won from the man. The only thing better than a congenial golfing buddy was a congenial golfing partner who couldn't beat you.

Jim watched as Althea Lyndon picked up Nora, as their redheaded granddaughter was now nicknamed, slung her on her hip and headed for the kitchen and a wet napkin to clean chocolate icing off the child's mouth. What a woman. Only Althea Lyndon could look like she was ready for a formal tea party at the Plaza, and still tickle a baby's belly and make that baby laugh in unholy glee. And she handled the child like a pro. Nora was giggling as her grandma pretended to scold her for getting icing on her pretty new dress, one of the dozens Althea seemed to produce on every visit.

Jim lifted a hand to touch Nora's chubby little thigh as Althea walked past, then blinked at sudden, unexpected tears as he rejoiced, as they had all rejoiced, when Nora had come through her second and last surgery like a champ. *Love.* What an amazing thing. It moved mountains. It built bridges. And it gave life to a little girl who was now going to grow up healthy and happy.

Elly was in the house, nursing Robbie, but she'd promised to bring the baby out to him in a few minutes, so he could take his turn spoiling the child. Five months old, and the kid had the hands of a basketball player—and the feet, too, as Elly had pointed out to him. He also had his mother's smile, and both mother and child smiled often.

"Hi, Pop-Pop," Susie said, sitting down beside him, fanning herself with a napkin. "Wanna get lucky with Mom-Mom tonight? After we send all the Indians home, of course."

He chuckled, turned his head to look at his wife of, now, more than thirty-one years. She looked like a new bride. "I suppose I could be talked into it," he said, deliberately leering at her.

"It's a date!" Susie said, then jumped up, already heading for the kitchen. "Althea's in there, isn't she? I promised her I'd help get Nora down for a nap. We sing a mean duet, you know. See ya, Pop-Pop."

Jim continued to sit, feeling that he was rather at Command Central, and watched over his family. Catherine was sitting at the edge of the pool, holding three-month-old Griff, Jr., dabbling his little feet into the water as Griff swam laps. He smiled as he remembered the photographic proofs Catherine had showed him earlier, the ones of her, Griff, and the baby. The ones Griff had said were going to be on the next round of billboards and taxi boards and bus stop benches. And with Catherine's full approval.

As a matter of fact, Griff had confided in Jim as Catherine had taken the pictures to show her mother, the whole thing had pretty much been Catherine's idea. Then he'd told Jim the new slogan Catherine had made up: "*Families* deal here with certitude." His oldest daughter was really something, and she and Griff were a definite partnership.

Pete slid into the chair Susie had vacated, sitting low on his spine, his long legs splayed out in front of him. "Playing patriarch again, Jim?" he asked, waving his hand to indicate the scene in front of them. "Mind if I sit here awhile? You're like an island of calm in the middle of this ocean of family fun and frolic."

"How's Abby?" Jim asked, watching as his youngest daughter stooped to play with Robbie, then stood up, pressed both hands to her back, rubbed at her muscles. She was wearing an absolute tent of a dress, all fire-engine red, and with a cutout of a stork holding a baby and blanket sewn on the front of it. She looked cute as a bug. A rather pot-bellied bug.

"Dilated two, Larry said, when we visited last week. He said it could happen anytime now, but Abby doesn't believe him. She says she's going to be pregnant forever. I'm beginning to agree with her.''

"Is she sleeping all right?" Jim couldn't help himself. He was a doctor, yes, but he was a father first.

Pete nodded. ''Nature's way of resting up for the big push, I suppose. It'll be fine, Jim, I promise. Abby's healthy as a horse, even working. She says she has a lifetime of columns ahead of her, now that she's going to be a mother. I don't know about you, but that's the only thing that scares me. I still haven't quite gotten over her helpful hints for a more romantic honeymoon. Of course, neither have the guys at the hospital. They've still got one of her columns tacked to the bulletin board outside the O.R.''

Jim chuckled, watching as Abby picked up the long-handled skimmer, began walking around the pool with it. "She's her mother all over again.''

"Umm-hmm," Pete said, also watching his wife. "Except maybe for this one thing, Jim. Even pregnant, Abby can get this…little *hitch* in her walk sometimes. She walks, and warning bells go off in my head, and the next thing I know I'm hanging curtains in the nursery, or spending my only afternoon off going antiquing. I can't describe it, but…well, never mind.''

"A certain hitch, you said? Ah, Pete, trust me in this. I understand." And then his smile faded, and Jim jumped up from his chair, began running toward the pool, Pete at his heels.

"Pete? Dad?" Abby was asking, looking down at the cement pool surround. "Is this what I think it is? Did my water just break? Well, how about that!''

Jim had delivered dozens of babies over the years. Hundreds. Pete had served his time in the obstetrics department. There should have been no problem, no panic. Everything going off like clockwork, everything calm, totally under control.

And it was, once Susie, Althea, Elly and Catherine took over.

Griff was sent to dry off, change, pull his car up into the driveway, as they'd brought the minivan today, and there'd be room for more people.

Rob found himself holding Robbie in one arm, Griff, Jr., in the other and listening to instructions that both children had to be put down for naps—after their diapers were changed, of course.

Susie and Althea led Abby inside the house, helped her change as Catherine loaded the front seat of the minivan with towels, and Elly poured Pete a drink of ice water, told him to sit down, put his head between his knees.

Richard Lyndon, who had been napping on the living room couch, was roused, given orders to call the doctor—his number was on the pad next to the telephone—and alert him to meet everyone at the hospital.

Jim, the calmest, most organized, most cool and confident guy in the world, walked to the furthermost part of the backyard, took several deep breaths. He didn't know what was wrong with him. He'd been at the hospital when both Robbie and Griff, Jr., had been born.

But then, damn it, he'd met his daughters at the hospital, once they were already there and in good hands, safe. He hadn't taken a pregnant woman to the hospital since he'd driven Susie there to have Abby and, he then remembered, he hadn't been much more helpful then, or when Catherine and Elly were born, than he felt now. One of the obstetrics nurses had told him that doctors were always the worst when it came to watching their wives in labor. He hadn't been the least unusual.

He gave himself a mental shake and then wiped his eyes before returning to the house. What he found was his youngest daughter, lying in the bed she'd slept in before she was married. "What's going on?" he asked, back in control of himself once more as he looked at Pete, who was heading into the bathroom off the bedroom.

"Dilated two, my sweet aunt Mary. I'm going to punch Larry flat on his nose, next time I see him," Pete answered tightly. "Come on, Jim. Looks like we're going to deliver a baby, and let me tell you, this is *not* my idea. Although you could ask your daughter why she's been having pains all day and didn't tell anyone."

"I thought it was false labor, Dad," Abby said, looking very small as she lay on the bed, Susie holding her hand.

"False labor, huh?" Jim answered, grinning at his daughter, now definitely in control of himself. "And, having had six babies, you'd know the difference?" He looked across the bed at Susie. "Someone's called for an ambulance?"

"Catherine. It's on its way, but I don't think this baby wants to wait. Abby says she wants to push."

Jim turned around, intending to go to his car, take out his medical bag, but Elly was standing right behind him, holding it out to him. Behind Elly was the rest of the world. Well, not literally, but it certainly seemed so. "Out," he said, making shooing motions with his hands. "All of you—except you, Susie.

Catherine, give me those sheets you're holding, then you can leave, too.''

Less than an hour later, as Althea served coffee and cake to the ambulance attendants in the kitchen, Jim opened the bedroom door and motioned for Susie to join him in the hallway. They stood together in the doorway for long moments first, looking at their baby hold her baby.

"She's beautiful, isn't she?" Susie said, sniffling.

"She certainly is," Jim agreed as he watched Pete sit down on the edge of the bed, gently run a finger over his daughter's fuzzy blond head. "And so's our new granddaughter. Are you happy now, Susie? Only a little over a year ago, you said you wanted grandchildren. Now we've got four. And, much as I didn't know how I was supposed to be able to help you get those grandchildren, I think, with this last one, I've just done it."

Susie stood on tiptoe, kissed his cheek. "And did it splendidly, darling," she told him. "You and Pete both were splendid. And Abby was magnificent. Now, let's leave the new family alone for a few minutes before they have to go to the hospital, all right?"

He watched as his wife, his bride, his love, moved down the hallway ahead of him. "Am I still going to get lucky tonight?" he called after her softly, so that she'd be the only one who heard him.

She looked back over her shoulder, laughed and continued to walk away from him, toward the kitchen. He watched her go, watched her walk. Saw the little hitch.

"Oh, yeah," he said, chuckling quietly. "I definitely do love that little hitch...."

*   *   *   *   *

READER SERVICE™

The best romantic fiction direct to your door

Our guarantee to you...

*The Reader Service involves you in no obligation
to purchase, and is truly a service to you!*

*There are many extra benefits including a free
monthly Newsletter with author interviews,
book previews and much more.*

*Your books are sent direct to your door
on 14 days no obligation home approval.*

*We offer huge discounts on selected books
exclusively for subscribers.*

*Plus, we have a dedicated Customer Care team
on hand to answer all your queries on
(UK) 020 8288 2888
(Ireland) 01 278 2062.*

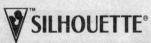